SHILOH

SHILOH

TEXAS BOUDREAU BROTHERHOOD

By
KATHY IVAN

COPYRIGHT

Heath – Original Copyright © March 2021 by Kathy Ivan

Cover by Elizabeth Mackay

Release date: March 2021
Print Edition

All Rights Reserved

SHILOH – Texas Boudreau Brotherhood

"In Shiloh Springs, Kathy Ivan has crafted warm, engaging characters that will steal your heart and a mystery that will keep you reading to the very last page." Barb Han, USA TODAY and Publisher's Weekly Bestselling Author

Kathy Ivan's books are addictive, you can't read just one." Susan Stoker, NYT Bestselling Author

BOOKS BY KATHY IVAN

www.kathyivan.com/books.html

TEXAS BOUDREAU BROTHERHOOD

Rafe

Antonio

Brody

Ridge

Lucas

Heath

Shiloh

Chance (coming soon)

NEW ORLEANS CONNECTION SERIES

Desperate Choices

Connor's Gamble

Relentless Pursuit

Ultimate Betrayal

Keeping Secrets

Sex, Lies and Apple Pies

Deadly Justice

Wicked Obsession

Hidden Agenda

Spies Like Us

Fatal Intentions

New Orleans Connection Series Box Set: Books 1-3

New Orleans Connection Series Box Set: Books 4-7

CAJUN CONNECTION SERIES
Saving Sarah
Saving Savannah
Saving Stephanie
Guarding Gabi

LOVIN' LAS VEGAS SERIES
It Happened In Vegas
Crazy Vegas Love
Marriage, Vegas Style
A Virgin In Vegas
Vegas, Baby!
Yours For The Holidays
Match Made In Vegas
One Night In Vegas
Last Chance In Vegas
Lovin' Las Vegas (box set books 1-3)

OTHER BOOKS BY KATHY IVAN
Second Chances (Destiny's Desire Book #1)
Losing Cassie (Destiny's Desire Book #2)

Hello Readers,

Welcome to Shiloh Springs, Texas! Don't you just love a small Texas town, where the people are neighborly, the gossip plentiful, and the heroes are...well, heroic, not to mention easy on the eyes! I love everything about Texas, which I why I've made the great state my home for over thirty years. There's no other place like it. From the delicious Tex-Mex food and downhome barbecue, the majestic scenery, and friendly atmosphere, the people and places of the Lone Star state are as unique and colorful as you'll find anywhere.

The Texas Boudreau Brotherhood series centers on a group of foster brothers, men who would have ended up in the system if not for Douglas and Patricia Boudreau. Instead of being hardened by life's hardships and bad circumstances beyond their control, they found a family who loved and accepted them, and gave them a place to call home. Sometimes brotherhood is more than sharing the same DNA.

This book is Shiloh Boudreau's story, and Shiloh gave me heart palpitations along the way while writing his book. It was a difficult book to write, because I was dealing with not only telling Shiloh's story, but bringing Lucas' sister Renee back home. I hope I did both of them justice. Add to that the fact I was writing this will dealing with all the pandemic stuff going on...well, let's just say Shiloh's book was a labor of love.

If you've read my other romantic suspense books (the New Orleans Connection series and Cajun Connection series), you'll be familiar with the Boudreau name. Turns out there are a whole lot of Boudreaus out there, just itching to have their stories told. (Douglas is the brother of Gator Boudreau, patriarch of the New Orleans branch of the Boudreau family. Oh, and did I mention they have another brother – Hank "The Tank" Boudreau?)

So, sit back and relax. The pace of small-living might be less hectic than the big city, but small towns hold secrets, excitement, and heroes who ride to the rescue. And don't you just love a Texas cowboy?

Kathy Ivan

EDITORIAL REVIEWS

"In Shiloh Springs, Kathy Ivan has crafted warm, engaging characters that will steal your heart and a mystery that will keep you reading to the very last page."

—Barb Han, *USA TODAY* and Publisher's Weekly Bestselling Author

"Kathy Ivan's books are addictive, you can't read just one."

—Susan Stoker, NYT Bestselling Author

"Kathy Ivan's books give you everything you're looking for and so much more."

—Geri Foster, USA Today and NYT Bestselling Author of the Falcon Securities Series

"This is the first I have read from Kathy Ivan and it won't be the last."

—Night Owl Reviews

"I highly recommend Desperate Choices. Readers can't go wrong here!"

—Melissa, Joyfully Reviewed

"I loved how the author wove a very intricate storyline with plenty of intriguing details that led to the final reveal…"

—Night Owl Reviews

Desperate Choices—Winner 2012 International Digital Award—Suspense

Desperate Choices—Best of Romance 2011 –Joyfully Reviewed

DEDICATIONS AND ACKNOWLEDGEMENTS

I love it when fans tell me they wish Shiloh Springs, Texas, was a real place, because they want to live there. Trust me, if it was real, I'd be your next door neighbor, because I want to live there too!

To my sister, Mary. She knows why.

As always, I dedicate this and every book to my mother, Betty Sullivan. Her love of reading introduced me to books at a young age. I will always cherish the memories of talking books and romance.

More about Kathy and her books can be found at

WEBSITE:
www.kathyivan.com

Follow Kathy on Facebook at
facebook.com/kathyivanauthor

Follow Kathy on Twitter at
twitter.com/@kathyivan

Follow Kathy at BookBub
bookbub.com/profile/kathy-ivan

NEWSLETTER SIGN UP

Don't want to miss out on any new books, contests, and free stuff? Sign up to get my newsletter. I promise not to spam you, and only send out notifications/e-mails whenever there's a new release or contest/giveaway. Follow the link and join today!

http://eepurl.com/baqdRX

SHILOH

CHAPTER ONE

The pounding, throbbing beat of the music matched the thrumming behind his eyes. *Bam, bam, bam.* Even the floor beneath his feet reverberated with the deep bass of the music. Flashing strobe lights illuminated the club's dance floor, bodies gyrating to the techno song blasting from the speakers. At least, he thought it was a song. He couldn't be sure, because there was nothing melodic about the clash of confusion and noise bombarding his eardrums.

Shiloh Boudreau stood close to the bar, nursing his bottle of water, wishing he'd opted for a beer instead. Couldn't do that, though, because he was working. He scanned the crowd again, looking for his mark. Earlier, he'd spotted the woman he sought easing through a door leading backstage. When he'd tried to follow, one of the club's security guards stopped him in his tracks.

So here he was, forced to cool his jets at the bar, waiting for her to reappear. Would she? The itch on the back of his neck, the one he got when something was about to happen, had the little hairs standing at attention. Acting on a hunch, because that's all it was, he slid the half-empty bottle onto the bar and headed for the exit. The minute he was through the front door, he sprinted toward the alley.

Son of a gun, I'm too late!

He watched the city bus pull away from the curb, saw her shining auburn hair highlighted in the interior lights, as she took a seat toward the back. He'd missed her by mere seconds. Somehow, some way, she managed to stay two steps ahead of him. If he didn't know better, he'd swear somebody tipped her off whenever he got close.

Too bad she'd didn't know who she was messing with. He was a Boudreau, and they didn't know the meaning of giving up. If she thought he'd simply turn tail and head back to Texas, she'd didn't have a clue. This case wasn't about a paycheck. It was a family quest, and he'd promised his brother he'd find Renee. Long-lost sister, separated from Lucas when they were youngsters, and put into the foster care system.

Lucas had been one of the lucky ones. He'd been placed at the Big House with the Boudreau clan. Renee simply disappeared into the system, and all records pertaining to her were mysteriously lost.

He flinched when she gave him a jaunty wave as the bus pulled away. No way could he manage getting back to his car and catching up to the rapidly departing bus. Parking had been a bear, and he ended up finding a spot several blocks away from the club. Some P.I. he was, he hadn't even gotten the number off the bus to see what areas it covered.

Giving a heavy sigh, he started back for his car. Might as well head back to his hotel room, get a good night's sleep, and start over in the morning. Renee O'Malley might be slicker than a greased piglet, but she'd find out soon enough she was dealing with a Boudreau. Quitting wasn't in his vocabulary, and he tended toward being tenacious as a bloodhound once he scented his prey.

He made it to the hotel and unlocked the door. Reaching into his duffle, he pulled out the bottle of aspirin and shook two into his hand, downing them without water. Sitting on the edge of the bed, he rested his head in his hands, frustration making it head pound. He'd been so close this time. When he'd first agreed to head to Portland, he'd jumped at the chance, thinking he'd catch up with Renee, or as she'd been calling herself, Elizabeth. What a joke.

The woman gave new meaning to the term elusive. First thing he'd done was head to the address Heath's newest recruit claimed he'd met Elizabeth Reynolds. After seeing a photo, everyone was convinced she was Lucas' missing sister, Renee. Lucas would have come himself, but he'd been neck deep in an investigation in Shiloh Springs. If he'd pulled out, illegal gambling would have gotten an even bigger foothold in and around their home town.

All his cases lately bored him. Working as a private investigator might sound all fun and exciting, but mostly it was mind-blowing boredom, mixed with sporadic thrills. If he admitted the truth, he was getting burned out both mentally and physically. When Lucas called, it seemed like the perfect escape. A trip to Oregon couldn't be considered a hardship, but more importantly, he'd be finding a missing member of the family.

Instead, he'd been chasing a ghost. A beautiful, elusive woman who intrigued him, without ever saying a word, which only made the chase more interesting. Let her run. He'd catch her. And when he did, she'd find herself in Shiloh Springs before she could say boo.

Scooting up on the bed, he put his back against the headboard and pulled out his phone, scanning his e-mail for messages. Nothing important enough to warrant his attention. On impulse, he dialed Lucas.

"Hello."

"Hey, bro. Thought I'd check in, find out how things are in Shiloh Springs."

"Do you realize what time it is, idiot?"

Shiloh winced when he remembered the time difference between Texas and Oregon. That couple of hours made it after midnight back home.

"Sorry. Just got back to the hotel and thought you might like an update on Renee."

"You've talked to her? How is she? Does she remember me?" The excitement in Lucas' voice struck at Shiloh like a knife to the gut. Now he had to tell his brother he'd struck out—again.

"Your sister is slippery as an eel. Every time I get close,

she somehow manages to elude me. I got within about six feet of her tonight, at a techno club downtown. By the time I got across the stinking dance floor, she'd slipped out the back door into the alley, and jumped on a bus."

"How's she doing this? It's like every time we get close enough to talk to her, she's in the wind. I want to know why she's running. To be this close, it's killing me."

"Dude, I almost didn't call, because I hate disappointing you. This game of hide and seek is going to end. I'm not giving up until you are face to face with your sister."

He heard Lucas' sigh, and wished for the millionth time he had better news. Every time he called, he'd told him the same thing. Renee outsmarted him at every turn, which told him she'd been doing this song and dance for a long time. Nobody got this good at eluding a hunter, unless they were used to being hunted. The thought literally made him sick to his stomach. Who preyed on a helpless woman? He knew the answer, which didn't help the overwhelming depression shadowing him.

"I know you're doing everything you can. I feel like I've failed her. Every record I've searched trying to locate her for years has either disappeared, been destroyed, or leads to dead ends. I'll rest easier once I know she's safe and happy. Even if she doesn't want me to be part of her life, I can accept that, as long as I know she's not in trouble."

"Yeah, me too. I'm going to start searching again in the morning. I've got another lead where she might be. I won't give up. I promise."

"Bro, I can't ask you—"

"Stop. I'm here because I want to be. I don't have anything else pending now, so this is a mini-vacation."

"Liar. You'll never know how much it means, you looking for Renee. The story's coming out Sunday, so I may head up there right after that, and help you search."

Shiloh knew his brother would be on the next plane out if he managed to run Renee to ground. "Listen, you're in the middle of moving back to Shiloh Springs. You and Jill are starting a new life, a second chance to get things right. Focus on that, and I'll handle things here. I give you my solemn promise, you'll be the first person I call when I've found your sister."

"But I can help you search."

"Lucas, buddy, I've got this. I'm afraid if she realizes two strange men are looking for her, she'll bolt. She's done it before. When I catch up to her, we can both figure out who's been chasing her and handle the problem."

"I—okay, fine. Call me any time, day or night, when you find her."

Shiloh rubbed the bridge of his nose between his thumb and forefinger, wishing the aspirin's effect would kick in.

"I will. Get some sleep."

"You too."

Shiloh disconnected the call and picked up the TV remote. Might as well see if there was anything worth watching. It was going to be a long night.

Renee shivered beneath the vent on the bus, its icy blast chilling her to the bone. She drew in a ragged breath and pushed the hair out of her eyes. That had been a close call. Too close. Whoever this guy was, he was good. It had been sheer dumb luck she'd spotted him leaning against the bar, or he'd have caught her. This wasn't the first time she'd seen him, and he was getting on her last nerve. Why couldn't he leave her alone? She wasn't hurting anybody. All she wanted was to have a little corner of the world to call home.

She was tired. So tired it was getting hard to think straight. Sleeping was as elusive as fairy's breath on the morning dew, and the hour or two she managed at night was filled with dreams. Mostly nightmares, but recently they'd been filled with visions of the dark-haired stranger from tonight. Hot, sweaty, not suitable for work-style dreams.

Who did he work for? Darius and Eileen didn't mind hiring freelancers. Thus far, she'd managed to elude her pursuers, but how much longer would her luck hold? She'd struggled to stay one step ahead of them, though this last time she'd cut it a little too close for comfort.

Cincinnati had been a blessing, a respite from living on the run. Who knew why, but they hadn't caught up to her there for almost two years—the longest she'd managed to stay in one place.

Luckily, the bus only held a handful of people this late at night, for which she was grateful. Nobody sat beside her, so she didn't have to make useless chitchat. When she'd jumped aboard, evading the stranger riding her tail, she hadn't even looked to see where it was headed, her only thought to get away from the club, and him, ASAP.

Picturing the handsome stranger in her mind, she wondered how much Darius paid him to find her. Somehow, she had a hard time picturing him as a hired killer. Oh, Darius would make sure killing her was the last resort, but she'd bet it was on the table, especially if Eileen had anything to say about it. Eileen wanted her dead and in the ground. Renee wouldn't be surprised if Eileen wanted the pleasure of being the one to put a bullet between her eyes personally.

She coughed as the stench of sweaty bodies wafted toward her, and caught the eye of an older man, huddled in a seat two rows ahead of her, wearing a tattered pea-green army jacket. His greasy brown hair held more than its share of gray and cascaded to the top of his shoulders, straggly and dirty. A dingy, faded duffle occupied the seat beside him, and she'd bet it contained all his worldly possessions.

Breaking free of his gaze, she glanced out the window, pleasantly surprised when she recognized familiar landmarks. Finally, one good thing from this horrible night had gone right. One of the few friends she'd picked up since moving to Portland lived only a couple of blocks away, and she knew

Tina wouldn't mind letting her bunk on her couch for the night.

She climbed off the bus, shivering against the chilly wind blowing from the north, and wished she'd stopped to grab her sweater, the one she'd left hanging on the back of a chair at the nightclub. Though calling the place a nightclub didn't really do justice to the place. It was one step up from being a dive bar. Its only saving grace? Their dance floor, where people actually got out of their seats and danced.

It had been a foolish impulse, going to the club, but she'd craved human contact. The urge to simply be around others, even people she didn't know, compelled her out into the real world. Even if she only made it through a couple of songs, maybe a dance or two, at least she'd feel something besides the loneliness plaguing her for so long.

Wrapping her arms around her to ward off the night's chill, she walked faster, hoping to make it to her friend's apartment before she turned into a human popsicle. Tina had worked with Renee at a local coffee shop, close to her old apartment. The charming spot wasn't one of the big chain stores, more of a mom-and-pop shop, but it had a friendly and loyal clientele, and she'd liked the atmosphere and the people. Too bad she'd been forced to quit, the instinct that kept her out of trouble pinging louder and louder. Whenever that happened, she listened, knowing she'd be hitting the road sooner rather than later.

She climbed the three flights of stairs to Tina's apartment, bypassing the elevator. Tina groused all the time about the unreliable monstrosity, Renee remembered, complaining it broke down more than it worked. And she really didn't want to be stuck in an elevator between floors. Not tonight. All she wanted was to curl up beneath a comfy blanket and seek oblivion in sleep. Tomorrow, she'd assess her situation, and decide if she could buy a little more time, or if she'd be forced to hit the bricks.

She chuckled quietly as she walked toward Tina's place. *I must be more tired than I thought if I'm thinking in cliches. And really lousy ones. I sound like a flatfoot from an old 40s movie.*

It took mere moments before she was settled onto Tina's overstuffed sofa with its enormous cushions, sipping a cup of hot cocoa. Tina tossed her a pillow and spare blanket, and once Renee promised to explain things the next morning, went back to bed.

Yeah, right. I'll have to come up with a believable story, not only for why I'm here, but why I'll be leaving Portland.

Sitting quietly on the corner of the sofa, she stared out the window, watching the sunrise, her thoughts drifting to a brown-eyed man, wondering if he'd be the death of her or her salvation.

CHAPTER TWO

S hiloh showered, dressed, and was out the door right
after the sun rose. He hadn't gotten much sleep, and
what little he managed was filled with crazy dreams of Renee.
Somehow, despite all the information he'd garnered about
her, he couldn't bring himself to call her Elizabeth or Liz or
Lizzie or any other derivative she might've used. All his life
he'd thought of her as Renee, Lucas' baby sister. Though,
after seeing her, he had to admit she definitely wasn't a baby
anymore.

Pulling up the collar on his jacket against the brisk
morning chill, he fleetingly wished he was back in Texas. He
disliked being cold, and autumn in Texas remained his idea
of perfection. Lovely cool mornings, warm afternoons where
more times than not he didn't even need a jacket, and cooler
temps in the evenings. So far, Portland had been cold, damp,
and pretty much miserable.

He walked a couple of blocks, bypassing the large coffee
shops chains, and headed for a local place the desk clerk had
recommended. There was something about dealing with
places like that, small stores run by families or local folks, he

appreciated. Probably the small-town boy in him. He always made a beeline for Daisy's Diner, or Jill's bakery, or even Gracie's coffee shop whenever he came back to Shiloh Springs. And not just because he considered the people who ran them extended family.

Walking through the front door, he drew in a deep breath, sighing at the scent of fresh beans being ground, and he quickly took his place in line. A middle-aged woman took orders at the counter, working with an ease and friendliness he knew probably came from years of experience. She greeted everyone with a smile, calling most by name. A good sign; repeat customers generally meant good quality.

"Good morning, welcome to Roaster's Retreat. What can I get for you this morning?"

"Morning. A large coffee, two creams, please."

"Got it. Would you like anything else? My husband, Carlos, made fresh-baked cinnamon buns this morning with an orange cream cheese glaze. Can I interest you in one?"

When his stomach rumbled at her words, he grinned. "Absolutely."

"Perfect. Here's your number. I'll have that ready in a jiff."

"Thanks."

He spotted an empty seat against the wall, huddled practically in the corner, and he swooped in and grabbed it before it disappeared. The quaint coffee shop had a homey feel, with sepia-tinted photos of what he assumed were old shots of Portland framed and hanging on the pale green and cream-colored walls. Open shelving held antique coffee paraphernalia, wooden coffee mills, and tin coffee pots and cups. All-in-all, a charming and warm place where he wouldn't mind spending an hour or two, if he had the time. Too bad his schedule today was full—looking for Renee.

"Here you go. Let me know what you think about Carlos' cinnamon buns. It's a new recipe he's trying out, and we're trying to decide whether to add them to the menu. Personally, I think they're a winner, but he's on the fence."

"If it tastes anything like it smells, I'd say you're right." Shiloh took a huge bite of the breakfast treat, and immediately wanted another. He chewed, savoring the burst of flavor with the mixture of spicy cinnamon contrasting perfectly right with the bite of orange and the sweetness of cream cheese.

"Well?" She grinned at his thumbs up because he was still chewing. "Awesome. I'll let Carlos know you liked it."

"Honestly? It's one of the best cinnamon buns I've ever eaten. Don't tell my soon-to-be sister-in-law, because she opened a bakery in my hometown recently, but these are way better." Shiloh gave her a cheerful grin and broke off another bite.

"Really?" The woman shifted from foot-to-foot, her expression thoughtful. "I know Carlos would love to have his own bakery, but we've got our hands full right now, running this place. We've got one barista who's shifted to part-time work, and our other one up and quit a few weeks ago. I hated losing Elizabeth, because she got to know the customers, took an interest in each one. Treated everybody like they were her best friends. Such a shame."

A surprising tingle raced down Shiloh's spine at the name Elizabeth. Nah, too much of a coincidence. What were the odds this lady's Elizabeth might be the same person he was looking for? Then again, most of the information they'd gained over the last few months had come about because of coincidences. He couldn't discount the possibility he might be in the right place at the right time to get a bead on Renee.

"You've got quite a place here. I got a referral this morning from the desk clerk where I'm staying. He sang your praises." He took a sip of his coffee and nearly swooned. "This is some mighty fine coffee. I'll definitely be back while I'm in town. Sorry to hear you're shorthanded. Bet you get a lot of repeat customers with coffee this good."

She grinned and glanced back toward the front counter, appearing torn about having to wait on customers and wanting to chat a bit longer. Shiloh hoped for option two, because he intended to dig a little bit, follow his hunch.

"We do a lot of repeat business. I'm planning to talk with Tina, my part-timer, and see if she can manage adding some additional hours to her shift. Can't hurt, right?"

"True. Listen, mind if I ask you something? You mentioned the barista who quit, her name was Elizabeth? I only just got into town, and I'm looking for my friend. She wasn't home this morning, but she told me she worked at a family-run coffee shop. I couldn't remember the name. Wouldn't it be a hoot if your Elizabeth and mine ended up being the same person?"

"Huh. Mighty big coincidence, you ask me."

Shiloh could read the suspicious vibes rolling off the now wary woman. He needed to put her at ease ASAP, or he'd lose any chance of getting the info he needed.

"Sorry, I didn't mean to overstep. Here," he dug out his wallet and pulled out the photo he had of Renee and handed it to her. "This is my friend's picture. Well, the latest one I've got. I'm Shiloh, by the way. Shiloh Boudreau, all the way from Texas."

She studied Renee's picture, a look of fondness on her face, and her lips curled up in a wistful smile. "Looks like it might be your lucky day, Mr. Boudreau."

"Shiloh, please."

"This is our Elizabeth, the one who worked here."

"Wow, that's amazing. I thought I'd give her a call this morning. She doesn't know I'm in town. It was a last-minute business thing, and I thought I'd surprise her."

"Good luck with that. The number I have for her has been disconnected."

Her words confirmed what he'd already discovered. The cell phone Renee had been using had been shut off with no forwarding account. His best guess? Burner phone she'd tossed or used all the minutes for and hadn't added more.

He rattled off the number he had, and the woman nodded. "That's the one I've got. Sorry."

"Me, too. Guess I'll have to tell my folks I couldn't find her." He stood and placed a generous tip on the table. "Appreciate your hospitality, and I'll definitely be back."

He smiled and stepped away, ready to head for the door, when she laid a hand on his arm. "Wait. The other gal who works here, Tina? She and Elizabeth got real chummy. I haven't asked, but maybe she'll have Elizabeth's new number. Want me to check with her?"

Bingo. Maybe Lady Luck decided to smile on me this morning after all.

"Is Tina working today? Maybe I can stop by while she's here and ask her myself."

She nodded and grinned at him. "Tina's coming in at ten a.m. She's covering the late morning shift. You want to talk to her, come back then."

The front door opened, and a large group of people piled inside, the chilly breeze sweeping along behind then before they got the door closed. Another reminder he wasn't home.

"Thank you again, ma'am."

"Ma'am," she chuckled. "You definitely ain't from around here. I've got to go serve these customers. See you later, Shiloh."

He walked outside and looked up at the sun peeking out from behind a gray cloud. "Looks like my luck might be turning around. Watch out, Renee O'Malley, I'm coming for you."

Renee put two slices of bread into the toaster, and filled both coffee mugs, adding cream and sugar to hers. Tina took hers black and strong, and Renee suppressed her shudder. She'd always teased Renee about her liking a little coffee with her cream and sugar, but she needed them to cut the bitterness.

The toast popped up and she slathered it with butter and honey. She'd heard the shower cut off, which meant Tina would be out soon, sticking her nose into Renee's business the minute she'd had her first sip of coffee. Too bad she hadn't come up with a plausible story to give her. How do you tell your best bud you're running for your life, and a hired gun has tracked you down? It sounded like the inconceivable plot of a bad romance novel, and she starred as the too-stupid-to-live heroine.

"Morning."

"You're up early. Don't you have the late morning shift?" Renee handed over the mug of black and cradled the other in her hand.

"Yes, but I don't have to be there until ten. Which means you get to spill your guts, girlfriend. And don't tell me there's nothing to say because I didn't buy that before, and I'm not gonna listen to any lies." Reaching into her bathrobe pocket, she pulled out a quarter and tossed it to Renee.

"What's this?"

"You know the old song? Well, here's a quarter, and I'm someone who cares. So, sister, spill the beans. You were pale as a ghost last night. I figured you needed sleep more than questions."

"And I appreciate that."

"It's morning, the sun is shining. Time to pull up your big girl panties and fill me in on all the details."

Renee glanced past Tina and looked out the tiny kitchen window over the sink. There was no view to speak of, but she could make out a patch of blue sky in the distance. Maybe the sun shone out there someplace, but even the thought of a rainless day couldn't cheer her up.

Tina pulled a chair out from the tiny kitchen set, plopped down onto the seat, settled her mug on the tabletop, and crossed her arms. From her mulish expression, Renee knew she wasn't taking no for an answer—not this time.

"It's…complicated."

"Pshaw. I deal with complicated every day. Pretty sure nothing you say will surprise me." Tina's eye roll had Renee chuckling.

"Alright, you asked for it. Let's start with the fact my name isn't really Elizabeth."

"Like I didn't already know that? Do I look like I live under a bridge? I can't tell you how many times I've called you Elizabeth, and you've totally ignored me or acted like you'd never heard the name before. I figured, hey, it's your business if you wanted to move to Portland and change your name. Believe me, you wouldn't be the first person to want to start over."

Renee stared at Tina, unable to believe she'd known all along. And she'd been using the name for a couple of years, you'd think she'd be used to it by now.

"It's been so long since I used my real name, I almost forgot it. Years. I think I was four when I got put in the first foster home. They called me Anna there. At that age, the system thinks you're young enough and malleable enough it's not a big deal to give you a new name. Although it's usually the last name that gets changed, when or if you get adopted. Not your first name."

Tina studied her intently, looking at her for so long Renee wondered if she'd drifted off into her own little world. Wouldn't be the first time; Tina tended to be a bit flighty sometimes.

"You don't look like an Anna."

"My real name is Renee. I haven't been called that in forever. Not since they separated me from my big brother. I can still hear him screaming my name as they took me away."

Tina sat up straighter in her chair, her mug halfway to her lips. She lowered it slowly back to the table. "You have a brother?"

She nodded, picturing Lucas' tearstained face the last time she'd seen him. Social workers held him back as he struggled to break free. Remembered screaming his name over and over as they strapped her into the van which carried her away from the only family she had left.

"His name is Lucas. I…haven't seen him since I was four years old." Tears threatened to spill, and she fought to keep them contained. Crying never helped; a lesson she'd learned at an early age at the end of a belt.

"Why'd you get separated? No, wait. We can talk about that later. Right now, I want to know why you showed up on my doorstep, looking like hellhounds were nipping at your heels."

"Remember you mentioning I wouldn't be the first person to come to Portland to start over? Pretty much what I did. I thought I could outrun my past. Looks like I was wrong."

"Well, crap. How much trouble are you in?" Tina picked up her cup again, drinking the rest of her coffee, before getting up for a refill. "I've got a little money socked away, if you need it."

"Thanks, but no. I need to lay low for a bit. Maybe lay a false trail, so the guy who's tailing me thinks I've left town."

Tina leaned back, taking a bite of her now-cold toast, scowling before she tossed it atop the napkin. "Wow, it's worse than I thought. Somebody's followed you to Portland, and you're hiding. Why?"

Renee stood and walked across the miniscule kitchenette and stared out the window. Now came the hard part. "I can't tell you. I know it's asking a lot, because I'm asking you to trust me without knowing everything, but I refuse to let you get involved in my problems."

"But—"

"Not gonna happen, Tina. Once this guy leaves, I'll be okay, I promise."

Tina snorted. "Right, by okay you mean you're gonna take off again. I can read it all over you. I thought we were friends."

"We are," Renee protested, wincing at the volume of her shouted cry. "I won't drag you into my problems. This is my mess, and I'm going to fix it, once and for all. I just need a few days." She met Tina's gaze, shoring up her resolve. It was past time for her to take her life back. The running and hiding, the living her life always on the edge, had to stop. "I could use a favor, though."

"Name it."

"I can't go back to my apartment. I'm positive this guy knows where I live. Can I stay here for a day? Two at the most. Long enough so I can put my plan in place?"

Tina stood and walked over, wrapping her arms around Renee. "I know we haven't known one other long, but I feel like you're my sister from another mister. Whatever you need, it's yours. Money, clothes. Well, except for my new boots. Touch those and you'll lose a few fingers."

Renee gave a watery laugh. "Got it, don't touch the boots."

"You know you're going to tell me everything. I'll try to be patient for a bit, but I'm going to pester, cajole, and wheedle it out of you. I have ways of making you talk. Be prepared." Tina gave a witch's cackle and another rough squeeze and pulled free. "Now, I've got to get dressed and head to work. You think of anything else you need, call me at the shop."

Renee walked to the living room, grabbed her purse, and pulled out a handful of cash. She'd learned a long time ago to always have money on hand in case she needed a quick getaway. "Can you get me a disposable cell phone? I had to toss mine yesterday."

"No problem." Picking up her mug, Tina headed for her bedroom, and Renee rinsed out her own mug, and put it in the dishwasher, already figuring out a plan to get Darius and Eileen to back off once and for all.

Closing her eyes, she took a deep breath, and internally stiffened her resolve. She'd had enough. Enough running. Enough hiding. Enough of everything keeping her from having a real life. It was past time to quit running and take a stand.

CHAPTER THREE

Pulling his rented sedan into the visitor's parking at the apartment complex where Renee lived, Shiloh climbed out and surveyed his surroundings. Deep in his gut, he doubted she'd come back here, especially since he'd spooked her enough to run. The tenants had garage parking, and he'd check it out after he tried her apartment, but he hadn't been able to determine if she even owned a car. He doubted it. Too many possessions made it harder to pick up and run, without leaving a trail a blind man could follow.

The complex appeared well-maintained, though not brand-spanking new. He'd bet it had been built in the past ten years. A high-rise, it boasted at least eight floors, and he knew from his research, and from Heath's source, they had an Olympic-sized pool, a gym, and spa to rival most of the newer complexes.

Walking in the front entrance, there was a spaciously appointed lobby area, and off to the left he spotted the gym, and smiled when he saw rows of elliptical machines, treadmills, stationary bikes, and several weight stations. Not a bad amenity to have. Nicer than the one in his apartment complex back in San Antonio.

The elevator ride to the fifth floor was uneventful, and he exited at the end of the hall. Moving with determination, he strode down the carpeted hall, stopping in front of apartment 512. He glanced up and down the hall, making sure no unsuspecting tenant stepped out, and pressed his ear against the door.

He didn't hear a sound. No television. No radio. Nothing to indicate anybody was home. Tempted to pick the lock and get a look around, he didn't dare. Getting caught in a strange city in a place he didn't belong wouldn't look good on the old resume. Besides, Ridge would laugh his butt off if he got caught.

When his cell phone rang, he wasn't surprised to see the caller ID was his twin's number. "Busy here, bro."

"What are you doing? I can feel the tension strong enough it's giving me a headache."

They'd always shared a bond, closer than any of his other brothers. Not surprising since they were identical twins. Most of the time they'd learned to block their emotions when they got too strong. Other times, they bled through no matter the circumstances.

"I'm contemplating a little B & E."

Ridge chuckled. "Lemme guess. Renee's apartment? Wait, of course it is. It's not likely you've turned into the friendly neighborhood cat burglar."

Shiloh leaned against the wall, a few steps from Renee's

front door. "I'm sorely tempted, just to get a quick look around. I saw her last night. Got close enough I could almost reach out and touch her."

"Seriously?" Surprise colored Ridge's voice, tinged with excitement. "Why didn't you talk to her? See if she remembers Lucas?"

"Something spooked her, and she rabbited. Raced out the back door of the nightclub and hopped on a bus before I could stop her. Figured it was a long shot, but I'm at her apartment, checking to see if she might've come home during the night."

Ridge sighed. "You find anything about why she's running or who she's hiding from?"

"Nope. Near as I can figure, she's running scared. And by scared, I mean terrified of her own shadow."

"I don't like it, either. This is the closest we've come to finding her in forever. And we've got some good sources between Antonio with the FBI, Dad and Gizmo's connections through the Army, all the years Lucas has been searching, and my pipeline of informants. That's not counting the endless hours I know you've put in working Renee's case, and not telling anybody."

Shiloh started at the sound of the elevator dinging and walked a couple of feet away from Renee's front door, not wanting to arouse suspicion. A man moving around in the hallway on the phone wouldn't attract a lot of attention. Standing in front of a single woman's apartment door, people would notice that.

"How'd you know...never mind. Of course you knew I was looking for her. There's this compulsion to find her. It's getting stronger every day. I can't explain it, but I've got this feeling she's in real danger, and if I don't find her, something awful is gonna happen."

"Want me to come there? I can be on a flight by tonight."

Shiloh pinched the bridge of his nose between his thumb and finger, feeling the beginnings of a tension headache. Or maybe it was the same one from last night, rearing its ugly head again. For some reason, his anxiety was riding high today, growing stronger when he thought about Renee. Something about the woman called to him on an instinctive level, and everything within him screamed to find her. Find her and keep her safe.

"Not now. If things look like they're about to get hairy, I'll call you. Right now, you'd be spinning your wheels. I'm following up on a hunch in a couple hours. Let's see how that plays out."

"Alright. If things change, call. I'll be on the first flight."

"I know. Give Maggie a kiss for me. I'll talk to you later."

Disconnecting the call, he gave a lingering glance at Renee's door, turned and slowly walked toward the elevator. He heard it ding as he approached, and watched a pretty brunette walk past, barely giving him a second glance.

Entering the elevator, he hesitated for a second before punching the ground floor button, and the doors closed. He was halfway across the lobby when he realized he probably should have looked to see which apartment the brunette headed for. Too late now.

He climbed behind the wheel, pulled the seatbelt across him, and glanced at the clock. Close to an hour left before he'd head back to the coffee shop and hopefully get a few answers from Tina. If he was lucky, she'd give him a clue where to start looking for Renee.

Renee heard what sounded like a kick against Tina's front door, and hesitantly walked toward it, intent on looking through the peephole. Right as she reached the door, she heard Tina's voice.

"It's me. Open up, I've got my hands full."

Swinging it open, Tina stared at her over the mound of clothing clutched to her chest. Striding past Renee, she dumped the pile onto the end of the sofa, turned and grinned.

"Sheesh, girl, I didn't ask you to empty out my closet. And why didn't you use the suitcase, I mean it was right there."

"I just did a grab-and-go. You're lucky I remembered to empty your underwear drawer, or you'd be going commando." Tina flung herself onto the sofa beside the pile of clothing. "I wanted to get in and out as quick as possible, in case somebody was watching your place."

"Right, and nobody would be suspicious of you walking out with armloads of clothing." Renee did a deliberate eye roll, and Tina tossed a throw pillow at her.

"There was this one guy, little old dude coming out of the gym, when I got to the lobby. Wanted to know if I was moving in or out, and could he get my number." She chuckled. "I told him it was donations for charity."

Renee sorted through the pile, grimacing at the wrinkles. Of course, wrinkles could be ironed or she could toss them in for a few spins in the dryer. At least she'd have clothes on her back if she needed to bolt.

"Did I say thank you?"

Tina gave her a toothy grin. "Nope." She bounded off the sofa. "I'll take it as said, though, because I've gotta book. If I run, I might make it on time for the job. I wasn't able to get everything you asked, but I'll make another run by your place this afternoon after work."

Renee gave her a quick hug, before Tina grabbed her purse, slung it over her shoulder, and was out the door. She wasn't sure what she'd have done if Tina hadn't been willing to help. Probably would've ended up sleeping in an alley, because she couldn't chance going back to her place last night. Of course, it wouldn't be the first time she'd camped out in the great outdoors, and unfortunately probably wouldn't be the last.

"I need to get to the bank." She wasn't about to be caught without ready cash. Truth was, she'd been careless, keeping the same name she'd used in Cincinnati. Hustling a new ID, at least the good stuff, cost money, and she'd had to leave most of hers behind, because the accounts had been frozen.

Pulling a pair of slacks and a knit blouse from the stack, she headed for Tina's bathroom to grab a shower, and then she'd change and head out. Luckily, Tina had given her a key earlier, so she'd run her errands, and put out a few feelers. See if she could figure out who the dark-haired stranger from the club was, and if his untimely arrival spelled trouble.

Half an hour and one cup of coffee later, she was out the door. First stop would be the bank. She didn't have much, but it would buy her a bus ticket south. Maybe San Francisco. Los Angeles if she could swing the price. Someplace with lots of people, because she'd found it was easier to get lost in the bigger cities. The frenetic pace, the energy, and the lifestyles of folks living in the city made it easy to blend into the background. She'd perfected being invisible when she wanted. Right now, that's exactly what she needed, to become a chameleon, unable to be spotted in the teeming masses.

The lady at the bank didn't question it when Renee wiped out her entire checking account, leaving only ten dollars. It would have caught somebody's attention if she'd emptied it. Instead, simply writing a check for cash was quick, easy, and didn't raise any eyebrows.

Next, she hopped on a bus and headed for her friend Nico's place. She knew this time of day he'd be sitting at the counter at his greasy diner in a not-so-upscale part of town. When she'd first decided to stay in Portland, after some judicious digging, she'd learned he was *the* go-to guy for obtaining quality ID. Fakes, of course, but impeccable; the kind that passed cursory examination without arousing undue suspicion from the government. He'd performed magic with the driver's license and passport using the Elizabeth Reynolds name, the one she'd been using for a couple of years. Guess her lack of forethought was coming back to bite her in the butt.

She drew a couple of stares from people climbing off and on the bus at various stops, and for the most part she ignored them, keeping herself inconspicuous. It took thirty minutes to get to Nico's, the cash burning a hole in her wallet. She hoped he'd give her a break, at least leaving her enough to get out of town.

Exiting the bus in a hail of exhaust fumes, she covered her mouth and coughed, then walked through the glass door. The overwhelming smell of greasy fried food permeated the air, making her a little queasy. Nearly the entire menu contained fatty, deep-fried items. Heaven forbid somebody wanted to order a salad, because they'd be out of luck at Nico's.

Nico sat in his usual place, the red vinyl-covered stool nearest the cash register, stooped over a cup of what she hoped was coffee. If it had been later in the day, she knew the coffee morphed to whiskey, the stronger the better. He didn't even glance up when she slid onto the stool beside him.

"Hey, Nico."

He spun his stool around, and faced her, his eyes widening. "Well, well, hello pretty lady. Didn't expect to see you round here so soon. Guess that means you're in trouble."

"I think they found me."

He shook his head, his unwashed hair sticking to the side of his face. Though his face was unlined, Renee had a feeling he was younger than he looked, except for his eyes. Those dark brown eyes held an old soul. One who'd seen the ugly side of humanity and managed to survive, despite the darkness people wrought.

"That's too bad. I hoped you'd find a measure of peace, at least for a while."

"Me, too. I'm going to have to leave, and…"

"You need new papers." Nico picked up his cup and tipped it, swallowing down the contents, before standing and walking around the counter.

"Yes. Except I'm kind of low on funds. I promise I'll get the money to you, but it might take a couple weeks." Renee reached inside her purse, ready to pull out her wallet, but his glare stopped her hand mid-motion.

"You know the rules. Cash only. Payable on receipt. No discounts. I'm no bargain basement sale. You want 'em fast and you want 'em good, that's a premium." Nico slid a fresh cup of coffee across the countertop, along with the cream and sugar. "No exceptions, honey. Not even for friends."

Renee honestly hadn't expected anything different, though she had to try. She needed ID good enough to pass scrutiny, especially if she wanted to get a job once she landed in California. But she gave it her best shot, because Nico's prices were high and his clientele paid without question simply because he was that good.

"I understand." She gave him a gentle smile, letting him know there were no hard feelings. "How much?"

Her stomach clenched when he tossed a number at her, because she hadn't expected it to be so high. When she first hit Portland, it had been half that amount. Biting the inside of her cheek to keep from crying, she wondered if she could get by with just the driver's license. Nope, it wasn't worth the risk. She needed the passport too, so she could sneak across the border if she couldn't shake her new shadow. Maybe she'd head north instead of California. Crossing into Canada might finally be far enough away from Darius and Eileen they'd stop hunting for her.

"Alright. That's gonna wipe me out, but I've got to have them. How soon can you have them ready?"

"You still have the old ones?" At her nod, he continued, "Hand them over and I'll use those photos, it'll save you a bit. Probably take a couple days."

Renee swallowed and took a deep breath. A couple of days. Tina would let her stay that long. If she was careful and kept out of sight, it might be enough time. Maybe.

"I can do a couple of days."

Nico leaned on the counter and stared at her, assessing her, maybe judging her, but he was a hard character to read. He was surly and gruff—and that was on his good days. Narrowing his eyes, he pointed a finger at her.

"Two days. I'll get it done. Want me to call you?"

She shook her head. "I had to get rid of the cell. I've got a burner coming tonight. I'll be back in two days."

Huffing out a sigh, he muttered, "Late afternoon, definitely before dark. I don't want you in this neighborhood after dark."

Standing, she held out her hand and waited. He looked at it long and hard, before wrapping his big paw around hers. "Thank you, Nico. I'll never be able to repay you for all your help."

"Stay alive, that's payment enough. Figure out a way to get whoever's after you off your trail permanently."

"I'm working on it."

Without another word, he disappeared into the kitchen, and Renee knew she'd been dismissed. Clutching her purse against her side, she walked outside, taking in the grime and soot coating the buildings. An aura of desperation permeated her surroundings. Hunching her shoulders, she scurried toward the bus stop, knowing it was past time to get back to Tina's apartment.

An eerie feeling washed over her, leaving goosebumps trailing along her skin. The sensation of being watched overwhelmed her, and she furtively glanced around, doing her best not to draw attention. Maybe it was the place; it wasn't the safest section of the city. She'd been careful not to leave a trail, taking a couple different buses to get here after she'd left the bank. Had it been enough, or had she picked up an unwanted tail?

When the bus pulled to a screeching halt, she climbed aboard, and settled onto a seat about halfway back. Nobody climbed on at her stop, and she exhaled a long sigh and lowered her head.

She was safe. For now. How long that might last was anybody's guess. Yeah, it was time to move on to the next town, stay one step ahead of Darius and the tall, dark, stranger he'd set on her trail.

CHAPTER FOUR

Shiloh had a dickens of a time finding a parking spot even though it was after ten by the time he got back to the coffee shop. Fingers crossed he'd find the mysterious Tina working her shift and willing to answer a few questions.

Opening the glass front door, sounds bombarded him from every side. Dozens of voices, conversations filled with laughter, rock music coming from the speakers high on the walls, and the sound of orders being yelled out from the windowed area behind the counter. Every table in the place held patrons getting their morning java jolt. He shook his head and barely kept from rolling his eyes. Didn't anybody work in this town?

Scanning the crowd, he noted the woman he spoke to earlier, and when their eyes met, she nodded her head toward the right. Immediately he spotted the dark-haired woman passing cups to a couple of college-aged guys, one of whom had his gaze glued to her chest. He chuckled, remembering those days when hormones overwhelmed common sense.

Something about her looked familiar, though he only saw her from the side. The hairstyle she sported was short and sassy, curving under at the nape of her neck. Sleek and smooth, the dark color reminded him of the coffee they served here in the shop.

When she spun around and walked away from the table, that's when it hit him. It was the woman he'd seen getting off the elevator at Renee's apartment. No way running into her again was a coincidence. Maybe karma was smiling on him for a change.

Trying not to be confrontational, he stepped into her path and smiled. "Excuse me, are you Tina?"

She eyed him up and down, and gave him a flirtatious smile, her eyes twinkling with good humor. "I am. What can I do for you?"

"My name's Shiloh Boudreau, and I wondered if I might ask you a couple of questions? I was in earlier today, and Gertie," he motioned toward the owner, "mentioned you'd be working and might be able to help me out."

Tina gave him another smile, this one a mixture of sultry and sweet. Not an overly aggressive come-on, but enough to let him know she'd be interested if he wanted a little more than coffee and conversation. Another time, another place, he might have taken her up on her unspoken offer.

"If Gertie vouches for you..." She motioned toward a side door with an employee's-only sign affixed, and he followed her, praying she'd have the answers he needed. Finding Renee had, without him being consciously aware of when it happened, morphed into almost an obsession. He might downplay it, spout off about reuniting her with her long-lost brother, but somehow during his search that had become only a half-truth. Seeing her in the flesh, the fantasy converging with the mystery, manifested into something beyond a simple P.I. case.

Tina led him to a tiny back office with an old-fashioned metal desk with a faux woodgrain top, steel legs, and drawers. It dominated the space, leaving barely enough room for an office chair on one side, and a plastic folding chair directly across. One two-drawer filing cabinet sat in the corner, with a mountainous pile of papers atop it, threatening to erupt into an avalanche with the slightest gust of air.

"Alright, Mr. Boudreau. How can I help you?" The dark blue of Tina's eyes appeared sincere, but he couldn't help spotting a mischievous twinkle in their depths.

Time to turn on the charm.

"Tina, I'm looking for someone. A friend of yours, Elizabeth Reynolds."

The change in her was instantaneous. The oh-so-subtle flirting, the thinly veiled interest disappeared as though it never existed. In its place her expression was completely walled off and guarded.

"Sorry, can't help you. If that's all, I need to get back to work."

"Please, Tina, I'm not trying to hurt Elizabeth." Reaching into his pocket, he pulled out a business card, realizing he probably should have started with that. "I'm a private investigator from Texas, and I—we—have been looking for her for a long time. Years, in fact."

She glanced at his card before tossing it onto the desk. "Like I said, sorry, I can't help you."

"Can't or won't?"

"Does it matter?"

He scrubbed a hand over his face, knowing he'd taken the wrong tack. "It matters. I only want to talk to her. There are things she needs to know, life-changing things. Could you at least give her my card? Ask her to contact me?"

Tina studied him so intently it felt like she looked into his very soul. Whatever she saw must have swayed her, at least the tiniest bit, because she relaxed enough to lean against the wall. "Give me something, Mr. Boudreau. One good reason I should tell her anything."

Ah, she does know where Renee is or knows how to get in touch. That's at least a step in the right direction.

"The reason I want to talk to her is…you know, this is difficult to sum up in a few minutes of conversation. Do you get a lunch break? Maybe I could take you out and explain why I need to talk with Elizabeth. I promise the reason isn't about bad news. Just the opposite, actually."

Tina ran a hand through her hair before pushing it behind her ear. "I don't usually take a lunch, but lemme ask Gertie. Since she knows you, maybe she'll give me a break."

Shiloh let out the breath he'd been holding and smiled, hoping she didn't read the panic he held at bay. Right now,

Tina was his biggest lead to finding Renee. He couldn't afford to let her slip through his fingers.

"Be right back."

He watched her step through the partially open doorway and moved to where he'd have a better view of the front of the coffee shop. Tina spoke with Gertie, waving a hand around and then pointing back toward the office. At Gertie's nod, the knot of tension in his gut unfurled, and he exhaled slowly.

Tina pushed the office door fully open and motioned him through. "Gertie's gonna give me a lunch break today. I don't know what you did to charm her, but she's in a really good mood."

"She seemed pleasant when I talked with her this morning."

Tina's eye roll spoke volumes. "Trust me, that's not Gertie's norm. Anyway, there's a Chinese buffet about a block and a half west of here, on the opposite side of the street. China Palace. Meet me there at one thirty."

"Thank you, Tina."

"Your story better be good, Mr. Boudreau, or I guarantee you'll never find Elizabeth. I'll make darn sure she's so far underground, you'll be knocking on Satan's front door before you dig deep enough."

"Understood. And call me Shiloh."

She chuckled and made a shooing motion. "Go on, get out of here before Gertie changes her mind."

With one last look, Shiloh headed out the front door and slid behind the wheel of his rental. Having a couple hours' free time, he decided following up a couple of old leads might be a good idea. Plus, he should probably check in with his office, see if anything needed his attention. He doubted it. The new addition to the company was a former Navy SEAL. He had a firm handle on all the ins and outs of the clients, and came highly recommended from Gizmo, his father's former Army buddy.

Pulling out his phone, he noted two missed calls. He'd turned it off before heading inside the coffee shop, not wanting or needing any distractions.

Dialing his brother's number, he wasn't surprised when Lucas picked up on the first ring.

"What've you got?"

"What, no hello, how are you? What's the weather like in Portland?" Shiloh felt the smile curving up his lips at his brother's frustrated sigh. "I've got a solid lead. I'm going to talk to somebody this afternoon who knows where she is."

"Seriously? How much do you trust this lead?" Shiloh could hear the underlying fear in Lucas' voice. While he trusted Tina would show up for their lunch meeting, he didn't want to make false promises of answers he might not get.

"All I can say is she's a solid lead. She seems very protective of Renee, or Elizabeth as she knows her. But she slipped up when we were talking, so I know she knows how to get in touch with your sister. I'm close, bro. We're going to find her."

"I'm frustrated because this is the closest we've been in years. I'm afraid to get my hopes up. What if she takes off again?" Lucas sighed. "I just want to make sure she's alright. That she's happy. Except my gut's screaming at me that she's running from something big enough she's scared, and I can't help her. I feel useless."

"Hate to admit it, but I think you're right. The good news is, once I catch up to her, get a chance to talk with her, I can assure her that we'll have her back no matter what. Whoever is after her, we'll stop them." Shiloh's gut clenched even thinking about Renee in trouble. His intuition screamed she was in danger, and that it was closer than any of them realized. Finding her felt like an itch beneath his skin, driving him with an insatiable urgency he couldn't quench.

"Does she look like the picture?" Lucas' tone had taken on a wistful quality, and it tugged at Shiloh's heart. He had all his Boudreau brothers, and he had his twin, Ridge. Even thinking about losing any of them made him cringe. Lucas had lost his flesh-and-blood sister, a physical part of him. The whole time they'd been growing up, Shiloh knew it had eaten at Lucas about living without her. The not knowing, wondering if she was alive or worse, if she'd ended up with people who hadn't loved and cared about her—or worse.

"Bro, she's beautiful. That pic Heath sent doesn't begin

to do her justice. You look enough alike, there's no mistaking you're related."

"I've got things cleaned up here, and I can head out to Portland and let you get back to your life soon."

"No!" Whoa, Shiloh hadn't meant for that to come out quite so harsh. "I'm already here, and I've got it handled. I've established a few local contacts, so I've got a working base. You need to stay and be with Jill. Things at my office are covered since I hired on a partner. Let's play it by ear, and if I need you to come out, you'll be the first person I call."

"Promise you'll call if you find out anything. No matter how small, I want to know."

"You've got my word, bro. I've gotta go. I'll talk to you soon."

Shiloh disconnected the call and leaned back against the headrest, closing his eyes. The frustration and anger mixed with hope in his brother's voice made him want to cry. Or scream. He didn't want to let another day go by without finding Renee. She might well tell him to take a hike and refuse to meet Lucas, but he wasn't giving up without a fight.

Renee opened Tina's laptop and logged into her e-mail account. Over the years, she'd picked up a couple of contacts, friends, for lack of a better term. People who kept their eyes and ears open and alerted her when Darius and

Eileen got too close. She'd gotten complacent living in Cincinnati, and it had almost cost her. Escaping with the clothes on her back and her go-bag, she'd been one step ahead of them.

She kept an open e-mail account, and only a select few had the address. Assumed name, of course, because she couldn't be too careful. Staying under the radar meant learning a few tricks to maneuver around the internet, including bouncing her signal all over the globe. So far, she'd been able to outwit hackers and trackers, though she had a gut feeling Darius would eventually hire somebody skilled enough to hunt her down digitally. Which was why she rarely got online, not unless she had to. Better safe than sorry. Or dead.

No updates from her contacts. Which meant both good news and bad news. Good, because she'd avoided Darius and Eileen for another day. Bad because she didn't know who the stranger was who'd been at the club watching her. Did he work for them? Somehow, she hadn't gotten the same hunter/stalker vibe she'd gotten from the others who'd managed to track her down in Cincinnati, Kansas City, and Miami.

Closing her eyes, she pictured him, the stranger from the club. Tall, she'd guess at least six feet. Not musclebound like some of the jocks she'd worked out with in her apartment, but he wasn't weak. Instinctively, she knew better than to underestimate him. Dark hair almost the color of a crow's feathers, it was cut in a shorter business style, with a little curl at the ends. She'd bet if he let it grow out, it would have a lot of waves. Most startling, though, were his eyes. They were a deep, rich brown, reminding her of her favorite chocolate ice cream. Eyes she could get lost in. Nope, she was too smart to fall into a trap just because somebody had a pretty face and a killer smile.

Stop it. You don't have time to daydream about a total stranger, especially one who might be working for Darius. Step up your game. Be sharp. Be ready. And don't be afraid to run for your life.

There would be enough to give Nico, but didn't leave a whole lot left over. If, and it was a big if, the stranger wasn't there because he worked for Darius, she'd need to look for a new job soon if she didn't want to live on the streets.

Renee jumped at the unexpected sound of the landline ringing, her hand flattening against her chest. Great, now she was jumping at the slightest noise. She stared at it, wondering if she should pick up the call. The answering machine clicked on before she'd taken two steps, and Tina's voice came on, calling her name.

"Elizabeth, if you're there, pick up. I need to talk to you."

Sprinting across the room, she grabbed the phone. "I'm here."

"Good. Listen, this guy came into the coffee shop this morning, asking questions about you."

Renee's stomach plummeted and she closed her eyes, steeling herself for what she knew was coming. "Tall, dark, good looking? Deep brown eyes?"

"Yep. Is he the guy from last night?"

"Sounds like. What did he want?"

Tina hesitated a second before she answered. "Dude says he's a private investigator—from Texas. He swore he wasn't here to hurt you, but he wants to talk to you."

"Tina, I can't."

"Well, I wanted to give you a head's up. I'm going to meet him at one thirty, find out everything I can. I didn't tell him anything and I won't. But I figure the more info you have…"

"You're meeting him?" Anxiety warred with intrigue deep in Renee's thoughts. She really wanted to find out more about the stranger, because just the quick glimpse or two she'd gotten the night before made her want to stay at the club. Talk to him. Get to know him. Shaking her head, she wiped away that silly notion. She didn't have time for relationships or even being attracted to a man. Not now. Maybe not ever. Her life was too messed up, unstable. How could she even consider pulling anybody into the nightmare that was her life?

"Yeah. Lunch at the China Palace. Don't you want to know why a private investigator from Texas is looking for Elizabeth Perkins? I know that's not your real name, so why is he calling you that? Do you have a connection to Texas you haven't told me about?"

Renee swallowed past the sudden lump in her throat and fought the sudden urge to burst into tears. There was one connection to Texas, though she'd done her best to lock it up tight and not think about him, because he was lost to her.

"Tina, please, don't tell him anything about me. Promise."

"I promise. That's why I called you first. If you want me to bail on meeting him, I will. Gotta say though, I didn't get the impression he's the type who'll give up without getting the answers he's looking for. I told him if I didn't like what he had to say, I'm outta there no matter how cute he is." Tina chuckled and Renee could picture her, tucking a lock of hair behind her ear, grinning like a loon.

"You're a good friend, Tina. If anything seems off-kilter about this dude, book it out of there. It might be nice to actually know why he's looking for me, instead of running into him without a clue what he's after."

"I've got you covered. I'll talk to you later, girlfriend."

Hanging up the phone, Renee nibbled on her lower lip, going over everything Tina had said. Had Darius and Eileen sent a hired gun to bring her back? Or maybe they'd opted for a final solution this time and hired a hitman. Just the thought made her insides clench, and her hands shake.

Life shouldn't have to be lived like this. Always on edge. Always running, never settling down. Always trying to stay one step ahead of the hunter. She was tired of being the prey.

Standing, she walked to the little entry of the apartment, and picked up her purse and the windbreaker hoodie she'd borrowed from Tina. Within seconds, she was out the door. She was tired of being the victim, of being at the mercy of everybody else. That stopped today. Exiting the apartment building, she glanced left and right, and then started walking toward her destination.

The China Palace.

CHAPTER FIVE

D arius Owens stared at the computer screen, a scowl marring his otherwise handsome face. He hated when he received bad news, and for the past couple of months, every time he checked his accounts, that's all he saw. Of course, he blamed his wife because she couldn't keep her flapping lips shut. On the bright side, she'd learned her lesson. Never trust anybody. Nothing good ever came for sharing your secrets.

Reading the e-mail again, his hands fisted on the desk, resting on either side of the keyboard. He was sick and tired of incompetence, especially when he paid out the nose for supposedly the best of the best. Mercenaries didn't come cheap, especially ones who were purportedly some of the best trackers in the world, skilled at finding people who didn't want to be found. Yet Elizabeth continued eluding him like a puff of smoke.

"Darling, what's put you in such a foul mood?"

At the sound of his wife's voice, he glanced up. Eileen stood in the doorway, her blonde hair coiffed to perfection—as always. The woman cost him a bloody fortune in stylist bills every darned month. Between that and her Botox injections, and those little nips and tucks, she remained youthful appearing. Almost as beautiful as the day he married her. Too bad the inside didn't match the outside package, because she was a poisonous viper, and everybody did well to avoid crossing her. He'd learned the hard way to stay on her good side.

To the world, he ran their company with skill and aplomb. No one outside the inner sanctum knew Eileen was the real power. He'd been on the wrong side of her viscous temper enough times, and he'd learned to kowtow to her on most things.

Except when it came to Elizabeth or Joanna. Or whatever she called herself now. Hence the not-very-helpful e-mail from their hired gun. The mercenary managed to track her from Cincinnati to the West Coast, and felt pretty sure he'd narrowed it down to Northern California or Oregon. He'd already ruled out Seattle.

"Darius?" Oh, right, she'd asked him a question.

"Nothing to worry about, dear."

Her eyes narrowed as she leaned against the doorjamb, her ankles crossed in those impossibly high five-inch heels she tottered around in. While they did amazing things for her legs, making them look a mile long, he held his breath every time she climbed the massive front staircase. One of these days he expected to find her sprawled across the polished marble at the base with a broken neck because of those ridiculous shoes. Oh, well…

"Have you heard from Bruce?"

He barely refrained from rolling his eyes. Of course, she knew the name of their hired tracker. If he didn't know better, he'd swear she had the office bugged. That or his cell phone. While she might appear the vacuous blonde Barbie doll, nothing could be farther from the truth. She was one of the most intelligent people he'd ever met, a trait which attracted him to her in the first place. Who knew under her beautiful façade lurked the heart of a female hyena?

"I got word from him earlier today as a matter of fact. I was reading his e-mail when you got here."

"Tell me he's found her." There was a distinctly predatory edge in her tone, and it sent a chill down his spine.

"He's narrowed her location down to Northern California or Oregon."

Picking up a vase from a table just inside the doorway, Eileen flung it against the wall. It splintered into a million little pieces. Her high-pitched screech of outrage caused him to wince. "That's not good enough. It's taking too long. I thought Bruce claimed he could find anybody."

She stalked into the room and perched on the edge of his desk, her blue eyes shooting daggers his way. Even though there were times when he despised her, there were moments when she was magnificent and reminded him why he'd chosen her to be his bride.

"My love, he's close. He's thinking he'll have a definitive answer to where Elizabeth is within the next forty-eight hours." He knew the smile curving his lips was almost as vicious as hers. Finding Elizabeth was the number one item on his to-do list, and he wasn't about to let the troublesome woman slip through his fingers again.

"I don't like waiting." Eileen's exaggerated pout almost made him chuckle. Poor woman hated delayed gratification, and she'd been disappointed a lot recently. Ever since Elizabeth disappeared. He ground his teeth, thinking about how she'd managed to slip through their fingers more than once. When they found her...

"Patience, darling. I'm convinced he'll find her. As a matter of fact, I'm going to contact the pilot, and have him get the jet prepared."

Rising from the corner of the desk, where she'd sat moments before, she turned and leaned forward until her face was within inches of his.

"What a lovely idea. The minute you hear from Bruce, you'll let me know, yes?" At his nod, her smile grew, though it never reached her eyes. "I think I'll go pack a bag. I wouldn't want anything to delay us once we know where sweet Elizabeth is now."

She blew him a kiss and walked out of the office. Letting out a deep sigh, he turned back to the open e-mail on his computer. Re-reading the e-mail from the mercenary, he felt his heartbeat speed up, because he'd just lied to his wife. The e-mail contained a one-word answer, and it caused his adrenaline to skyrocket.

Portland.

CHAPTER SIX

Shiloh arrived at the China Palace several minutes before the appointed time. While his head told him Tina would show, he was on pins and needles, wanting to get the answers that might lead him to Renee. A sense of urgency filled him. Glancing down the street, he spotted Tina heading in his direction. When she got closer, he waved, watching her grin when she spotted him. She really was a pretty gal, and at a different time in his life, he'd probably have done a little flirting, maybe gotten a kiss of two. But right now, he wasn't interested.

"Sorry, things were a little crazy at the shop. Hope I'm not too late."

"You're right on time."

He pulled open the door and the fragrance of authentic Chinese food hit him, and his stomach growled in appreciation. Inside, he noted the massive rows of buffet tables, with steaming containers of deliciousness. Several people moved through the lines, picking out their favorite entrees, and from the look on their faces, they were enjoying their meals.

Once they were seated, Tina faced him, her expression

curious. "I'll admit, I've been thinking about our meeting this morning. You said you're a private investigator. I'll tell you upfront, after you left, I called the number on your business card. When I asked about you, they confirmed you own the company. Impressive, but I'm not gullible or stupid, so I also checked you out online. You know some interesting people, Mr. Boudreau."

"Please, call me Shiloh."

"Okay, Shiloh." She grinned. "What's it like to rub elbows with the rich and famous?"

He knew exactly who she meant. A couple of years back, he'd done some work for a professional football player who'd lived in Dallas, although he'd since moved to Las Vegas to play there. They'd become friends when he'd been working Jax's case, and he still called a couple of times a year. He'd also worked for a celebrity couple who'd been filming in the Austin area, and the wife had picked up an overzealous fan who'd bordered on stalker-type behavior. The police ended up involved, and the fan was serving time.

"Most of my clients are ordinary folks who simply need a little help when they're in trouble."

Tina studied him, her elbows on the table, with her chin rested on her interlocked fingers. Her eyes sparkled with mirth. "Why do I find that a little hard to believe, Mr. P.I.?"

Shiloh did a cross my heart motion. "I swear, most of my cases are small potatoes. Cheating spouses, insurance fraud. Most of the time it's kind of boring."

"Now I really don't believe you. Anyway, I'm starving. Let's grab some food."

They meandered through the line, and he loaded his plate with a little bit of everything, with a large heaping of teriyaki chicken, one of his favorites. With the first bite, he felt like he was in nirvana. His taste buds exploded at the sweet, tangy flavor.

About halfway through their meal, he knew he couldn't put Tina's questions off much longer. He didn't have any problem answering her questions, since she seemed on the up and up. Especially if it meant he'd find out about Renee.

"I know you're curious, so go ahead and ask me anything. I'll answer your questions, and then I'll ask mine. Sound fair?"

Tina nodded, and laid down her fork. "I don't know where to start. Why are you looking for Elizabeth? Is she in some kind of trouble?"

"Nothing like that. It's…personal. I'm trying to find her because—well, she's been—you know what, maybe I should tell you what I know about Re…Elizabeth Reynolds. Then you can quiz me."

Picking up her fork, she motioned for him to keep talking, while she popped a shrimp into her mouth.

"The woman I'm looking for goes by the name Elizabeth Reynolds now, but her real name, the name she was born with, is Renee O'Malley. When she was a young girl, she and her brother ended up in foster care in Texas." He watched

Tina's eyes widen with each word spoken. If nothing else, she listened intently and didn't attempt to interrupt him. "In the system, Renee and her brother ended up separated. Lucas O'Malley was placed in a wonderful, loving home with a family called the Boudreaus."

"From the name, I'm guessing they're some relatives of yours."

Shiloh nodded. "My parents. Douglas and Patricia Boudreau. They are the finest people I've ever met. Amazing foster parents to a rowdy bunch of hellions the system couldn't handle and turned them into the best brothers and friends in the world."

"You said foster parents. They weren't your biological parents? I mean, you have the same last name."

"Yes, they're my foster parents, although I've never looked at them as anything other than my folks. It's a tradition in our family on our eighteenth birthday to legally change our last name to Boudreau. Those they could adopt, they did. The ones not eligible to be adopted for whatever reason, still changed their name legally. We're all Boudreaus."

"That's so cool. Sounds like they're pretty awesome."

"If you'd ever met them, you'd agree. Anyway, Renee and Lucas somehow got separated after they'd been through intake, and Lucas ended up with us. When Douglas and Ms. Patti found out about Renee, they immediately started trying to find her, to bring her into our home with her brother, but something went wrong. Records went missing. Nothing in the computer systems, and we couldn't find Renee. It was like she'd vanished without a trace. Lucas was devastated, and swore he'd find her someday. He's been searching for almost twenty years."

"Twenty—holy smokes! And somehow you think Elizabeth Reynolds and Renee what'd you call her, O'Malley, are the same person?"

"Everything we've been able to uncover points to that fact."

Tina started to say something, then her gaze darted past him toward the door. Glancing over his shoulder, he froze at the sight of the beautiful redhead standing just inside the entrance. Without hesitation, she stormed over to their table, and moved around to stand behind Tina. Her jade green eyes sparked with anger.

"Okay, buster, you're looking for me? Well, here I am. And I want some answers. Who sent you?"

Shiloh slowly rose from his chair, never breaking eye contact with her. And it was her, there wasn't a doubt in his mind. Renee O'Malley in the flesh.

"Elizabeth, it's not what you think. I mean, yes, he's looking for you, but he's not one of the bad guys. He's—"

"Trust me, Tina, they're all bad guys in one way or another. I'm sick to death of running. Of hiding. Never settling down, never making friends because I'll have to leave them behind. He's" she gestured toward Shiloh, "just another in a string of people who've made my life a living, breathing nightmare."

Shiloh pulled out an extra chair at the table and gestured for her to sit. With a weary sigh, she slid onto it, and raked her fingers through her hair. He couldn't help wondering if it felt as soft as it looked. He was almost tempted to lean closer and see if she used scented shampoo, to inhale and mark her scent into his senses.

"Hello, Renee."

The bunching of her muscles at the mention of her real name was the only evidence she heard him. Both hands clenched into fists on the tabletop, and he itched to grab them, smooth his fingertips across the skin he knew would be softer than silk, and try to bring her a little comfort. But it wasn't his place, not now anyway. Maybe when she got to know him.

"How do you know that name? I haven't heard it since I was four years old."

At her admission, he felt a squeezing in his chest, a yearning to pull her close, let her know she wasn't alone anymore. She had a readymade family waiting to bring her into the fold. To love her unconditionally. But it was far too soon for that, it would probably make her run away even faster.

"From Lucas. Your brother."

At the sound of her brother's name coming from the stranger's lips, Renee's head began spinning. The ringing in her ears made her slam her hands against them, instinctively wanting to block out his voice. Deny the ache in her heart at the mention of Lucas' name. The memories were far too painful.

"I don't believe you. Lucas is dead."

"No, he's not. He's alive and well. Lives in Shiloh Springs, Texas. He's been looking for you his whole life, Renee."

"That's a lie. They told me he died. He went into a foster home and they killed him. They…I don't believe you."

Without another word, Shiloh pulled his cell phone from his pocket, and scrolled through his photos, finding one of Lucas and Jill, taken the day her bakery opened on Main Street. He handed it to Renee.

"That's Lucas and his fiancée, Jill. It was taken a few weeks ago."

He couldn't help noticing the slight tremble in the hand holding his phone, or the way her eyes devoured the picture. Watched her fingers slide across the screen, making it bigger. He wondered what emotions spilled through her. A heartbreaking sob emerged from her lips, and her eyes brimmed with unshed tears.

"How is this possible? I've thought he was dead. If I'd known, I'd have searched harder for him."

"He's never stopped looking for you, Renee," Shiloh said

her name again, wanting to reinforce it, make her realize she didn't have to hide anymore. "That's what I was just explaining to Tina. Lucas is part of my family. But he's worried about you. Did you know all the records regarding you from the time you went into the system disappeared? It was almost like you never existed. He never gave up. None of us did. Momma and Dad did everything they could, petitioned the state, but it was like you'd vanished in the night without a trace."

"I—I wasn't in foster care long. I don't want to talk about that. Tell me, was he happy? You said he's part of your family? Did he get adopted?"

Shiloh knew she wanted to know everything, but that was too long a story to tell while sitting in a restaurant, especially where prying eyes and ears could overhear details Renee might not want others to know about—not if she was still running from dangerous people.

"I know you've got lots of questions, and I'll answer them all. But I think we need to move this conversation somewhere with fewer prying eyes. Is there some place you'd feel more comfortable?" When Renee and Tina exchanged a glance, he continued. "If you don't mind, how about we move this back to my room?"

"I'm not sure that's the best idea."

"Let me finish. I know you don't trust me, and I under-stand and don't blame you. My room would be a neutral place, where you can leave any time. Plus, this way I won't know where you're staying, in case you decide you want nothing else to do with me." He gave the women a grin, letting them know he'd have no hard feelings either way.

Tina and Renee exchanged another long look, and Renee sighed. "Fine, but we'll get there on our own. Where are you staying?"

Shiloh rattled off the name of his hotel and his room number, feeling almost giddy. Seeing Renee face-to-face, hearing her voice, did strange things to his insides. He didn't have time to explore that now, he was too close to achieving his goal. Thinking about Lucas, he couldn't wait to tell him the good news.

"Gertie was in a good mood and let me have the rest of the day off, so I'm free."

Renee's mouth dropped open. "Wait, Gertie was in a good mood? How'd that happen?"

Tina jerked her thumb toward Shiloh. "She's been over-the-moon ever since she met him this morning. He charmed the socks off her. Never seen anything like it, girl."

Shiloh bit back a chuckle when both women turned their attention on him. What could he say, the ladies loved him.

Renee shook her head, shooting a glance in his direction. "Tina and I will meet you, because I want to hear about Lucas."

"Sounds like a plan. Let me take care of the check, and we can meet there in say…fifteen minutes?"

"Works for me." Tina stood and latched onto Renee's

arm, and tugged her to her feet. "I'll drive. Meet you there."

Shiloh watched the two women walk out the front door, feeling like he'd been swept up in a Texas tornado. Everything felt topsy-turvy and twisted around, but through it all one thing shone through.

He'd found Renee.

Seated in the passenger seat of Tina's Prius, Renee scrubbed her hands over her face, trying to make sense of the last few minutes. Was it possible Lucas was alive? Then again, why was she surprised? She'd been lied to her entire life, what was one more?

"You okay?"

"I don't know. Everything inside my head is spinning. It's like I'm looking through a kaleidoscope, with whirls of information scattered around in by brain, and I can't make sense of most of it. This Shiloh Boudreau tells me my brother is still alive. How is that possible? When I was old enough and first had access to a computer, I looked for him and found nothing. Do you think he's telling the truth?"

"My guess, and I'm only going by gut instinct here, is yes. Why would he lie? I mean, what's he got to gain?" Tina tossed her cell phone into Renee's lap. "It'll take a couple of minutes to get to his hotel. Go online and see if you find anything about your brother now. Shiloh mentioned the name of the town he lived in. What was it again? I remember it had his name in it."

"Shiloh Springs. In Texas." Fingers shaking, she typed Lucas O'Malley into the search bar, and watched as several sites popped up under it. Scanning the different URL sites, she spotted the name of a prestigious paper in Dallas that listed her brother, along with several articles he'd written. Clicking on the link, the first thing that popped onto the phone's small screen was a photo.

The breath seized in her chest as she stared at the familiar face. Oh, he was older now, mature, his face showing character and a touch of humor with his crooked grin. Drawing in a deep breath, she exhaled slowly, and touched his picture with her fingertip. She remembered that smile, one he'd worn so often when they were younger. He had the same hair and eye color as hers.

"It's him. Lucas." Tears streamed down her cheeks, and she leaned her head back against the headrest. "I've been such a fool. When I didn't find anything when I first looked, and was told he died, I stopped looking. I don't get it. Why'd they lie?"

"Don't know, but I'm guessing Shiloh's gonna have answers to a lot of your questions. But are you prepared to answer his? I got the distinct impression he's not somebody who's going to go away without getting what he wants."

"If all he wants to know is about my connection with Lucas, that's fine. He doesn't need to know anything else."

"Yeah, right," Tina murmured under her breath, but Renee still managed to hear it.

"Look, girlfriend, if he's who he says he is, helping out Lucas, I'm not dragging him into my mess."

Tina pulled the car into the parking garage of Shiloh's hotel and after a couple of minutes pulled into a spot. Turning in the seat, she looked at Renee and sighed. "You know I want you to be happy, right?" At Renee's nod, she reached forward and clasped her hand. "Part of wanting you to be happy is knowing you're safe. I know, I know, you can't tell me what you're running from or who's after you. But my question's this. Do you have to do it all alone? Maybe talk to Shiloh. I mean, the dude's gotta be a pretty good P.I., since he found you."

"I guess."

"I checked him out earlier," Tina broke off at Renee's snicker. "Not like that, perv. Okay, maybe I did check him out that way, too. I mean I called his office in San Antonio and spoke with his partner. Looked at his posted references. They all look legit. Listen to him, that's all I'm asking. If you think you can trust him, hire him. I've got some money saved up, so we can pay him a retainer, and let him investigate the crap out of whoever's after you."

Renee felt the waterworks threatening to start again. Her emotions felt like a roller coaster, dipping and rising so fast, she feared she might get whiplash.

"Have I told you lately what a good friend you are?"

Tina grinned. "I'm the best, and don't you forget it. Now, let's go meet with Mr. Sexy and find out more about your brother."

CHAPTER SEVEN

Shiloh glanced around the hotel room, slapping the lid of his open suitcase closed and tossing it into the closet. Maid service hadn't been through yet, so the bed was unmade, but otherwise things didn't look too bad. And why in the world was he fussing over a hotel room anyway? He knew why; he wanted to make a good impression on Renee. They'd gotten off to a rocky start already, and he wanted her to like him. How pathetic was that?

At the knock on the door, he ran a hand through his hair and checked his breath. Shaking his head, he muttered a curse under his breath and pulled the door open. Renee and Tina stood on the other side. Renee's expression contained a mixture of skepticism and hope, and he fought the urge to pull her into his arms and assure her everything would be alright. Reuniting her with Lucas was a no brainer. Fixing her other problem—whoever she was running from—that might take a bit more effort.

"Come in, make yourselves at home."

"Thanks." Tina sauntered through the open doorway like she owned the place, and he knew her eyes didn't miss a trick. Renee took a step forward, watching her friend, and if he hadn't been watching both women closely, he'd have missed the subtle nod Tina gave. Guess he'd passed whatever test they'd concocted.

"Why don't you ladies take the chairs by the table? Can I get you anything? Room service? It's on me, since we didn't get to finish lunch."

"No, thanks. I'd rather get this over with." Renee's voice was barely above a whisper, and he didn't miss the underlying anxiety in her voice. Not that he could fault her being overwhelmed. He'd hit her with a lot of information without a lot of warning. Kind of a one-two punch.

"Where would you like me to start?"

Renee met his stare, never flinching or looking away. "Tell me about Lucas."

Shiloh smiled, thinking about his brother. "He's awesome. I know he was in foster care for a little while before he came to live with the Boudreaus. Actually, he was there before me and Ridge. Did I mention I have a twin brother?"

Tina's chuckle filled the room. "I can't image two of you. The girls in Texas must go gaga when you both walk into a room."

"Not so much anymore. Ridge met a lovely woman named Maggie. They're engaged and planning a wedding."

"Off the market, huh? Too bad." She gave him a flirtatious wink, but there wasn't really any spark between them, and he knew it was an automatic reflex with her. Kind of like

Heath. He'd flirted like crazy with every woman he met. Until he found Camilla.

"I know Lucas got labeled as a troublemaker in foster care. Gave them fits when he first got shuffled into the system. Douglas, he's our dad, has a reputation of taking in some of the harder cases. He's got a couple of contacts in the Texas Child Protective Services, and when they get somebody who's a 'special case', they'll call him."

"What do they consider a special case?" It was the first time Renee had spoken since he'd begun talking about Lucas. Shiloh watched her fingers tug at the bottom of her shirt, pulling at a loose thread, toying with it like a lifeline. It had already unraveled a couple of inches, and he wondered if she'd pull the whole thread loose before they finished.

"Douglas and Ms. Patti have made a home for boys, usually preteens or early teenagers, who've been through troublesome pasts. Drug addicted parents. Abusive parents. In my case, I had a father who was murdered because he was in the wrong place at the wrong time. My mother and Ms. Patti were friends for many years. When she was diagnosed with cancer, and knew she was dying, she implored them to take Ridge and I into their home and their family."

"Didn't you have anybody else, family who would have taken you in?"

Thinking about the Calloways, his biological grandparents, he fought to keep the grimace off his face. As far as he was concerned, they might carry the same DNA, but he'd never call them family.

"Let's simply say living with the Boudreaus was a miracle for me and Ridge."

"Sounds like there's a lot more to your story than the abbreviated version you're sharing." For once, Tina didn't have the teasing, flirty tone in her voice. He simply nodded. His history wasn't something he was ashamed of, but it also wasn't something to be tossed around in casual conversation. Most of the locals in Shiloh Springs knew it; shoot, they'd lived through it with them. While there wasn't an out-and-out feud between the Boudreaus and Calloways, they weren't all warm and fuzzy, either.

"Maybe I'll share that story another time. Right now, let's get back to Lucas. Douglas got a call from one of his contacts, saying they had a young boy who could use his help. Lucas was younger than the boys he and Ms. Patti usually brought into their home, and from the way Douglas tells it, he debated long and hard before agreeing to meet the kid. Said it took him less than five minutes after that to sign the paperwork and bring him home."

As he told his brother's story, his gaze stayed locked on Renee, studying her expressions. Though she tried to hide it, she listened with rapt attention, soaking up every word about her older brother. It would be obvious to anybody with half a brain cell that she'd never forgotten Lucas. A knot formed in the pit of his stomach, thinking about all the years they'd lost because of some incompetent boob in CPS splitting up the siblings.

"Lucas had a rough couple of weeks in the beginning. Momma said it broke her heart watching him alternate between moping around like a lost soul and getting into knockdown, drag outs with Antonio and Liam."

"More brothers?" This question from Tina, and he nodded, shooting her a grin.

"There are quite a few of us. Let's see there's Rafe, Antonio, Brody, Liam, Lucas, Dane, Ridge, Heath, Chance, Joshua, me, and of course Nica. She's the baby of the family. There were some others, ones who ended up aging out of the system and leaving for greener pastures, and a few who didn't—adjust—to living at the Big House."

"That's a big family. Are all of you…"

"Adopted? Yes and no. Not everybody could be adopted, for varying reasons. The ones who could and wanted to be got adopted. Those who couldn't be adopted legally changed their name to Boudreau as soon as they turned eighteen. Everybody except Lucas. He's still an O'Malley."

"Why?" Ah, finally, Renee spoke. He knew she'd been paying attention to every word.

"Lucas wanted to make sure if you ever came looking for him, you'd be able to find him. He kept the O'Malley name, though everybody in Shiloh Springs considers him part of the Boudreau clan. He's my brother as much as any of the Boudreaus. That's the thing, even though none of us share the same blood, the same DNA, we're family. It doesn't matter to any one of us what he calls himself, he's our brother."

He watched a single tear slid down her cheek, followed by another and then another. The breath caught in his chest at the sight, and he reached for the box of tissue on the dresser, handing it to Renee. Pulling a couple free, she wiped at her eyes, blotting away the wetness.

"Renee, I didn't—"

"It's okay. I'm happy he had a good life. When I got a little older, and fully understood what happened to us, that's all I wanted—for Lucas to be happy."

"He is. He's in love with a good woman, and he's moving back to Shiloh Springs. Trust me, that fact alone has made Momma ecstatic. I think she wants all her young'uns in one place." He reached forward and gently clasped one of Renee's hands in his. "Would you like to talk to Lucas?"

Renee's eyes widened, staring at him with a mixture of wonder and, if he wasn't mistaken, fear. Which didn't make any sense, because Lucas would never, ever do anything to hurt his sister.

"I can't." Her words were barely above a whisper, and Shiloh glanced over at Tina, who shrugged. Guess she didn't understand any more than he did.

"Renee? Is it okay to call you that or do you want me to call you Elizabeth? I've always known you by Renee, but if you'd rather…"

She gave him a watery smile. "Renee. I haven't been

called that in a long time. For a while I was Sarah. Then Emily. The last couple of years I've been Elizabeth. I'd like you to call me Renee."

At her almost timid smile, it felt like a fist squeezing in the center of his chest, and his heartbeat pounded loud enough he could heart it. "Renee. I know you've been moving around a lot, changing your name. I don't know the reason, but whatever it is, let me help you."

"You can't."

"Believe me, there's nothing too bad we can't fix it. You've got a big family, even though you don't know us well yet. We'll help you, find a way to keep you safe. I'll do anything to make sure nobody ever hurts you again."

Renee tugged her hand loose and stood, putting several feet between them, the gulf like a giant canyon, and he felt bereft without her hand in his. Like an almost invisible connection with her, one which went deeper than simple friendship or familial feelings.

"Nobody can promise me that. I'm glad we talked, and you told me about Lucas. It helps knowing he's healthy and happy. But I can't be part of your world. I mean his world. It's too late."

"Elizabeth, I mean Renee, please don't do this. Girlfriend, I know you. You're about to hit the road again, aren't you? Don't deny it, because you know you can't lie to me. Please, listen to Shiloh." Tina waved a hand in his direction, though she didn't even glance at him. "Look at him. Really, take a good, long, hard look. I don't trust easy. Heck, I rarely trust anybody, but there's something about Shiloh that makes me believe he's telling us the truth. Let him in. *Trust him.* If he says he and his brothers can help, I say let them. I worry about you. You're always looking over your shoulder. Always scared. I hate it. Please, please, let him—us—help."

Shiloh watched a myriad of emotions race across Renee's face, could almost hear the internal dialogue running through her head. Maybe he'd approached this whole thing wrong, but he'd been so anxious to find her, see her face-to-face. He couldn't—wouldn't—let her slip through is fingers now. If he lost her…

"You don't understand, I can't drag either of you into my mess. I will not put your lives in danger, and they will be if I stick around."

Before Shiloh could open his mouth, a cell phone rang. Wasn't his. Tina pulled hers out of her pocket and mouthed the word "sorry" before answering. He only half-listened, most of his focus on Renee. The instincts he trusted when working a case were blaring like an alarm bell. The minute she left this meeting, she'd run. It didn't take a rocket scientist to figure that one out. How could he stop her?

Tina disconnected the call, and he noted how pale she'd become. Whatever the caller said, it wasn't good news. He hoped it wasn't serious because he couldn't afford to let his attention be split. Right now, he needed every ounce of concentration focused on Renee.

Tina turned to face Renee and took a deep breath. "That was Gertie. She said somebody just came by the coffee shop looking for you. Said he was pretty pushy when she told him she didn't know anybody named Elizabeth Reynolds. Claimed he had an aura about him she didn't trust."

"No, no, no. I waited too long. I—I have to go." Renee turned to Shiloh and grabbed both of his hands. "Tell Lucas I'm glad he had a good life, and I want him to be happy. But he's got to stop searching for me."

"Renee, come with me. You need to get out of Portland. I'll take you to Texas. You can stay at the Big House, at least until you've got time to make better plans than running in panic. Being unprepared leads to mistakes and gives the upper hand to whoever's after you. I promise you'll be safe in Shiloh Springs." He squeezed her hands a little tighter when she tried to pull free. "Trust me."

"I...Shiloh..."

Tina interrupted Renee before she could object again. "Go with him. If you're going to leave anyway, take him up on his offer. It'll give you time to get a new ID, pick a place where nobody will find you. Shiloh Springs sounds like a good place to start over."

"Oh, Tina. I'm so sorry I've pulled you into the middle of my mess."

"Make it up to me by letting Shiloh help you. Between him, his brothers, and you, figure out a way for you to be safe." Tina pulled Renee into a hug, and Shiloh knew their bond wouldn't break despite putting distance between them. He had the feeling he'd be seeing a lot more of Tina, probably sooner rather than later.

"Renee?" Drawing her attention back to him, he waited for her answer.

She closed her eyes and drew in a shuddering breath, before opening them. "Okay. What do we do?"

"Leave it to me, sweetheart. Say your goodbyes while I make a couple of calls."

Turning his back to her, he breathed a sigh of relief. It had been close, but he hadn't been about to let her run again, not without him. This was better, though. Getting Renee to Shiloh Springs solved a lot of things, including reuniting her with Lucas.

Pulling out his cell phone, he texted the one person he knew could move mountains—his momma.

CHAPTER EIGHT

Renee sat beside Shiloh, her hands clutching the armrests of the plane's seat. She was a lousy flyer, always had been, but somehow this flight caused an army of angry aliens to fight inside her stomach, clawing to escape captivity. Drawing in a deep breath, she blew it slowly out through her mouth, then repeated the action, imagined the plane safely on the ground, and her getting off this giant tin can of death.

"It won't be long now." Shiloh's voice pulled her from her thoughts of doom and despair, and she glanced at him, felt his calm demeanor wash over her, and loosened her grip on the armrest. She wouldn't be surprised if she left behind claw marks from where her nails dug into it.

"Sorry I'm being such a baby. I hate flying."

"Must have made it difficult moving from place to place."

She shook her head, thinking about all the ways she'd maneuvered and finagled to stay clear of the friendly skies. "Not really. Buses, trains, they tend to keep their wheels on the ground. I drove when I could, walked when I had no other choice. I rarely got on a plane, mostly because I couldn't afford it. But also," she waved her hand, indicating the confines of the plane's cabin, "claustrophobia might play a role, too. I'm sure I've got some kind of complex about being in tight spaces without a clear way out."

Shiloh reached between their seats and clasped her hand, and she felt the warmth and strength in him when his hand touched hers. What must he think of her, acting like a scaredy-cat, simply because she hated knowing her feet weren't firmly on the ground? Millions of people flew every year, and hardly anybody plummeted out of the sky. Seriously, what were the odds the one time she boarded a plane, it would plummet from thirty thousand feet? But while her brain told her everything was okay, her imagination played havoc with her subconscious.

"We'll be landing in Houston in about twenty minutes. Think you can hold out that long?"

She gave a halfhearted chuckle. "Not like I've got much choice, do I? What am I gonna do, open the door and step outside for some fresh air?"

She noted the corners of his lips curling up at her joke. "Everything's going to be okay. Once we land, we'll pick up my car from long-term parking and drive to Shiloh Springs. Momma's got everything set up for you. The guest room's ready, and between her and Dad, they'll make sure nobody sets foot on Boudreau property without their say so."

"Shiloh, I'm scared." The words spilled out before she could stop them.

"I know you are, sweetheart, but I promise I'll keep you safe. Once you're settled, we're going to sit down, just you and me, and you will tell me what's got you running scared. Then we'll fix it."

She shook her head, both in denial and to keep thoughts of Darius and Eileen from lurching to the forefront. Dealing with them wasn't on her top ten list, even on her best days. Today, they didn't rank in the top one hundred. The only bright spot in ages was meeting Shiloh. While she still wasn't sure how she felt about the dark-haired, maybe brother-by-almost-adoption, he made her feel things. Things she'd never experienced before. The thought alternately excited and terrified her. She couldn't afford to let her feelings, her whirlwind of swirling emotions, run roughshod over her intellect. Managing to stay one step ahead of Darius and Eileen kept her alive this long. She wasn't ready to toss in her chips yet.

"Will Lucas be at your parents' ranch?"

Shiloh chuckled. "I wouldn't be surprised if he's standing at the end of the front drive waiting for you. Momma said she's kept him corralled at the Big House, but even she might not be able to keep him away once you get there. He's been waiting a long time to reunite with you, and I expect he's going to vacillate between excitement and sheer terror that he'll be a disappointment because he didn't find you sooner."

"I...I want to see him, too. Everything's happening so

fast, I'm not sure what to expect. Lucas is a memory, you know? A good memory, but I'm afraid I've built him up to be something he's not. In my head, I know he's a grown adult with a life I know practically nothing about. But I don't picture him that way. To me, he's still a freckle-faced kid, standing there screaming while the foster care people took me away. It's been twenty years. I'm not sure how I'm supposed to act around him."

"Simply be who you are. Renee O'Malley."

Her fingers tightened around his hand, clammy and cold, and she welcomed the warmth his touch provided, because thinking about meeting Lucas made her want to throw up.

"I don't even remember who Renee O'Malley is any-more. Like Lucas, she's been gone for a long time. Maybe that's part of the problem. I've been so many people in the last few years, I don't know who I am anymore."

Shiloh's deep brown eyes burned with compassion and understanding. He leaned forward and brushed a soft kiss against her forehead. It was the lightest touch, soft as a butterfly's wing, a whisper of sensation against her skin, yet she felt it deep in her core, filling her with warmth.

"We'll figure that out, too. I'm going to make sure all your problems disappear, and you can be anybody you want. I promise."

With a contented sigh, Renee leaned against Shiloh, and placed her head on his shoulder, feeling something she hadn't dared feel in longer than she cared to admit.

Safe.

Once they'd disembarked, Shiloh steered Renee toward the front exit. He'd left his car in long-term parking when he'd flow to Portland to search for her, figuring if he had to stay too long, his business partner could pick it up. Though he'd probably grouse and give him grief for a few days for making him drive from San Antonio to Houston, he was turning out to be a surprisingly good choice for the PI company. Placing his hand on the small of Renee's back, he held her backpack and his duffel in the other hand when he spotted a familiar face. Nope, make that a couple of all-too-familiar faces.

His brothers stood by the exit, crowded around like conspirators in a bad spy novel. They leaned close, whispering, eyes scanning the debarking passengers. *Way to be subtle, guys.* When he locked eyes with Chance, who gave a sheepish grin, Shiloh barely bit back a laugh. Could he really blame them for wanting to get a glimpse of the woman they considered their sister? After all, they'd grown up with the same stories Lucas told about Renee. They'd all been part of the ongoing search for the missing O'Malley girl. Heck, if he'd been back here in Texas instead of in Portland, he'd probably be standing with his brothers, waiting to welcome Renee to Texas, too.

"I hate to break it to you, but we've got company."

He felt the slight stiffening of her spine at his words, her gaze whipping around the crowded airport. Leaning closer, he nodded toward his errant brothers, adding, "The three doofuses standing over there are my brothers. The blue-eyed blonde is Chance. The one with ditchwater brown hair? That's Dane. Wonder why he's here? He runs the ranch, and you usually can't pry him away from the spread without a national disaster occurring. The third clown is Antonio. I had no idea they'd be here. Sorry."

Renee's eyes widened as she watched the three men walking toward her. So different in outward appearance, Shiloh knew anybody who didn't know better would never think they were related. Still, he'd told Momma he didn't need anybody meeting them at the airport. Made him wonder how these three snuck away without her knowing. Only thing missing from this merry group was his nosy sister. If Nica showed up...

"Hey, little brother!"

Little brother? Seriously, Chance is only four months older than me.

"What are you guys doing here? I hold Momma we didn't need a ride."

"My fault. I couldn't wait to see our sister." Antonio gave Shiloh the side eye, and reached out his hand to Renee. "I'm Antonio Boudreau. I can't tell you how thrilled we are to finally meet you."

Renee slowly held out her hand, and Antonio enveloped it between his. Her eyes were wide, and she had that I'm-about-to-head-for-the-hills look, which was the last thing Shiloh needed or wanted her thinking about. Just like his brothers to ignore everything except what they thought best.

"I bet this is all a bit overwhelming," Antonio smiled, and he felt Renee relax against the hand Shiloh still held against her lower back. "Momma doesn't know we're here."

"She does now," Chance added, holding up his cell. "Looks like we're in for a world of trouble when we get home."

"I'm sorry. I don't mean to cause problems."

"Sugar, don't you worry your pretty head about it. We," Chance gestured toward himself and the other two lunk-heads standing beside him, "couldn't wait for you to get to Shiloh Springs. The whole family is beside itself, knowing you're finally coming home. Momma's not really mad. She's probably more frustrated that we snuck out without letting her tag along."

"Enough of this standing around, we should probably hit the road." Dane reached forward and took the bags from Shiloh, and he turned them loose, glad he had his hands free in case he needed to wrap them around Chance's neck. Dude better stop shooting those flirtatious glances toward Renee, or he'd…

What? I don't have any claim on her. What I feel toward the beautiful redhead is new and unexplored, and I'm not sure what it means. Maybe she doesn't feel the same. Even if she's clinging to me like I'm the only life preserver in the ocean, I'm just the only person she knows here.

"Lucas is gonna have a conniption when he finds out we snuck away from the Big House. Dad's got the grill going, so you'll have plenty to eat when you get home. Momma's been keeping Lucas running around, helping with odd jobs to keep him occupied, though he's about worn a hole in the floorboards in the hall. Jill's there, too."

Shiloh closed his eyes and counted to five before speaking. "Tell me everybody's not at the Big House. I told Momma to keep things low key. Renee's already been through a lot and hitting her with all the Boudreaus at once is more than any person should have to endure."

From the crestfallen expression on his brothers' faces, Shiloh knew he'd guessed right. Probably every Boudreau within a hundred-mile radius would be sitting front and center when they pulled onto the long driveway to the Big House. He could picture the front porch of the Big House packed with wall-to-wall bodies, all scrambling to get the first look at their special visitor.

"I'm sorry, sweetheart. Let's get the car and start heading toward Shiloh Springs. Once we're on the road, I'll call Momma and tell her to clear 'em all out."

"No, don't do that." Color washed into Renee's cheeks as she spoke. "It's kind of sweet, everybody turning out to meet me." She looked at his three brothers, studying them for a moment. "Thank you for coming. Shiloh's told me a little about each of you, but I hope you'll bear with me while I learn which name goes with which brother. The last couple of days have been…overwhelming, but in a good way."

Chance stepped forward and took Renee's hand and laid it in the crook of his arm, and patted her hand, shooting a wicked grin at Shiloh. "I'm glad you're here. You take all the time you need to get acclimated. Now, let's get you home. Momma is gonna love you, I promise."

He started walking toward the airport's electronic doors, Renee in step with him, and Shiloh fought the urge to race after them, rip Chance's arm off and beat him over the head with it. What in the heck was his brother up to?

"She seems nice. Can't get over how much she looks like Lucas." Dane fell into step beside Shiloh, matching him stride for stride. "I talked with Dad before we left. He's in agreement; we find out who's after her and take care of it. He can line up reinforcements if we need them."

Reinforcements. Shiloh smiled at the term. That was Douglas Boudreau speak for calling in his former Army buddies for a little extra muscle. Of course, a couple of them worked better with their brains than their brawn. If there was tracking involved, human or otherwise, they'd get a kick out of it.

"I haven't gotten the whole story from her yet, but she's definitely running scared. She was getting ready to hightail it out of Portland because she thought I was a mercenary sent after her."

"That bad, huh?" Dane's jaw tightened. "We'll make sure the ranch is secure. After Jamie got kidnapped, I had the whole place wired. Cameras, alarms, the whole shebang. Nobody's coming onto our land without us knowing."

Shiloh studied the determined set of his brother's shoulders, and his expression was one he rarely saw on Dane's face. He knew little Jamie's kidnapping shook the whole family. Jamie's father escaped from prison and grabbed that precious little angel right from under their noses, and wanted a million bucks for her return. A cold shiver raced down his spine. His father had offered himself in exchange for Jamie. Although he knew the family had money, between his father's construction company, Momma's real estate business, and the money from the ranch and cattle, they weren't hurting for cash. But if Evan had managed to get Douglas out of the country...

"When'd you do that? Dad didn't mention it."

A guilty flush crossed Dane's face. "I didn't tell him."

Shiloh glanced up and spotted Renee walking between Antonio and Chance. They were both animatedly talking to her at the same time. She kept looking from one to the other, and he grinned. If she stuck around, she'd have to get used to listening to more than one conversation at a time. Happened every day around the Boudreaus.

"What do you mean you didn't tell him?"

"Dad's been busy running Boudreau Construction. He

and Liam have been up to their eyeballs with problems on the job sites. Besides, I run the day-to-day operations at the ranch. Part of that is security. I made a decision, one that benefits the family, and keeps everybody safe. I had Ridge help because I wasn't going to cut corners. There's closed circuit cameras located along the pastures, alarms, infrared. You name it, we've got it. There's even a command center set up at my place to monitor things twenty-four/seven." Dane shot him a glare. "With our brothers getting engaged, planning weddings, and bringing kids into the equation, I'm not about to let anything happen. Never again."

Dane's voice was laced with a hard edge, something Shiloh couldn't ever remember hearing in the normally easygoing man. He blew out a long breath. Dane was right. They couldn't take chances with the women they'd welcomed into their clan. While Jamie was the only youngster, he knew it wouldn't be long before more kids were added to their family. The thought of them being in danger was unacceptable.

"I know a bit about security systems. Let me look at it once Renee's welcome party's over. Maybe I can spot any weaknesses."

Dane chuckled, slapping Shiloh's back. "You are just like your brother. He designed the entire system, top to bottom. Went over everything with a fine-tooth comb, and yet every time he comes to the Big House, he's looking for ways to upgrade things. Pretty sure you won't find any issues."

Shiloh nodded. "Ridge is good at what he does."

"But you're still gonna take a look, aren't you?"

He simply raised his brow, and Dane chuckled. With a grin, he trailed behind Chance and Antonio, his eyes glued to Renee. When she laughed at something Chance said, he felt a weight lift off his chest. She was going to fit right in with the Boudreaus.

Only one obstacle stood in the way of her finally finding some peace. Figuring out who hunted her, and eliminating the problem—once and for all.

CHAPTER NINE

"I can't believe you're finally here." Strong feminine arms wrapped around Renee, and she couldn't help hearing the soft sniffle as Shiloh's mother pulled her close. "We've waited a very long time to welcome you home."

Home. Such a simple word, but filled with so many emotions they nearly choked her. The concept seemed simple, yet never having lived anywhere she'd consider an actual honest-to-goodness home, a feeling of awe suffused her. Closing her eyes, she returned Ms. Patti's hug, allowing the feeling of warmth to wash over her. Taking a deep breath, she breathed in the subtle scent of vanilla coming from the woman holding her, along with more homey smells. Citrusy fragrances she recognized, similar to the cleaning products she'd used. Wood smoke she assumed came from the grill one of the brothers mentioned. The scent of fresh-baked bread.

"Momma, don't hog her. We all want to welcome Renee to the family."

At the feminine voice, Renee opened her eyes and glanced over Ms. Patti's shoulder, noting a young woman

87

dressed in a pink button-down shirt tucked into dark jeans. Long blonde hair pulled up in a high ponytail swayed with every movement, and golden-brown eyes studied Renee.

Taking a step forward, the young woman tugged on Ms. Patti's shoulder, and brushed a quick kiss against the older woman's cheek. The smile she flashed at Renee held warmth and welcome, and Renee felt the coil of tension deep inside begin to unfurl. She'd been a bit leery of her welcome, despite Shiloh's repeated assurances that the family would greet her with open arms. A little niggling doubt crept in during the drive from the Houston airport, which had been peppered with questions from Shiloh's brothers.

"I'm Nica. All these big lugs are my brothers. Don't worry," she added, threading Renee's arm through hers, "you'll get use to the overload of testosterone around here. If they get too aggravating, bop 'em on the head, and they'll back off."

"Um, okay?"

Nica chuckled and led Renee into the kitchen. The space was large and open, with a big window over the sink allowing light to flood the space. Every surface seemed to be covered with huge amounts of food. Platters piled high with corn on the cob, bowls filled with potato salad, coleslaw, and homemade rolls stood alongside cookies and brownies, and one of the prettiest cakes she'd ever seen outside a professional bakery.

The kitchen was also filled to overflowing with bodies.

Men and women ringed the open spaces along the walls, and she spotted a little girl with lopsided pigtails nibbling on what looked like a chocolate chip cookie. Tiny streaks of chocolate rimmed her lips with her next bite.

"Renee, meet the family. Family, meet Renee."

Chuckles met Nica's announcement, and Renee let go of the last bit of nerves and tension. The love in this family was a living, breathing thing. There wasn't a shadow of doubt this home was a happy one. Her heart overflowed with happiness at the thought Lucas had grown up here, amidst the love and laughter and comradery. He'd had a good life.

But one question lingered. Where was he? Looking around the kitchen, she searched for the brother she hadn't seen since she'd been ripped away from him so long ago. No auburn hair. No jade-green eyes. Where was he?

Nica leaned against her side and whispered, "He's out back. We," she swept an arm, indicating the family, "thought your first meeting should be private. Just the two of you, without a bunch of prying eyes."

"I…"

She felt a familiar arm slide around her waist and lifted her gaze to meet Shiloh's. "It's okay, sweetheart. I'll be right here. Lucas has waited forever to find you again."

"I want to see him, too. I'm scared. No, that's the wrong word. Nervous, anxious. What if he's disappointed?" Her words were barely above a whisper, and she hoped he couldn't feel her body tremble.

"Never gonna happen. He adores you. He's right outside, probably pacing back and forth, wearing a rut in Momma's vegetable garden. You can do this. Go out there and put him out of his misery. I promise everything's going to be okay."

Renee took a deep breath and nodded. Now if she could only get her feet unglued from the floor. Taking one tentative step, she reached deep for strength and then took another. With each one, her mind raced, whether it was from nerves or anticipation, she wasn't sure. When she reached the back door, she straightened her spine, pulling on all the courage she had. Deep inside, she knew Lucas wouldn't hurt her. She was simply afraid she'd built the anticipation into something so big the reality could never match her expectations.

With one final deep breath, she reached forward with a somehow now steady hand and turned the knob, opening the door. Pulling it inward, she glanced outside, and spotted a man standing several feet away with his back to her. Watched his body stiffen at the sound of the opening door, he surprised her by not turning around.

Sunlight glinted off his deep auburn hair, its color an almost perfect match for hers. He was tall, probably six feet, standing with his feet braced apart. Tension radiated from him in waves she could also visualize, matching her own trepidation.

"Lucas?"

He spun around immediately at the sound of her voice, and she inhaled at the first sight of her brother in over twenty years. Though he'd aged from the little boy she remembered into a fully grown man, she instinctively knew she'd have recognized him anywhere. At the smile beginning to crease his lips, her heart squeezed, and her anxiety disappeared.

"Renee? It really is you!"

He sped across the distance separating them, skidding to a stop about a foot in front of her. With a heavy indrawn breath, he lifted his hand and reach toward her, only to stop before touching her. His gaze caught hers, and she couldn't help wondering what he saw when he looked at her. Could he see the little girl who'd cried for months after Child Services tore them apart? Had he screamed and fought, trying to make them bring her back, fighting a battle he couldn't win? Because that's what she'd done, day after day, never accepting the lies she'd been told about giving her a happy home. She never believed for one second she was better off without her big brother, although she'd been fed so many lies by both her foster families and her adoptive parents.

"I can't believe this is really happening. A few days ago, I didn't even know you were still alive. Today, you're standing in front of me."

"It's a miracle." Lucas took another step closer. "I've missed you so much, peanut."

Her breath caught in her chest at the nickname. One she hadn't heard in what seemed like forever. Lucas had called her that as a kid, because she'd loved snacking on those crazy marshmallow circus peanuts their parents would buy by the bagful. He'd tease her even as he took wet cloths and wiped her sticky hands and mouth. Then he'd pull her close and make elephant noises and tickle her, pretending he was stealing her secret stash of the sweet treat.

"I haven't heard that name in years."

"Renee, I—I have to…"

Without another word, Lucas pulled her into his arms, hugging her tight enough she let out a little squeak. Without thinking about it, her arms reached around, hugging him just as tight. His ragged inhaled breath proved his emotions ran as deep as hers. Feeling his arms around her felt right, and she sighed, leaning her head against his chest. Being with Lucas again felt like coming home.

She wasn't sure how long they stood there, simply holding each other, without uttering a single word. Memories from her childhood sprang forth, one after the other, a kaleidoscope of colors swirling into each other. Like the time he'd crawled into bed with her during a vicious thunderstorm, huddling beneath the covers, holding a flashlight because she'd been afraid of the dark. Or the time he'd pushed her on the swing in their backyard. She'd fallen off and skinned her knee. He'd cried, thinking he'd hurt her. The cavalcade of images from the past rushed forward, one after the next, and she couldn't stop the tears streaming down her cheeks.

After what seemed an eternity, yet could only have been moments, she dragged in a ragged breath. Taking a step back, she dropped her hands to her sides. Lucas' cheeks were wet with his own tears.

"Ah, peanut, please don't cry."

"They're happy tears, I promise."

"There're some chairs around the side, if you want to sit. I want to know everything. Where you've been. What you've been doing. Did you have a good life? Everything."

Renee gave a watery chuckle at Lucas' rapid-fire questions. "I want to know all about your life too, although Shiloh's filled me in on some of it. Looks like you landed on your feet. The Boudreaus seem like good people."

Lucas grin lit his face, his green eyes shining. "They're amazing. Don't get me wrong, I loved our parents, and think about them every day. Just like I thought about you. There wasn't a day that went by I didn't think about you. I—we looked for you. Douglas and Ms. Patti spent years trying to find you."

Renee couldn't miss the way his eyes glinted like steel as he spoke. She didn't doubt his sincerity or the truth in his words.

"When I was old enough, I searched for you. I couldn't find anything. My guardians told me the state of Texas said you were dead." She didn't try to disguise her contempt when she mentioned her guardians. Pitiful excuses for human beings. The truth about them was bitter and ugly, and had no place in this happy reunion with her brother.

"They lied. I'd love to know why, though."

"We'll probably never know." Renee pasted a smile on her face and cupped Lucas' cheeks. "I'm thrilled to see how erroneous their information was, and you're alive—and from what I've heard—happily in love."

Another grin from her brother. "I am. You probably saw Jill in the kitchen. She can't wait to meet you."

Renee glanced over her shoulder, and bit back a laugh when she spotted several faces peering through the kitchen doorway. "We'll have plenty of time to talk later. I think your family is getting restless. Plus, I hear I'm going to get some real Texas barbeque."

"Dad's spent all morning getting the grill ready. Nothing he likes better than throwing steaks onto a sizzling hot flame. Claims it's his God-given right as a Texan male." He studied her face, adding, "We will talk later. I know you're in trouble, or you wouldn't have kept running and changing your identity, staying off the grid." He raised his hand when she started to interrupt. "Doesn't matter what it is, I'll help you. We'll help you. You are my family as much as the Boudreaus are. I know you've had a lot of stuff dumped on you the last couple of days, and knowing Shiloh, it most likely wasn't done in the most diplomatic fashion."

"Not true. He's been kind." She knew that wasn't the

most descriptive word to use when she thought about the man who'd barreled into her life, turning it upside down. Still, he had been kind. Patient. Understanding. But he also occupied her thoughts, even when he wasn't around. The man was an enigma, larger than life, and if she was being honest, he fascinated her. Made her want things she had no business wanting. It scared her, because for the first time, she wanted to stop running. Find out if what she felt was real, something that could grow and blossom into something greater.

"Never heard my brother called kind before. Lots of other words, but..." At her chuckle, Lucas reached out and clasped her hand. "I'm glad he found you and brought you home."

"I might not be able to stay. You need to realize that up front. If things get too dangerous for you or your family, I'm outta here. Nobody else is getting hurt because of me, Lucas."

"Give us a chance, Renee. I know you've been bombarded with a lot, and it's all a bit overwhelming. But you'll find the Boudreau clan protects its own. Whoever or whatever is threatening you, making you afraid, well, they've met their match if they think to go up against us. I give you my solemn word, you are safe here."

"Okay." She squeezed his hand. "We'll take things one day at a time. Now, let's head back inside and get this party started."

Renee allowed Lucas to lead her back inside the Boudreau home, hoping he was right and she could finally end this nightmare. But if he was wrong, she'd run far and fast before she'd allow Darius and Eileen to get their hooks into her newfound family.

Darius meticulously stacked the files, lining each corner up even with the one behind it. He realized he was more than a tad obsessive compulsive, but his extreme caution kept him alive when others had failed. Knowing everything had a place, a purpose, maintained order in his otherwise chaotic existence. Eileen was no help. She liked money and power. It didn't matter how she obtained it, as long as the coffers were full and law enforcement remained blind to where it came from.

Marrying her seemed like a coup at the time. He'd snatched her out from beneath his cousin's nose. Truthfully, it hadn't taken much effort, because Eileen might look like the typical flighty blonde, but nothing could be farther from the truth. She was a great white, a monster focused on her prey, and nothing and no one got in her way. Once she'd decided Darius had the ambition and drive to take her places, she'd walked away from her fiancée without a backward glance.

"Darling, how much longer are you going to be? We're

due at the Fosters' in half an hour." Eileen leaned against the doorframe, her beauty silhouetted by the chandelier's light. No matter how long they'd been together, she still fascinated and enchanted him. He'd never grow tired of not only her physical allure, but her astounding mind beneath the beautiful exterior. People underestimated her, to their detriment. Like the predator he'd thought of earlier, she'd chew them up or devour them whole before they even knew what hit them.

He tapped the corner of the file folders. "Let me put these in the safe, and I'm done, my love."

Straightening, she walked into his study, hips swaying with each step. "Have you heard from Bruce?"

Darius grimaced at the name. Using a mercenary, a gun for hire, rubbed him the wrong way. Elizabeth proved smarter and more elusive than he'd anticipated. She'd evaded his best efforts for several years. Part of him felt proud, because she'd fulfilled every instinct he'd had about her from the beginning. Cunning, intelligent, and clever, she'd slipped beneath his guard and managed to fool him into thinking she wanted to be part of his inner sanctum. To work with him, be guided by him, groomed as a rightful successor. Instead, she'd garnered enough information about the inner workings of his organization to take him down, have him thrown in federal custody for the rest of his natural life. Of course, his lovely Eileen would be right there with him, because she was neck deep and a willing participant.

"Not since the last time he called. If I haven't heard from him within the next twenty-four hours, I am seriously considering finding someone else. I don't trust him. Hiring unknown mercenaries, I can't be sure where his loyalties lie."

Eileen slid around in front of him and ran her bright red nail down his shirtfront. The brilliant splash of color against the bright white reminded him of blood. A premonition maybe? Shaking his head, he raised her hand to his lips, pressing a kiss against her palm. While he adored everything about his wife, he wasn't blind to her faults. Knew if and when an opportunity presented itself, she wouldn't hesitate to put a bullet between his eyes, and walk away without a backward glance.

"Darling, he's come through for us before. Elizabeth," she sneered, "might have eluded him, but he's determined to find her. I wouldn't count him out just yet. Remember, he came through for us with our little problem in Wyoming."

Darius nodded. She was right. Bruce had handled the situation in Wyoming. No muss, no fuss. At least nothing that could lead back to him. As far as he knew, the bodies still hadn't been discovered.

Turning, he punched in the combination and placed the files inside. With a quick move, he closed the door, and spun around, pulling Eileen into his arms. "What would I do without you, my love?

"Let's hope we never have to find out." Her hand cupped his cheek and she smiled, her loveliness snatching his breath away. Deep inside, where all his most carefully guarded secrets lay, he knew she'd betray him one day. Avaricious and without a moral compass, she'd been the perfect foil for him in every aspect.

Everything hinged on finding Elizabeth. She was the key to his survival. If Eileen managed to get her hands on the other woman first…

"Darling, what's wrong?" Her saccharine sweetness set his teeth on edge. Only a little while longer, and he'd have the upper hand again, but until then, he had to bide his time. Eileen would finally learn where her real place was in the grand scheme, and it wasn't at the top of the pyramid. It was beneath his boot heel.

"Nothing, my love. Time to go."

CHAPTER TEN

Standing beside his father at the oversized barbecue grill, Shiloh's gaze kept darting to Renee. He couldn't seem to help it. Sitting surrounded by his family, she tossed her head back and laughed at something Jill said. Watching her could quickly become the highlight of his day, and he realized the thought didn't bother him at all. Seeing her in the midst of his family, the way she fit in with ease, only solidified and acknowledged Renee was special.

"Son, unless you want everybody to know how you feel about that young lady, you need to stop watching her like a wolf about to pounce on a tasty bunny."

Shiloh turned his head and looked at his dad's grinning face and shrugged. Guess he wasn't exactly being subtle about his interest in Renee O'Malley. He couldn't bring himself to call her by the name she'd used in Portland. She was Renee, the girl he'd heard about all his life. Little sister to his brother. Always considered a part of the Boudreau clan, everyone looked on Renee as the sister of their heart, if not by blood.

Except he didn't feel brotherly toward her. What he felt

was somehow deeper, stronger, and he wanted her with every fiber of his being.

"That obvious, Dad?"

"To me, yeah. You're lucky everybody else is preoccupied with Renee, or your brothers might have noticed."

Shiloh drew in a deep breath, needing the moment to figure out what he could say. His dad noticed everything going on with his sons, from a bad mood to a bad breakup. Offered sage advice when asked for, and kept his opinions to himself unless he felt they could help. Shiloh couldn't remember a time his father's words of wisdom steered him wrong.

"I'm not sure what's going on. She fascinates me, unlike anybody I've ever met. She's smart and funny."

"Pretty as a picture too."

"Yeah, she's beautiful. If she was anybody else, I'd probably already have asked her out. But she's not just anybody; she's Lucas' sister. She's an honorary member of our family."

Douglas checked the doneness of a steak and flipped it over. When his eyes met Shiloh's, they were serious, his expression stoic. "You're right. She's part of our family. Lucas' sister, the one we've been searching for and hoping to find ever since your brother came to live with us. Doesn't mean you can't have feelings that aren't...familial. Look at Brody and Beth. I had a similar conversation with him not all that long ago. He was worried about making his feelings for her known, because he didn't want to make things difficult for Rafe and Tessa. Afraid if he dated Beth and things didn't work out, it'd drive a wedge between him and his brother, because Rafe is marrying Tessa."

"I didn't know that."

Douglas flipped over another steak and moved around a couple of burgers, the scents coming from the cooking meat eliciting a growl from his stomach. He hadn't eaten all day, except for a quick snack before getting on the plane, and he was starving. Nobody manned a grill like his dad. Momma might rule the roost when it came to her kitchen, but when it came to fixing the beef, it was all Dad.

"Took him the longest time to decide she was worth taking a risk on. Personally, I knew they were a good match. He looked at Beth the way you're looking at Renee. Difference is he knew Beth for months before he asked her out. You've only known Renee what, a couple of days? My opinion, for what it's worth? Give her some time. Let her get settled. Little gal's been on her own too long, and she's never been able to settle down and build a life." Douglas grinned, the laugh lines beside his eyes crinkling. "Court her. Do what Ridge said he was gonna do with Maggie. Woo her, but give her space, too. She's gonna be skittish for a bit. Let her realize she's home. We'll take care of whatever's kept her moving, eliminate the danger. Then you can sweet talk her into staying."

Shiloh glanced across the patio, watching his family interact with Renee. Rafe and Tessa sat to her left, with Nica on her right on the big outdoor sofa situated on the corner of the patio. Momma, Brody, and Chance sat in chairs across from her. Beth was perched on Brody's lap, his arm around her. He leaned forward and whispered something in her ear, and Beth glowed. There was no other word for it. Seeing them together, there was no denying their love and devotion to each other.

"You're right, Dad. I'll give her time. She's had so much thrown at her in the last couple of days. The timing could've been better, but I'll wait. Figure out who's after her, because she was getting ready to hightail it outta Portland. She's running scared, and I'm going to find out why and solve her problem. Then I'm going to figure out if what I'm feeling is real, or if it's all tied up in the excitement of the moment. Finding her, helping her, I—I want to give us a shot."

"You know I'll help. So will all your brothers. The faster we get a handle on things, the safer everybody will be. Now, I think it's about time to call everybody over for supper."

Reaching underneath the enormous grill, Douglas pulled out an old-fashioned chuck wagon iron dinner bell, one of those triangle-shaped ones with a separate striker hooked to the top. Grinning at Shiloh, he struck the bell several times, repeating the motion over and over. Shiloh noted his family staring, open-mouthed at his dad.

"Where'd that come from?" Shiloh pointed to his dad's new toy.

"Gizmo sent it to me a couple weeks ago. It's an antique

one. Said he found it in some shop. Figured I'd like it."

"Something tells me nobody else knew about your new toy."

"Nope," Douglas added, sliding the bell back onto the shelf under the grill. "Figured I'd surprise 'em."

"I think it worked."

The food from inside lined a long rectangular table, covered with a couple of plastic tablecloths. Shiloh couldn't remember a time that table hadn't been around. Even before they'd built this newer backyard patio area, the table had held pride of place on the old one. It was big enough to seat at least twelve with room left over, and as young'uns they'd shared many a happy meal surrounding the old table. That was one of the things he hated about living in San Antonio—these family get-togethers, where everybody gathered 'round the old gal and swapped stories. Shared what was new in their lives, gossiped about the town's goings on, and spent time as a family. He'd never admit it, but he missed times like this.

As his family started across the patio, Shiloh spotted somebody coming around the corner of the house. Recognizing first the woman and then the man, his spine stiffened with rage. What were they doing here? He knew darned well nobody invited them, because every one of the Boudreaus knew how he felt about the Calloways.

His grandparents. At least biologically. As far has he was concerned, he wasn't any relation to them. Not since they tossed his mother out before he and Ridge were born. After she died, they hadn't even attempted to gain guardianship of them. Patti and Douglas Boudreau were his parents, his family, not the worthless couple headed toward them.

"Why are they here?"

"Don't know, son, but I'm aiming to find out." Douglas laid his tongs down on the small wooden table beside the grill, his movements precise, though Shiloh noted his hand ball into a fist afterward. Not that he blamed his father; the Calloways had been thorns in the side of the Boudreaus for decades. He wanted them gone before they brought a blight to the happy gathering.

Unfortunately, Douglas wasn't quite as quick as his momma. He watched her stomp across the paved area, stopping at the edge, with her hands on her hips. Willing to bet she'd have fire in her eyes, Shiloh walked over and stood beside Renee. He wasn't worried; he knew his momma was more than a match for Richard and Julie Calloway.

"Julie."

"Patricia."

"I don't remember inviting you to my home." Cold contempt laced Ms. Patti's words.

Julie Calloway glanced down for a second, and Richard moved to put his arm around his wife. Shiloh noted how pale she looked and felt a tinge of sympathy, though he didn't want to. They'd made their bed a long time ago.

"I apologize for interrupting your family gathering, but

Sally Anne said Rafe would be here. I—we need to speak with him."

"And you couldn't manage a phone call? You had to drive all the way out here?"

"Please, Patricia, I need to speak with Rafe. He needs to know—"

"Momma, what's going on?" Rafe walked over to stand beside his mother, and Shiloh noted how rigid his brother's posture was, his spine like an iron rod. It wasn't like Rafe to be so unbending, even to the Calloways. Had something happened he didn't know about?

"Rafe, could we speak to you privately?" Richard asked, and for the first time Shiloh noted how frail, almost fragile, the man seemed since the last time he'd seen him. With a shock, he realized they'd aged over the last few years, and time hadn't been kind.

Rafe nodded and took a step forward. "Let's go around to the front porch and let everybody else continue with their meal."

"No, son. Unless it's an emergency, they can contact you later. This is family time." Shiloh almost laughed at his dad, standing behind and slightly to the side of his momma. Douglas Boudreau was a mountain of a man, towering over Richard Calloway by several inches. Broad across the chest, and still in his prime, he posed an intimidating sight.

When he chanced a look at Rafe's face, Shiloh knew something was wrong. Seriously wrong. Unless he'd been looking at him, he probably wouldn't have noticed the tic at the corner of his mouth, or the way he'd shifted his stance, squaring his shoulders as if anticipating a blow. Not physical, because there's no way Richard would have attacked Rafe. Not unless he had a screw loose, because he wasn't a match for the younger man. No, something else was going on, beneath the surface, and it piqued Shiloh's internal alarms. Whatever it was, it wasn't good.

"Rafe?" He started toward his brother, and Renee touched his arm, stopping him in his tracks.

"It's fine." Rafe turned back to the Calloways.

"It's not fine," Julie retorted. "Nothing about this is fine. Rafe, we just talked to Doc Jennings. He told us what's going on. I swear we're not behind this. We'd never—"

"Behind what? Somebody wanna tell me what's going on?" Momma's glare froze Julie in her tracks, and her hand rose, clutching at her throat. Her face turned pale, and Shiloh sprinted forward, managing to catch her as her knees crumpled. Lifting her in his arms, he carried her over and placed her gently onto the sofa.

"Are you okay? Can I get you some water or something?"

"No," she whispered, her gaze locked on Rafe. "I swear we had nothing to do with the petition." By this time, Brody was kneeling at the woman's side, taking her pulse and checking her respirations. Shiloh knew his brother carried emergency supplies in his truck. As a firefighter, Brody was always prepared to help in a crisis.

Julie clutched Rafe's hand, wrapping both of her smaller ones around his. "Doc Jennings said everybody in town thinks we're responsible. We're not! Today's the first we even heard about the petition."

"What petition?" Momma had moved over to stand by the sofa at Julie's head.

"They don't know?" A stricken look spread across the older woman's face. "I'm sorry. I didn't mean to make things worse. We, Richard and I, wanted you to know we had nothing to do with it."

Rafe patted her hand awkwardly with the one not held within her frail grip. "Everything's gonna be okay." He glanced toward his parents, before adding, "Most of the family doesn't know. Guess I've got some explaining to do. Are you going to be okay?" Though Rafe spoke to her, Shiloh noted he'd really asked the question of Brody.

"She's going to be fine."

Renee squeezed Shiloh's hand and whispered, "Do you think I should go inside, give your family some privacy? It sounds like there's something going on, and I don't want to intrude."

"You stay right where you are. I don't have any idea what's going on, but I think we're about to find out. Big brother Rafe's been acting kind of cagey the last couple of times we talked. Guess he's been hiding something from the family. Won't be any more hiding after today, though."

"I'm sorry, son." Richard gingerly sat next to his wife on

the sofa. "Didn't mean to bring more trouble to your doorstep. We got angry when Doc Jennings told us about the petition. Then when he said folks around town thought we'd started the doggone thing, it just burned my hide. Can't say we haven't had or differences with your folks over the years, but something like trying to get you kicked out of office? No. A hard no. You're doing a fine job as sheriff."

"Thank you, Mr. Calloway."

Shiloh couldn't believe what he'd just heard. People were trying to get Rafe kicked out of office? For what? There was nobody finer for the job. Plus, he'd been duly elected by the citizens of Shiloh Springs. Glancing around, he read the shocked expressions on his family's faces, except for one or two. Looked like he'd been out of the loop far too long if his brothers were keeping secrets from him.

"Richard, I think we should go." With a swiftness belying his age, Richard jumped up and helped Julie to her feet. His gentleness revealed the affection he carried for his wife, as he tucked her close to his side. While Shiloh might despise the man whose blood ran through his own veins, he couldn't fault their affection. Simply their motives.

When Julie's eyes met his, a pleading look in their depths, he refused to back down or break eye contact first. When they'd tossed aside their twin grandsons, uncaring and unfeeling, along with their mother, leaving them to their fates, they'd made their choice. If they regretted their mistake, so be it. They wouldn't be changing his mind. As far as he was concerned, they had no place in his life. He was a Boudreau, plain and simple.

Brody followed behind the couple as they walked away. That was just like his loving, caring brother. He'd chosen to be a firefighter, and now the fire chief, because he wanted to help people. Personal grudges aside, he'd do whatever needed doing, if it meant easing somebody else's suffering.

"Son," his dad's booming voice drew Shiloh's attention back to the situation at hand. Renee's fingertips gripped his arm tight, and he absently patted them, intent on finding out what Rafe had been hiding.

Rafe drew in a deep breath and exhaled slowly before answering. "A few weeks ago, I found out about a petition circulating throughout the county. It asked for my recall from holding the position of sheriff."

"Why didn't you say anything?" Though his father appeared unruffled, Shiloh knew the man well enough to know a seething volcano dwelled beneath his stoic exterior.

"First, I wanted to find out where it came from. Who thought I didn't deserve to be sheriff. Still haven't figured that one out. Then, I got mad."

Shiloh found himself nodding at his brother's words. Simply the thought of anybody thinking Rafe wasn't fit for the job—inconceivable. And it wasn't because Rafe was his brother. Before moving to San Antonio, he'd lived most of his life in Shiloh Springs, and Rafe was the best sheriff the county had ever had. Bar none.

"Decided I wasn't going to do a thing about it. If enough folks in the county decided I'm unfit for the job, I'll step down."

Several voices raised, overriding Rafe's voice, and although everybody spoke at once protesting Rafe's decision, Shiloh kind of understood it. It would've hit at his brother's pride, thinking anybody felt he wasn't doing a good job. It was a natural reaction. Not one he agreed with though. He planned on doing a little bit of digging to find out who was behind the stupid petition to recall the sheriff's position. If he hadn't heard the Calloways proclaiming their innocence, they'd be number one on his list of suspects. He glanced at Renee, and felt a twinge of guilt. Torn between wanting to figure out who'd act like a yellow-bellied coward and go behind Rafe's back, wanting him out of a job, and putting all his focus on Renee.

"You are not quitting." His dad's voice overrode the cacophony of everyone else.

"I don't plan on it," Rafe answered. "Sally Anne told me and Heath she saw one of the petitions and it barely had any signatures on it. Doc Jennings said the same. Pretty sure they won't get enough signatures to make it happen."

"I won't stand for this." *Uh, oh. Momma's riled. Whoever's behind this better run far and run fast.*

"Momma—"

"Don't you Momma me, Rafael Felipe Alvarado Boudreau! How dare you keep something like this from us?

From me!"

Rafe took a step back as his momma advanced toward him, hands raised to shoulder height, and Shiloh barely bit back the smile threatening to curve his lips upward. While he felt sorry for his big brother, he deserved to get hammered by his momma's wrath. He should've known better than to try and keep secrets from the one woman who had her finger on the pulse of everything happening in Shiloh Springs. It was an honest-to-goodness miracle that she hadn't already found out about the petition, especially if it had been circulating for more than a day. The town folk must've deliberately kept the news from her, which wasn't going to sit well when Hurricane Patti swept through Shiloh Springs.

"And you," she shook her finger at Heath, who raised both hands, a panicked look on his face, "you knew about this and didn't tell me or your father?"

"Hey, Lucas knew, too."

"Gee, thanks for throwing me under the bus, bro."

"Is it always like this around here?" Renee whispered, leaning closer, and Shiloh inhaled the light scent she wore.

"Truthfully? Pretty much. Although this is kind of a big deal, because Rafe should have come to us, told us what was happening, instead of trying to handle things alone. That's what family does. We have your back, no matter what."

"Must be nice."

He pointed toward his mother, and leaned in close, whispering in Renee's ear. "She might be tiny, but she's like a whirlwind when she's riled. Dad calls her his little Texas Tornado. She's a fierce warrior where her family is concerned. That woman has a heart as big as the whole state, and she's loyal and protective of those she considers hers. That includes you, sweetheart."

"I cannot believe the audacity of anybody in the town, much less the county, to even insinuate you aren't capable of doing your job. I want to know who started the petition, and I want to know yesterday. You got me, son? No more hiding. No more having hurt feelings because somebody else is being a jackass." Momma narrowed her eyes at Rafe, before shifting her gaze to envelop everyone. "Douglas, there's more here than a simple petition."

"Agreed." His father wrapped his arms around his mother's waist from behind and pulled her against him, and Shiloh felt the deep connection and love his parents shared. He wanted that, craved it with an intensity that shocked him.

She drew in a deep breath and squared her shoulders. "Alright, everybody, we aren't going to let this food go to waste." His momma turned and smiled at Renee. "I'm sorry your first day home got interrupted, sugar. Guess you got thrown into the deep end of the pool without warning. Fortunately, we all know how to swim, so you don't have anything to worry about."

"Welcome to the family, Renee." Douglas walked over and patted her on the shoulder, and Shiloh knew with that simple gesture, his dad had accepted her not only as part of the Boudreau clan, but also as the woman Shiloh cared about.

"Overwhelmed?"

"A bit. I don't like anybody who sugarcoats things. I'd much rather people are honest and upfront with their feelings than to put on a façade. I've had enough of that to last a lifetime."

Shiloh found Renee's admission telling, and it also made him curious. Somebody had hurt her badly in the past, and he never wanted to see her hurt again. Which meant getting the truth, the whole truth from her. The good, the bad, and the ugly. He needed to know everything, so he could eliminate the danger stalking her once and for all. Because he had the feeling she was about to become the most important thing in his life, and he didn't mind one little bit.

CHAPTER ELEVEN

The next morning, Renee walked down the stairs and headed to the kitchen. She'd slept later than usual. Everything seemed to hit her at once after she'd gone to the guest room, and she'd finally managed to block out the events of the past couple of days. For the first time in a long time, sleep hadn't evaded her. Instead, she'd gotten the best night's sleep in ages.

She followed the scent of bacon and coffee into the kitchen. After working in the coffee shop in Portland, she'd found herself craving that first morning jolt of caffeine. The quick shot of energy each morning helped her face each long day, and kept her on her toes. Well, that and the constant adrenaline rushing through her bloodstream at every sound.

"Good morning, Renee." Ms. Patti stood by the big farm sink, her hands encased in bright yellow rubber gloves, with soap bubbles glistening in the sunlight. Her welcoming smile reached her eyes, and Renee felt the older woman's warmth and acceptance filling her. Giving herself an internal shake, she refused to dwell on the bad stuff this morning. Today, she'd simply enjoy spending time with Lucas and his family, getting to know the people who insisted she was part of their family. Their clan, as Shiloh called them. She loved that word. It was old-fashioned but had a depth of connection that spoke to her.

"Morning, Ms. Patti. Something smells wonderful."

"Coffee's over there." She pointed to the pot and extra mugs sitting on the far counter. "I kept a plate hot for you in the oven. Help yourself, hon."

"You didn't need to do that, but thank you. I'm starving this morning. Must be all the fresh air."

"It's no trouble. I like cooking. Don't get to do nearly enough anymore, since all the boys are grown and have moved out of the house. I miss it, but don't tell them I said so, or they'll be showing up at all hours, wanting me to feed them."

Renee finished pouring her coffee, making it just the way she liked it, and grabbed the covered plate out of the oven. Heaped high with scrambled eggs, bacon, home fries, and a couple of biscuits, her stomach growled. The heavenly scents made her mouth water.

"I can't imagine cooking for so many people at once. I pretty much get takeout or pop a frozen meal in the microwave."

Putting the last dish in the dish drainer, Ms. Patti whipped off the rubber gloves and turned, leaning a hip against the countertop. "I can't imagine being alone all the time. I loved having a passel of kids around the house, always getting into something. Usually trouble." She grinned at her teasing remark. "I've always worked, running the real estate office and raising the boys, which was a full-time job in and of itself. And I loved every minute of it."

Renee took a bite of the scrambled eggs, almost moaning as the taste exploded in her mouth. She quickly bit into a piece of bacon, and closed her eyes, enjoying the first home-cooked meal she'd had in years.

"This is wonderful."

Ms. Patti merely shrugged and moved across the kitchen to sit across from Renee. Dressed in black slacks and a pale pink blouse with an apron covering the front, she appeared a typical housewife at first glance. Renee studied the petite woman, quickly determining the Boudreau matriarch was more than meets the eye. Especially after her display of frustration and anger the day before, when she confronted her son about keeping secrets from the family. Reminded her of a momma wolf protecting her cubs from danger, ready to attack any and all who posed a threat. She'd quickly realized the diminutive older woman's anger wasn't directed at her son, but at the people who'd tried to hurt him by taking his job away. There wasn't a shadow of doubt in Renee's mind whoever was behind the political petition would be answering to the Boudreau clan before long, and there would be a reckoning due.

"I'm glad we've got a couple of minutes to talk. Douglas took Lucas and Shiloh with him to the job site. He wanted a chance to talk with them, and give you a chance to catch a breath without them underfoot. I know this has been a lot for you to take in, upending your life and coming halfway across the country for a bunch of strangers. We also thought you might want to talk—and I'm a rather good listener."

"It's been more than I expected, but you've all been wonderful."

Ms. Patti gave an inelegant snort. "Girl, admit it, we've been a pain in your backside, everybody clamoring to meet you, talk to you. Wanting to make sure you realize you're part of the family. I've gotta say, you've handled things well. I'd have run screaming for the hills five minutes after I got here." She smoothed her hand across the apron then met Renee's eyes. "I'm betting you've got questions.

Renee laid down her fork, her appetite suddenly gone. It felt like she was on a runaway train headed straight for a mountain, and the only way off was to jump. Swirling emotions threatened to crush her, nerves assailing her until her every instinct screamed to run. But she couldn't, wouldn't do that. She'd made up her mind somewhere between Portland and Shiloh Springs. If she wanted any chance at a normal life, she needed to take a stand. What better place to do that than the place it all started?

"Can you tell me about Lucas? How he ended up placed with your family?"

"That's a bit of a story. By the time Lucas came to live with us, we already had some of the boys living here. Rafe was our first. Then Antonio and Brody. Each one had their own circumstances and reasons for ending up in our home, and they weren't happy events for the most part. Douglas and I talked when we first took in Rafe. He came out of an abusive situation, and seeing how much understanding and compassion that young boy needed, we decided to find the boys who needed the most love and affection. A connection to home and family."

Ms. Patti stood and got herself a cup of coffee, then rejoined Renee at the table. Renee got the impression she'd needed a moment to compose herself, so she didn't ask another question, simply waited for the Boudreau matriarch to continue when she was ready.

"I'm not sure how much you remember about the time you and Lucas went into the system. I know you were really young."

She nodded. "I can't tell you much about the circumstances or what our lives were like. I only remember Lucas. He took care of me, watched over me. I think I'd just turned four when the state got us."

"Do you remember your Aunt Hattie?"

Renee tried thinking back to when she was a child. She remembered being scared. Remembered Lucas taking care of her. Remembered screams and shouting and anger.

"I really don't remember her."

Ms. Patti huffed a sigh. "Probably a good thing. Your mother had a hard life. I'm not going to demean or disparage who she was or her life choices. If you've got questions, you can ask Lucas. What I will say is the welfare system felt that your Aunt Hattie, your mother's sister, would be a good guardian to take care of you and Lucas. She was an alcoholic, a mean and nasty drunk who gave you little more than a roof over your heads. All she was concerned about was the money coming from the state every month, and couldn't have cared less what happened to you or your brother."

"How do I not remember her?

"Probably best you don't. Anyway, Douglas didn't hear about Lucas until after you'd been separated. He was having a horrible time adjusting. Fighting all the time. Refusing to stay with his foster family. Running away. Nobody knew why because they weren't told that he had a sister he'd been separated from. Might have made things a whole lot easier if they'd been upfront and honest about it from the get-go."

"Do you know why they separated us? I thought the state usually tried to keep siblings together."

"That's one of the things we've never been able to figure out. You *should* have been kept together, especially at your age. We, Douglas and I, didn't know about Lucas having a sister. When we found out, we immediately petitioned child welfare to have you moved into our home, only nobody could find any records of you even being in the system. Nothing. It was as it you'd never been through intake. When we kept pushing, we found out there was a fire and all the records were destroyed. You and Lucas used to live in this tiny town, only had about seven hundred people. They'd only just started inputting the records into computer databases. The fire was ruled suspicious, but nothing ever came of the investigation."

"That explains why I couldn't find anything on Lucas when I searched."

Ms. Patti shook her head. "Lucas has paperwork through Child Protective Services. Everything was in order, and he was assigned a case worker. That's how he ended up with us. We tend to get the difficult ones, the kids who have loads of potential but need a little extra attention. We've got a special connection with a case worker, who notified us about your brother. That's how he ended up with us. You on the other hand? There's not one shred of evidence you ever existed."

"What about a birth certificate? There must have been one."

Ms. Patti shook her head. "Nothing we could find. You'd think in this day and age, with all the paperless trails, a good computer expert could find something. But there was no evidence Renee Louisa O'Malley ever existed."

She pushed her plate away, hunger gone. Why would someone have erased her very existence? It didn't make sense. Although thinking about her childhood, maybe it did. She'd been shunted around from family to family, not staying any place for long. Of course, a lot of that stemmed from her own stubbornness and acting out. She'd been a holy terror to anybody and everybody in her path.

"I'm glad Lucas ended up here. He seems like he's grounded and has his own purpose in life. He says he's happy, and I believe him."

"Well, I can tell you he's been loved every single day since he came to live here. All my boys know they are loved and wanted. Not a day went by I didn't tell them that. They are my sons. My family. I don't care they don't carry my blood. They carry my heart. That's all that matters."

Tears pricked Renee's eyes, and she blinked them back. "He's lucky. All your sons are. Can I ask, why did you only foster boys?"

Ms. Patti leaned back in her chair, a wistful expression crossing her face. "It wasn't intentional, not at first. Rafe came to us first, after a car accident. Taking him in wasn't planned, and we scrambled around like crazy folks, trying to make sure we got everything done so he could come straight from the hospital into our house. Then Antonio and Brody came, and with three boys, we discussed maybe taking in a girl. We were willing, but every time Mrs. A contacted us, it was for a troubled adolescent male." She smiled. "Mrs. A is the person who'd call us when she found one of her 'special boys' who needed us. Douglas and I were told we couldn't have children, and my husband has so much love to give, we'd take on the troubled ones."

"Nica's adopted, too?"

"My little troublemaker? No, she's our miracle. With a houseful of rambunctious, rowdy preteens and teenagers, I had my hands full. Against all odds, I ended up pregnant. Talk about a shock. The doctors still haven't come up with a good explanation, but we ended up with our blessing." She leaned forward and whispered, "First and only time I've ever seen my husband pass out. That man is stronger than a mountain, but two little blue lines in a piece of plastic knocked his knees out from under him."

Renee laughed, trying to picture the larger-than-life man she'd met the day before being flummoxed by anything. After seeing the way he looked at Ms. Patti, the gentle way he held her hand, or put his arm around her, she believed it.

"Anyway, we're getting off topic. Lucas barely spoke to us when he first came here. Cussed up a storm, sure, because anger was all he understood. Anger and grief. He fought with the other boys. Poor child had so many bloody noses and black eyes, you'd have thought we were the ones abusing him. He finally broke down and told Douglas why he was rebelling, not wanting to be here. Every instinct that child had was to find his sister. You."

"I looked for him too. I'll admit, I was a horrible child. You'd have probably kicked me to the curb too, the way I acted."

"Never!" Ms. Patti reached across the table and squeezed Renee's balled up fist. "We don't give up on someone because they're hurting. Sometimes the pain isn't on the outside, it's all bottled up on the inside, and the only way to express it is by exploding. Verbal, physical, same difference.

We'd have loved you the same way we love your brother."

Renee couldn't stop the tears this time. It felt like a dam breaking, the cracks in its façade going far deeper than superficial. All her life, she'd wanted to find Lucas so she'd have a place to belong. A sense of family she'd been missing, unknowingly searching for. A home to finally settle and call her own. A place like the Boudreaus.

Ms. Patti clamored from her chair, came around the table, and wrapped her arms around Renee's shoulders. "You are a part of this family now. I get it, we've done nothing but pile stuff on you from the moment Shiloh crossed your path in Portland, but we're so happy we found you. I know you've got to be dealing with sensory overload, and you take all the time you need. I swear I won't let anybody pressure you into doing or saying anything you don't want. I simply want you to know, you have a place here. A family who will support you and love you no matter what."

"I don't know what to say." She drew in a ragged breath, wiping away the last few tears. Ms. Patti was right; she felt like she was drowning, going under for the third time with everything she'd experienced. Her entire life seemed like one endless loop of lies and mistrust, secrets and fear. Mostly fear.

"You don't have to say anything. Well, that's not exactly true. You will eventually have to tell us who or what's got you on the run. Doesn't matter what it is, we'll help." Ms. Patti chuckled. "I've got boys with their fingers into so many things, one of them is bound to be able to help, no matter what your problem is. Sheriff, FBI, district attorney, security expert, private investigator. Douglas and I also have friends we can call on who have connections you wouldn't believe. We'll straighten things out, don't you fret."

"You don't even know me. I could be a serial killer."

"Honey, I'm a good judge of people. You've got a good heart. Now, finish your breakfast, because I'm pretty sure Lucas and Shiloh will be coming back soon."

Renee looked down at her plate, her appetite returning. "Thank you, Ms. Patti. For everything."

Eileen drew a brush through her long hair, then leaned forward, staring into the large trifold mirror of her dressing table. Was that a gray hair? She barely refrained from throwing the brush at the mirror, reining in her temper at the last second. Guess another trip to her personal stylist had to happen sooner than later. Appearance was everything in her world. Cultivating the beauty she'd been gifted with at birth took a lot of hard work and an even bigger amount of money. People expected her to be a beautiful airhead, a trophy gracing her husband's arm. Little did they realize who the real brain behind their expanding empire was, and that suited her fine. Let them think she was a plastic Barbie doll without a thought in her head except shopping and meeting her girlfriends for cocktails.

Smoothing a hand down her dressing gown, she smirked. She'd deliberately bought the sheer covering because it hinted at more than it revealed. Looking like something worn by a starlet out of a 50s movie, it belted tightly at the waist and had long billowing sleeves edged with feathers. The black complimented her coloring and emphasized her curves. Too bad Darius had a meeting this morning. He would have enjoyed the sight of her; glamor and glitz always made him smile.

Sliding her feet into matching mules, she stepped away from the vanity. Before she'd taken more than a couple steps, her phone rang. Her brow furrowed when she noted the name on the caller ID. At least he hadn't made the mistake of calling Darius first this time.

"What have you found out?"

"Good morning to you, too. Get up on the wrong side of the bed, darling?"

Gritting her teeth, she bit back the retort on the tip of her tongue. He was getting far too cavalier with their relationship, reading more into it than actually existed. Too bad she couldn't pull the plug and have him taken out of the picture. Not yet. He was too important in her quest to find Elizabeth.

"She abandoned the apartment. I saw the super opening her door. Pretended I was visiting somebody else, and wondered if the unit had become available. Guy didn't even hesitate to let me know the previous tenant skipped out. Broke the lease with a phone call. Told him to toss all her belongings because she wasn't coming back."

Eileen took a deep breath and counted to five, reining in her temper. No sense killing the messenger. "Any idea where she's headed?"

"Actually..." He drawled out the word, holding it like a tantalizing morsel of information. "I went to the coffee shop where she used to work. As always, my timing was impeccable. I heard one of the baristas mention to the owner Elizabeth was headed to Texas."

"Where precisely in Texas?"

"That's where things get a little dicey. The little brunette didn't mention specifics. I'm planning on following the pretty little bird back to her nest and spending a little personal time with her. Maybe some one-on-one conversation might persuade her to share Elizabeth's destination."

Eileen was smart enough to put two-and-two together. When she'd been looking for someone who could follow orders and get the job done, without questions, he'd fit the bill. Throughout their lucrative relationship, he'd proven adept at facilitating her needs and obtaining information through sometimes unorthodox means. Not that she cared how he managed to obtain the information. She simply demanded results, and Bruce complied—by whatever means necessary.

"Make it happen. I need to know where my lovely daughter is by whatever means necessary."

CHAPTER TWELVE

Shiloh ran his fingers behind Otto's ears, scratching the old donkey's head. Otto butted his head against his hand, urging him to keep scratching. He smiled, remembering little Jamie's excitement when she'd found Otto wandering around inside the pen by the barn. Never having seen a donkey in person, she'd immediately wanted to ride him. While most of the time the old codger wouldn't hurt a fly, nobody wanted to take the chance of putting a small girl onto the back of a fully grown troublemaker.

"Saw your momma looking out the kitchen window. Guess Renee's up."

Shiloh gave Otto a final pat and turned to his father. "I'm planning to talk to her today. The sooner she tells us what's going on, the faster we can handle it, and let her get on with a normal life."

"That's what we all want."

"She's amazing, isn't she?" Lucas stepped up to the railing and handed half an apple to Otto. "I feel like I'm dreaming and when I wake up, she's still going to be missing."

"She's really here." Shiloh squeezed Lucas' shoulder, and met his dad's gaze. "When I found her in Portland, she was terrified. Ran from me the second she spotted me in the club. If I hadn't talked her friend Tina into meeting me, I'm betting Renee would have been in the wind before I could catch her."

"Looks like we owe Tina one. If she helped Renee, we're in her debt." His father rolled his shoulders, before adding, "I've got people on standby, ready to help any way they can. Once you find out what Renee needs, count on us."

"Thanks, Dad." Lucas glanced at the house. "I want to go in there and talk to her, find out everything, but I think we overwhelmed her yesterday." He turned to Shiloh. "She's closest to you, especially since you've spent the most time together. Talk with her. Find out what I can do. She seems to trust you."

"Bro, it's only because I'm the one she's been around the most over last few days. Give her a chance. I know she wants to reconnect with you, but she's scared."

Lucas blew out a ragged sigh. "I know. I'm going into town and find Jill. I'm afraid if I stick around here, I'm going to scare her more, be too pushy. Tell her I'll be back. Call me if she—"

"Don't worry so much. She'll still be here when you get back." Shiloh gave him a little shove toward the house. "Go tell her goodbye. I'll be in in a minute. Want to talk with Dad first."

"Thanks."

As Lucas walked away, Shiloh leaned against the railing, taking in the ranchland in the distance. He knew Dane, had gotten up before dawn and headed out to the pasture to feed the cattle, like he did every morning before the sun even peeked over the horizon. Growing up, they'd all done their fair share around the homestead, everything from mucking the stalls to riding the fence line, and running barbed wire. It was a hot, thankless job, but in a way it made being part of the Boudreau family seem more real. Like he'd finally settled into his own skin, in a way nothing else had. Not that he wanted the life of a ranch hand; no, he craved adventure, action, being his own boss. Set his own hours.

"What's on your mind, son?"

"I'm not sure. Something about this whole thing with Renee, it's got me on edge."

"How so?" Douglas moved to stand beside him, leaning with his back against the railing, where he could keep an eye on the back door of the Big House.

"I can't describe it. I think she's beginning to trust me, but every time I see the fear in her eyes, I want to grab her and escape to someplace where nobody can hurt her." Shiloh knew he wasn't describing what he felt well, but couldn't seem to find the words to express how much he was starting to care for the pretty redhead.

"Understandable. You're a good man, and you can't stand seeing her frightened or hurting. It's part of who you are. Always has been. You want to rescue her, wrap her in cotton wool, and tuck her away to keep her safe. If it was your momma, I'd want to do the same. Problem is that Renee is a strong, independent woman. Smart, too. She'd have to be to have stayed one step ahead of whoever's chasing her for so long. You can't coddle her or take away her choices."

"All I know is it's tearing me up inside, thinking about what kind of life she's had. It couldn't have been all that happy; otherwise, she wouldn't be racing against the clock, trying to vanish. I keep picturing things in my head. Hard not to. We've seen some pretty nasty stuff right here at home."

Douglas lowered his head, his expression shuttered. Shiloh knew he was probably thinking about a few of the boys who hadn't adapted to life at the Big House. Sometimes, no matter how much love and affection you gave someone, they were too damaged or unwilling to grab onto what was being offered.

"They haunt me," he whispered, his voice soft and filled with anguish. "I wonder every day if there'd been more I could've done. Was I too hard on them? I pray for them every night, hoping they've found some peace in their lives and can begin to heal."

"Me too, Dad. You did everything possible, never doubt that. Momma, too. Sometimes, no matter how many good intentions, how many chances people are given, they can't accept a miracle when they see one. You and Momma, you've helped far more people than you'll probably ever know. I'm convinced the ones who wound up leaving here will one day realize what a blessing they got, having a chance to live here. Even if was only for a short time, I'm willing to bet it had an impact on them. We might never know how much, but I feel it deep down. You made a difference."

"I hope so." Douglas straightened and pulled his hat lower, shielding his eyes. "You go talk with Renee. Figure out what's what. I've got to get to the site. Foundations being poured today for the building, and I can't let Liam have all the fun."

Shiloh chuckled and swiped his hands over his jean-clad thighs. "He hates foundation days. Give him the construction end, putting up walls and roofs, and he's a happy man. Course he's gonna complain no matter what, just to get a rise out of you."

Douglas smiled at Shiloh's words. "I know. Why do you think I'm running late? By the time I get there, he'll be swearing a blue streak and the crew will be threatening to walk off the job. Happens every time."

"Go. When I find out something, I'll call."

Douglas gave him one of his patented cowboy nods and strode toward the Big House, his steps sure and even. Just like everything else about the man, placid and steady, he was the backbone of the Boudreau clan. The man held everything together with a calm steadfastness, and it was easy to forget sometimes that he was all-too-human and felt things deeply. Shiloh made a mental note, once he'd gotten things straightened out with Renee, and she was safe, he might investigate the whereabouts of the boys who ended up not staying with the Boudreaus. Maybe it would give his parents some closure, if they knew where they'd ended up, and how their lives turned out.

But for now, he had a job to do, and that entailed getting the real story from Renee O'Malley.

Renee walked out onto the front porch and leaned her head back, taking a deep breath of the fresh air. It was nice here, clean and open and bright. So different from all the cities she'd lived in her whole life. Hiding in plain sight usually worked best, where there were crowds of people milling around. Easy to get lost in the teeming masses. People tended to ignore you, unless you initiated the conversations, other than a brief hello, how are you.

It felt different here at Shiloh's home. When they'd driven through Shiloh Springs, she'd been a bit preoccupied, talking with his brothers. What she'd seen reminded her of what she imagined a small town in Texas would look like. Main Street charm with bright multihued awnings, flower baskets adding bursts of color, and old-fashioned light poles gave the whole scene an aura of nostalgia. She'd spotted the sheriff's station, a diner, and various other businesses as they'd driven through. If she had to put her finger on a description, she'd say it reminded her of Mayberry from that old TV show.

She walked across the porch, eased onto the swing. and pushed off with her foot, smiling at the easy back and forth motion. Tried to remember the last time she'd simply stopped and enjoyed herself amidst peaceful surroundings.

Huge live oak trees flanked the front of the house on both sides, with Spanish moss dripping like melted candle-wax from their stupendous branches. Lush green grass grew in velvety waves in front of the house, and off to the side a large area of gravel had been smoothed into parking spaces. Currently a couple of large pickups occupied them.

The screen door swung outward and Douglas Boudreau stepped through, taking up a good portion of the doorway. His ready smile made her feel a sense of welcome, and he walked over to stand beside the swing. Though he was a large man, well-muscled and broad-shouldered, he didn't make her feel threatened in any way.

"Everything alright?"

"Yes, thanks. You've all been most welcoming. Your home is amazing. Thank you for letting me stay."

"You're family now. I'm heading in to work. My wife had to go into town for a bit, to check on some things at her office. She'll be back in a couple hours. Shiloh and Nica should be around if you need anything. I also left my number on the console table in the entry if you need me."

Unfamiliar warmth spread through her. She wondered if this was what it felt like to be part of an actual family. Shunted around more times than she cared to admit, she'd never experienced what it was like to be part of a normal, functional family. She liked this feeling of acceptance, being a part of a group without having expectations placed on her. It made her kind of giddy.

He started down the porch steps, and she watched him walk to one of the two pickups. Giving her a brief wave, he pulled out and drove away, leaving her to her thoughts. They were a jumbled miasma, tumbling around inside her brain with no rhyme or reason, no cohesive pattern. The world she'd created, living alone, refusing to garner close friends, taught her to survive on her own. Yet within a few days, ever since meeting Shiloh Boudreau, her world had been turned topsy-turvy, upside down. Closing her eyes, she rocked the swing back and forth, listening to the sounds of the ranch and trying to figure out how she was going to tell Shiloh the truth. Would he hate her when he found out? It was a distinct possibility, and one she had to consider.

"Renee?"

She recognized his voice instantly, even with her eyes closed. A tiny smile escaped, and she slowly opened her eyes. "Good morning."

"Mind if I join you?"

She patted the cushion beside her. "Your family home is

beautiful. Peaceful and serene."

Shiloh made a scoffing sound. "It wasn't like this growing up. Picture eleven rambunctious, rowdy adolescent and teenage boys and one pampered princess on a Friday night. Fights over the bathrooms. Pushing and shoving because somebody looked at somebody else funny. We had more than our share of black eyes and bloody noses. Man, we were loud. And obnoxious. I don't know how Momma and Dad put up with us."

"They loved you."

"True. Ridge and I, we were the more fortunate ones. We knew our birth mother loved us unconditionally. We lost our father before we were born, but we had her for a while. Our mother was best friends with Momma—Ms. Patti—and when she found out she was dying, she made sure we'd be taken care of. Especially since our biological grandparents wanted nothing to do with us."

"Seriously? How could they turn their backs on their own flesh and blood?"

The look he gave her sent a shiver down her spine, focused solely on her, as if he wanted to make sure she garnered the importance of his words. She matched his stare, refusing to look away, knowing whatever he said meant something important.

"One of the lessons you learn, especially once you get involved with the Boudreau clan, become a part of our community, is family is more than blood. DNA might tell us who spawned us but love and commitment count for a heck of a lot more than any random sperm donor ever could. Ridge and I share an unbreakable bond because we're twins, and that's a connection nobody can take away. The Boudreaus are my family *by choice*. I have nothing to do with my biological grandparents. It's a conscious decision, a choice Ridge and I made a long time ago. Nothing's happened to change my mind."

She broke their intense staring match and leaned her head against his shoulder, feeling the rock solid muscles beneath the skin, the strength that was more than skin deep. "I feel sorry for them. It's their loss because you are a wonderful man. Although we just met, and I'm only now meeting your family, I can feel the Boudreau influence running deep in you. I'm sure your grandparents regret turning their backs on you."

He shook his head. "You saw them yesterday. They haven't changed. Probably only came to tell Ms. Patti and Douglas what they did, because they didn't want or need any more animosity directed their way. They aren't the most popular folks in Shiloh Springs."

"The Calloways? Those people who showed up here? They're your grandparents?"

"In name only. Ridge and I don't acknowledge them as family. They made their choice when they turned their back on our mother. Might seem vindictive, but we've done the same with them. Ridge and I both legally changed our name as soon as we turned eighteen." He grinned, white teeth flashing, and she saw the hint of a dimple in his cheek. "It's kind of a family tradition."

"I remember you mentioning Lucas hadn't changed his name. That he remained an O'Malley."

Shiloh grabbed her hand, twining their fingers together, and leaned back on the swing. "I remember after Ridge and I legally changed our names, asking him if he planned to do the same. He looked me dead in the eye and said absolutely not. Wouldn't budge on the subject. He wouldn't even consider the option. Not until he found you. Said if you were looking to reconnect with him, he wanted to make it easier, because you'd remember being an O'Malley."

She tried to breathe past the lump in her throat, the beginning of tears clogging it. "I barely remember being an O'Malley. I moved around so much in the beginning, and every new foster home wanted you to use their last name, even if it wasn't exactly legal. I didn't have any sense of self-worth or self-awareness. I got lost in the merry-go-round of shifting from home to home. A different roof over my head so often, like a revolving door you'd go in and come right back out again. I did remember having a brother, and always asked where he was, but nobody ever told me. The only way I know I'm Renee O'Malley is because I found some papers in a box when one of my foster moms died."

"I'm sorry."

Shaking her head, Renee replied, "Don't be. She wasn't

the nicest person. I admit I snooped through the box when she wasn't looking. I knew she was sick, and had gone to the doctor. I snuck into her bedroom because I knew she hid stuff there. Saw her stuffing things into a white box, and shove it in the closet. Me and another girl who lived there dug it out and opened it. I found an old picture of me. Guess I was about five or so. On the back was written my name and birthday."

Shiloh slid a bit closer, and tingles raced across Renee's skin. Something about him just did it for her. There was no explanation for it. She'd been attracted to other men before, dated occasionally, though not often lately. Getting close to somebody meant hurting them when she moved on to the next place. Feelings were complicated things, so it was simply easier to not let anybody too close. But something about Shiloh got under her carefully constructed fences, and she wasn't sure she wanted to keep him out anyway.

"I wish we'd found you sooner. The foster care system across the U.S. is messed up. They do their best and, in most instances, things work to help children in need. Families step up and help children in crisis. A perfect example are Douglas and Ms. Patti. They are proof it can work. It's unfortunate that a few rotten people slip through the cracks, and the kids are the ones who pay the price."

Renee remained silent, not wanting to add any ugliness to this moment. Having his arm around her shoulders and leaning into his side felt right. She knew reading too much into this crazy situation was asking for trouble, but was it so wrong to snatch this moment of happiness? They'd been rare, like precious pearls scattered across the ground from a broken necklace, and she wanted to have this one to secret away, because she knew it wouldn't last forever.

"You know we have to talk." The seriousness of his voice sent a shiver down her spine. Uh, oh. Guess the moment of truth had caught up to her. No more hiding.

"We are talking, aren't we?"

"You know what I mean, Renee. The longer we put it off, the better chance you're giving whoever's chasing you to catch up."

She inhaled a deep breath, catching the slightest whiff of soap, aftershave, and man. Slightly woodsy and totally masculine, it suited him. It would be so easy, so simple, to lean on him, let him shoulder the burden of Darius and Eileen, and escape from her problems. But that was the coward's way out, and she was finally tired of running. Hiding. Staying one step ahead of them, at the point of exhaustion, mentally, physically and emotionally.

Time to pay the piper.

"You're right. We should talk."

CHAPTER THIRTEEN

"I have an idea."

"What kind of idea?" Renee gave him a skeptical glance, probably trying to figure out what he had in mind. He'd just told her they needed to talk about all her deep, dark issues. No matter how they approached the subject, it was bound to be tense and bring up things she didn't want to share easily. Maybe if he could make things a little more comfortable, given them privacy so they wouldn't be disturbed, it might make things a little easier on them both.

"Wait here. I'm going to grab us both some coffee. Then I want to show you something special."

A slow blush heated her cheeks, and she looked away, but not before he read the laughter in her eyes, and caught the double entendre his words sparked. Using a knuckle, he tilted her head up. "Someplace special, okay?"

"Um, sure."

Moving quickly into the kitchen, he got two travel mugs from the cupboard and quickly filled them. He grabbed a couple of cookies and wrapped them in a napkin and slid them into his pocket. Quickly jotting down a note stating where they'd be in case anybody needed them, he headed back out. Within another minute. he was handing her one of the mugs.

"Come on. I think you're going to like this." He'd made the spur of the moment decision to show her Momma's secret garden with its hidden gazebo. It would ensure them privacy to have their long overdue talk, and he really wanted to see her expression when she saw what to most outsiders was considered a private family spot. Unless you were a Boudreau intimate, chances were good you hadn't found the place that was considered a closely held secret.

He grasped her hand and led her around the side of the Big House. Built out from the side of the house was a porch with a burst of colors from his mother's green thumb. A small table and chairs graced the space, a comfortable and easy place where he'd spent many a sunny afternoon with his momma, laughing and talking, sipping lemonade or sweet tea. Fond memories he cherished and tucked away for those lonely days when he was stuck far away in his one-bedroom apartment in San Antonio.

Continuing past the porch, a tall stand of pine trees marched straight and tall, clustered together like a mighty forest, keeping the bandits and marauders away. The wooded area had been a wonderful playground for him, Ridge, and Heath when they'd been rambunctious boys. He shot a surreptitious glance at Renee, watched her taking in all the woodland beauty, and he couldn't help thinking that she was prettier than all the natural wonders surrounding them.

"Be careful where you step. Some of the roots can be a little tricky." He held her hand as she stepped over one of the windy patches, kicking a couple of the bigger stones scattered along the path.

"Are you sure you know where we're going? If we got lost, I'm sure I won't be able to lead us back. I haven't been dropping any breadcrumbs."

"Don't worry, Gretel, I know the way."

Her cheeky grin lit him up inside. How could her simple smile make him feel like he was ten feet tall? It didn't make sense, but he'd worry about it later. Right now, he wanted her to see Momma's garden.

"It's not much farther. Trust me?"

"Absolutely." Her response was instantaneous, surprising him.

He heard her gasp as they rounded a large pine, and the hidden gazebo came into view. Surrounded by the tall pine trees, the dainty structure should have felt out of place. Instead, it felt like it had always been there from the beginning of time. The simplicity of the building complimented the natural beauty surrounding it.

Roses trailed along the posts, climbing ever upward toward the roofline, and the heady scent was intoxicating. The white painted structure stood as a testament to his mother's hard work, because something this beautiful hadn't been accomplished overnight. Shiloh remembered his mother spending hours and hours here, digging and planting, making things fit her vision. Rafe had helped her whenever he could, because he'd found an affinity and love for digging in the soil by her side. All the boys pitched in from one time or another, sometimes because they'd wanted to help. Other times, it had been their chance to have some one-on-one time with their mother.

Renee handed him her travel mug and walked all the way around the gazebo, her gaze filled with wonder. Her soft fingers stroked the columns, covered with roses, their heady fragrance mixed with the scent of pine. Stooping down, her fingertips traced across the top of the lilies and tall ornamental grasses planted around the base of the gazebo, and she lifted her face toward the sunlight. A shaft of light highlighted her within its glow, and Shiloh's heartbeat stuttered. She was perfect. Ethereal grace and beauty, and he was struck with the notion he didn't want to lose her.

"This is amazing. Warm and inviting, like stepping from the darkness into the light. So much work and love went into this."

"This is Momma's special garden. Her hideaway when raising a houseful of hellions became too much. She's worked on this and added to it over the years. Dad and us boys ran electric wiring from the house out here, so she has power to run lights in the evenings." He reached inside the opening and flipped the switch, turning on the tiny white fairy lights rimming the inside of the gazebo's roof. More twinkling lights were wrapped around tree trunks, adding to the magical scene.

"Come here." He kept his voice low, not wanting to break the spell the garden created. When Renee glanced at him, he crooked his finger, and motioned toward the entrance to the gazebo. Joining him at the opening, he heard her gasp and knew she'd spotted the gazebo's hidden secret.

"Is that a wishing well?"

"That's what I've always called it. Technically, it's simply a well, built so Momma wouldn't have to drag water from the house. It's too far to run hoses, not without a lot of trouble. She loves this better anyway."

"I can't blame her. It's like I've stepped back in time to some medieval fantasy. I should be wearing a long, flowing gossamer gown, and you," she pressed her fingertip against his chest, "should be wearing a suit of armor. You are my white knight, after all, helping me escape from the dreaded dragon."

She took a step further inside the gazebo, and spun around in a circle, arms lifted in the air, her laughter spilling through him. Loathe to spoil the moment, he eased onto the white-painted bench and watched her, enjoying her carefree attitude and the sense of freedom her movements displayed. Somehow, he doubted she had many unguarded moments lately, and he wanted her to know she was safe and protected with him at her side.

"Thank you for sharing this place with me."

The smile accompanying her words had the breath catching in his chest. Even though he knew he needed to guard his heart, he had the feeling it was a lost cause. Too late, because he was falling hard for the beautiful redhead.

"You are most welcome, my lady."

She took the few steps separating them, and eased down beside him on the wooden bench, and brushed her shoulder against his. It took every ounce of strength he had not to turn and pull her into his arms and whisk her away, someplace where he could protect her from anyone and everyone who'd wish her harm. But he didn't.

"I guess it's time."

He gave a simple nod.

"I'm not sure where to start."

"Start wherever it's comfortable for you. You've told me a little about how you grew up, moving from home to home. What changed?"

"Everything."

Renee glanced down at her hands, her fingers twisted together in her lap. Why was this so hard? Telling the truth shouldn't cause her stomach to clench and her muscles to tighten to the point of agony. But telling the truth to Shiloh meant revealing all her deep, dark secrets. Exposing the ugly underbelly she'd been dragged into, had willingly participated in, without any smoke and mirrors. The raw truth sometimes wasn't pretty, and hers definitely showed the worse for wear.

"You know a bit about my early years. A few of the families I stayed with were nice enough. Most of the time, they were in it to help kids. The added bonus of the checks coming in every month didn't hurt, either. The homes where it wasn't so nice—I don't want to talk about, it brings back too many memories. Suffice it to say, I survived."

"The sad part of all this is it should never have happened. You should have been here, living a good life, with a family who loved you. For that, my heart aches for the little girl you were."

"It wasn't all bad. I wasn't beaten or hurt. School helped. I loved going to classes, learning new things. Books, especially, were my lifeline. My escape from a not-so-shiny existence into lands of wonder and excitement. I borrowed books from the school libraries; practically every day I had my nose in a book." She stopped when she noted Shiloh silently laughing behind his hand. "What?"

"Remind me to introduce you to Camilla. I think you two are going to become fast friends."

"Camilla?"

He nodded. "Camilla Stewart. She's Heath's fiancée, and she's a writer. I think Nica said she writes something called romantic suspense, whatever that is."

"Seriously? That would be awesome." Internally, Renee

did a little jig, thrilled she'd get to meet a real live author in person.

"They're fixing to move back to Shiloh Springs in a few weeks. Heath works for the ATF in D.C. He's transferring to the Austin office. Camilla said she can work just about anywhere that has an internet connection and Wi-Fi. Momma's already lined up a rental place for them, for when they come and visit on the weekends."

"I love that your family is close. You don't know how rare that is. I've known people with family members who pretty much can't stand each other. Always bickering and arguing. Being around the Boudreaus is like a breath of fresh air."

"We have our moments. We're only human. Fortunately, Momma and Dad have a way of keeping us grounded and focused on the things that are important. Like family."

"Back on topic. I taught myself how to use the school's computer, and searched every database I could, trying to find Lucas. That's when I was told he'd died."

"See, I don't get that." She understood Shiloh's puzzlement, because she'd asked herself the same question over and over. "There should've been a pretty clear path to Lucas. Course, he wasn't in the spotlight at that age, so not in the media. But there would still be records. Birth certificate, something. If he'd died, there would have been something in the newspaper, an obituary or announcement. You didn't find anything?"

"There is a birth certificate. Even an intake form from when he was first taken into Child Protective Services." She paused a second before adding. "There was no mention of me in his report, nor any other family."

"That's what we found. Looking for you, it was like an empty void. Any record of your existence was erased. Renee O'Malley had no registered birth certificate. We checked the pediatrician's office records where Lucas went, and they didn't have anything. I've got a good computer expert who works for my PI firm. He couldn't find a trace, either. Destiny, a brilliant hacker who works for Ridge, conducted extensive searches of the dark web and couldn't find anything related to Renee O'Malley. I've talked to neighbors of your parents from the time you were little. The few we were able to trace remembered Lucas, but didn't remember the O'Malley's having a baby girl."

"How is that possible?"

Shiloh scratched the back of his head, and gave her a chagrined look. "It's perplexing. Maybe once we know your whole story, we can figure out who wanted you to disappear."

Renee gave him a tentative smile. "I guess I really can't stall any longer."

"Best to get it over with. Like ripping off a bandage. Painful at first, but it goes away quickly."

She gave him an open-eyed stare. "You rip off the bandage? Just like that?" The way her shoulders shook, he knew she was biting back laughter, easing the tension of the moment.

"Doesn't everyone?"

"Only macho, he-man types. Ladies peel back the edges and work it off gently." She laughed at his deliberately offended expression, and he grinned. Renee was turning out to have a wicked sense of humor, and he found himself drawn to her in ways it was difficult to explain. Sure, there was a physical attraction. She was a beautiful woman. But it was more than a simple chemical reaction of boy meets girl. He liked her intellect, her wit. Though reluctant, she hadn't backed down when it would have been easier to simply run away again. Heck, if he was honest, he simply liked—her.

"We really do need to talk about who's after you, Renee. Whatever it is, all of us will help. There's nothing to be afraid of, I promise."

"Don't make promises you might not be able to keep, Shiloh. Darius and Eileen have the money and the clout to do anything they want, without repercussions. They have powerful friends in high places."

"As do the Boudreaus. Talk to me, sweetheart." Shiloh took her hands in his, noting they felt like ice, though it wasn't cold outside. "No more hiding. No more running. We'll confront the bad guys together. You're not alone anymore. You've got a whole family you can count on."

"I thought I had a family before. Darius and Eileen were my family. Turns out I was nothing to them but a means to an end, a pawn."

"Tell me. You have to talk to someone. It's eating you alive, a little at a time. Brace yourself, and yank it off like the bandage. When you're done, you'll feel better."

Renee stared into his eyes for the longest time, and he wondered if she'd back out, decide not to let them—him—help. Finally, after what seemed an eternity, she nodded.

"You're right. It's time for it to end. I'll tell you everything."

CHAPTER FOURTEEN

Renee stared down at her hands, clasped tightly within Shiloh's. The icy cold that permeated her seemed to melt beneath his gentle, yet strong touch. She'd known from the moment they met he'd be instrumental in changing her life in ways she couldn't imagine. That change had to start today, by telling him the truth. She only hoped when he knew, he wouldn't turn his back and walk away.

"You know the first part, when I was young. I was shifted around from foster home to group homes in the welfare system, never staying long in one place. There were times when I almost wondered if I was going crazy, thinking I had a family somewhere who wanted me, who was looking for me. All I'd ever known was overcrowded houses with little food and angry kids. Moving from place to place became my norm. Until just before my tenth birthday; that's when everything changed."

She half-expected him to interrupt, but he simply nodded, indicating for her to keep going.

"I was living in a group home, I think it was in Kansas. I remember they'd get the smaller kids together and have us do shows when visitors came. It was weird how they'd dress us up in these school uniforms, and have us sing or read passages from books. I don't remember doing that at the other homes, only this last one. There were several families there on this day, men in suits and ties, and women in dresses or blouses and pants. Nice outfits. But this one couple stood out, even to me, as being different than the others."

"Different how?"

"I got the impression they were more important than the rest. Ms. Beavers, she's the lady who ran our group, acted like she'd kiss the ground they walked on if they asked. Anyway, these two, a man and a woman, paid attention to me. Asked me questions, let me sit with them, things like that. I felt…special."

Shiloh squeezed the hands he still held. "You are special, Renee."

She gave him the briefest smile. The bad stuff was coming soon. What would he think? It didn't matter, the truth had to be told.

"It wasn't long before I found myself moving in with Darius and Eileen Black. I remember feeling overwhelmed when I walked into their house. Mansion, really. It was the biggest place I'd ever seen, and I was going to live there. Get a room all to myself, not sharing with anybody. And it was beautiful, a little girl's dream room. A canopied bed with a pink ruffled bedspread and white lacy curtains on the windows, and I didn't have to share it. A toy box overflowing with more things than I'd seen in my lifetime. At ten years old, it was like my every dream all wrapped up in a big package with a bow on top. It even had a bathroom attached. I don't think I ever had a bathroom I didn't share with a whole bunch of people, so this was something really special."

Remembering those early years hurt; emotions threatening to choke her. She'd been happy there, having a brand-new family who loved her and took care of her. Gave her everything she'd ever dreamed about. Eileen treated her like a princess, having matching outfits made for them, right down to the shoes. She hadn't realized until years later she was nothing more than a puppet, a doll, something for Eileen to play with and mold into her own image. It almost worked, too.

"I had private tutors until I reached high school age. Then I was allowed to go to a private school. I guess most of this is unimportant, really, in the grand scheme. I simply need you to understand the connection between me and Darius and Eileen. For all intents and purposes, they are—were—my parents for the greater part of my life. I can't prove anything, but I'd bet money Darius is the one who made all my records disappear. He and Eileen told everyone I was his daughter from a previous marriage who'd come to live with them. I don't look like either one of them, but that didn't stop the lie, and nobody questioned it."

"I've never heard of Darius or Eileen Black. Pretty common last name, though. Where were you living?"

"Kansas City." She grinned and added, "Missouri, in case you were going to ask."

Shiloh simply rolled his eyes and she chuckled, using the moment of levity to ground herself, remember she wasn't still there, still in the grasp of two horrible people.

"Darius has several businesses in the city. All of them highly successful. Eileen does charitable work and fundraisers for the community. They're friends with the mayor and a couple of state senators. Darius is friends with a couple of highly-placed judges too."

"So, I guess he thinks he's pretty unstoppable, at least on a state level."

"Trust me, he is." She pushed past the memory of trying to expose what Darius and Eileen were doing. She'd gone to Charles, the man she'd been dating when she'd uncovered the truth, begging him to help her expose Darius. Instead of going straight to the authorities, he'd taken her back to Darius, telling him he needed to put a muzzle on Renee before she got them all arrested. That betrayal still stung because she'd cared for Charles. His actions killed what affection she'd had, turning it to loathing and hate.

"Nobody is above the law, sweetheart. We'll find a way to take him down, no matter how many high-powered friends he's got."

"Okay." She gave a noncommittal agreement, though she doubted it'd happen. Too many had tried and failed. "I should probably get to the bad stuff. Really bad stuff. After I graduated high school, I decided what I wanted to do with my life. I wanted some real-life experience before heading to college, so I talked with my parents, and we decided to let me take a gap year. Darius let me intern for him. I think he wanted me around so he could keep an eye on me. And I was like an overeager puppy, doing my best to please my master. I learned a tremendous amount, following him around, watching him interact with businesspeople from all over the country. Eileen wasn't happy about it. She wanted me to go straight to college after graduation. I'm not sure if she wanted me out of the house because I was older, and she didn't want to have anybody making her look or feel older. She's extremely vain about her looks, and I was cramping her style. People referred her to her Darius' trophy wife and she loved it, because it made her feel young and attractive. Having an almost 19-year-old daughter didn't figure in to that equation."

"Sounds like an idiot. I've never understood the mentality that says you have to keep trying to alter reality. Living and aging are natural facts of life; it happens to everyone. There's no changing or delaying the march of time. I've always said embrace who you are, and be proud of the life you're given. Looks fade, who you are inside lives on."

Renee chuckled, leaning against his side. "Eileen would've hated you. She does Botox, nips and tucks, whatever keeps her looking the perfect plastic princess."

"I prefer reality to artificial. A woman like you holds more appeal."

She felt a wash of heat flooding her cheeks and ducked her head, hoping he wouldn't notice. Shiloh wasn't flirting, he was speaking the truth, and it made her feel special. Oh, how she wished things were different. That she'd met him as part of a normal life. One where she could date him, get to know him. Maybe even have a relationship. All of that was moot, because the reality was she might never have a chance at a normal life. Not as long as Darius and Eileen were on her trail.

"Darius loves her, despite her flaws, or maybe because of them. They are far more alike than I'd ever imagined. Working daily with him opened my eyes to the facts. Not everybody who worked for him thought he walked on water; quite the opposite. I heard murmurs, rumblings of discontent. People weren't happy, but he paid better than anybody else in town, so job loyalty kept people long-term. Nobody said you had to like your job. You simply had to do it well. Darius has a home office because he tends toward being a workaholic. Running multilayered conglomerates isn't a nine-to-five proposition. Leaving the office didn't mean an end to the work day. I found the variety of businesses fascinating, so I didn't mind the long hours."

Shiloh was drawing tiny patterns with his fingertip on top of her hand, and it distracted her. He didn't even seem to be aware he was doing it, a faraway expression on his face.

She wondered if he was even listening. She'd been droning on and on, probably boring him out of his mind.

Great going, he's comatose from boredom.

"What kind of businesses?" His question startled me, and I realized I'd been sitting for a long time, not talking, lost in the swirling distraction of his fingertip on my skin.

"Um, he runs an insurance brokerage firm. Also, he owns several restaurants within Kansas City, high-end, upper-level clientele. A sporting goods emporium. He's also a partial owner of a couple sports franchises." She grinned when Shiloh sat a little straighter. "You might have heard of them." When she mentioned the names, his eyes widened in recognition. Men and their games, she mused.

"You're right, he's got his fingers in a lot of things. But this all sounds legit. Where does the not-so-legal stuff come into play?"

Oh, boy, here we go.

"Let me say up front, I never suspected they were up to anything illicit, immoral, or illegal. Not even a hint or a whisper, disgruntled employees aside. Until one evening, I was putting away some files in Darius' office. He and Eileen had gone out for the evening. They did that a lot, dinners with clients. Charity events with the city's finest. Dressing up in fancy gowns and wearing heels all night wasn't high on my list of things I enjoyed, so he'd let me stay home. A phone call came through on Darius' private line. I'm never supposed to answer that number; it's only for his most important clients. People who don't go through the normal channels. It was the way big business worked, he told me."

"Let me guess. You answered it."

"You think you're so smart, don't you? Of course I answered it."

Shiloh's shoulder moved under my head, and I knew he was laughing at me. Not that I blamed him; I'd been stupid and predictable. "There was a man on the other end, calling to say the meetup had been moved to the alternate site. I didn't have a clue what he meant, but I said I'd relay the message to Darius. I debated with myself about calling him, because he was going to be supremely pissed that I'd answered his private line. On the other hand, he needed to go to the alternate meeting place or he'd miss his appointment. In the end, I called him. I've never heard Darius utter a single foul word before, but he went on a tirade. The words spewing from him scared me. I mean really scared me, like go and hide from the big, bad wolf terrified. After a while, he seemed calmer and realized what he'd said. He apologized and thanked me for letting him know. Then he said we'd talk when he got home. I think that frightened me more than the verbal abuse."

"Did he tell you what the meeting was about?"

She barked out a harsh laugh. "It probably would have been best if I'd waited and let him tell me. But I've always had a curious streak coupled with a stubborn nature that doesn't like to be told what to do. I had the address. Why not go there and find out why Darius blew a gasket? I changed clothes, because Darius and Eileen had been dressed in formal wear when they left."

Shiloh leaned forward his elbows on his knees, and head in his hands. "You're telling me you went to the meeting place."

She nodded. "I had to. It was like I was compelled to go. Haven't you ever had the feeling if you didn't do something, bad things would happen?" At his shrug, she rolled her eyes hard enough it was a wonder they stayed inside her head. "I followed the GPS to the address I'd input. It took me outside of the city, to the north. There were rows and rows of shipping containers, maybe a dozen of them all stacked up on either side of this big warehouse-type building. All concrete blocks and metal, and no windows except high up by the roofline. It was a strange juxtaposition, because there were valets outside, parking cars. The mix of expensive Mercedes and BMWs were interspersed with older sedans and pickup trucks. Not what you'd expect to see for a high-end business function."

She knew she'd spiked his interest when he sat up straighter, shifting until he was facing her. Shiloh's brown eyes gleamed in the dappled sunlight spilling through the gazebo's walls. His attention seemed riveted on every word, as though he knew the big payoff was moments away. If only it was that simple, instead of the nightmare she'd lived with for the past several years.

"I almost turned around and went home. Something didn't add up. What kind of meeting took place in a rundown warehouse on the edge of town? But I couldn't chicken out. If this was part of Darius' business world, I needed to see for myself. Instead of giving my keys to the valet, I drove past and turned into an alley behind the building. The asphalt was cracked and full of potholes, and I was astonished my undercarriage made it ten feet without being torn loose. I ended up parking in total darkness, several feet from the building. There wasn't a hint of light except for the bit shining through the high windows. I made it to the back door, only to find it padlocked."

"I'm sure a girl scout like you didn't let that stop you."

"Okay, I won't tell you that when I lived in one of the homes, I learned how to pick locks. One of the other girls taught me, smarty pants." His laughter made her feel all warm and tingly inside, like a teenage schoolgirl with her first unrequited crush on her teacher. Been there, done that. "It was still pretty dark once I got inside, though there was lots of noise that grew louder the closer I got to the center of the warehouse. The lights got brighter, too. I snuck through an unoccupied doorway into what looked like a boxing arena, only not. There was a raised platform, square with ropes all the way around it. Picture a wrestling match, where the competitors fight. Except encircling that was a large chain-link fence reaching probably twelve feet high. The top was chain-link too. Like a giant cage. Dozens and dozens of people were crowded around the huge room. Some sat in cordoned off areas, with plush seating. They were dressed the way Darius and Eileen had been when they left the house. Formal wear. Suits and ties. Sparkling gowns. It was grotesquely obscene. Others stood behind barricades. Those folks looked more like regular people, dressed like working class people."

"Sounds like somebody's idea of a fight club. Illegal gambling is high all over the United States. Lucas wrote an award-winning article about it not too long ago." Shiloh smiled, the pride in his brother's work shining through.

"That's what I thought it was—at first. I'd at least have understood the thrill of the fight. The lure of betting, winning and losing. This…it was diabolic. Macabre. Two men fought inside the ring. The crowd cheered every hit, every punch. I'd never seen anything like this spectacle. There was a kind of blood lust permeating the air. This wasn't fighting. It was an annihilation. I watch someone open a portion of the fenced off area and toss in a baseball bat and a machete."

Shiloh's sharp inhalation pulled her from the vivid memory. She knew words alone couldn't begin to describe the horror playing out before her that night. The events transpiring shattered her innocence and sent her whole world into a tailspin she'd never recovered from. Not really.

"Renee—"

"No, let me finish it. I don't know if I can tell it again if

I stop." She drew in a ragged breath, letting the viciousness of the memory fade. "Both men fought like their lives depended on it. Little did I understand at the time, they *were* fighting for their very lives. I've learned these are called death matches. They've been around in the States for decades. Fighters willing to risk everything for the money these fights bring. And they bring in a lot of cash. Sometimes hundreds of thousands of dollars, and that's not even counting the illegal gambling. It's an insidious monster and people feed on the depravity of death."

She couldn't sit still another second. Walking around the well in the center of the gazebo, she looked at the loveliness surrounding her, in sharp contrast to the ugliness of her words. It was impossible not to see the irony, and she wasn't adept at explaining the desperation and malevolence she'd witnessed.

"The fighters grabbed the weapons, swinging them, attacking their opponent in a frenzied madness I refuse to remember. I lived with nightmares for months and months afterward. They still creep up on me occasionally. The mat soaked in blood. The sound of the baseball bat connecting. The snap of bone as it broke. It haunts me. And still the people cheered. I imagine it's what the Roman Colosseum must've been like with the gladiators. Combatants fighting for their lives and the glory of the emperor. It sickened me, yet I couldn't force my feet to move. Darius sat, chatting with some person seated beside him, occasionally glancing at the fight, but he seemed desensitized from it all. Eileen, though, I'll never forget the look on her face. She savored every blow, every drop of blood shed."

"Stop. Please, Renee, you're killing me."

"I can't. I have to finish telling it. I stayed until the end. The killing blow. Until there was a lone combatant standing within the cage, while the crowd roared their approval. After that, it was like the spell was broken and I ran. Climbed in my car, and sped toward home. I had to stop twice on the way, because I was sick to my stomach."

Shiloh stood and pulled her into his arms, and she realized she was shaking, though she hadn't shed a single tear. There weren't any left to cry.

"We'll get them shut down."

"You can't. I've tried everything. If a whisper about the fights gets to the police, the site is simply shut down or moved to another location until the heat's off, and then they start up again. I asked Darius about the fighters. Didn't their families try to find them? Who were they? How could they get away with killing? Do you know what he told me? Nobody missed them because they were homeless. Men they got from the streets, still in decent shape so they could endure the matches. Former military, veterans down on their luck or with drug problems, but still able to do battle and make a good showing of it. That's all it is to him—a show. A performance he can charge astronomical amounts of money for, and depraved, despicable people flock to them like it's a bloody circus."

"I promise we will stop the Blacks. Stop the killings. No matter what it takes, this will end and you'll be free."

"Free? Don't you understand, I'll never be free. I have blood on my hands. Blood money paid for everything. My clothes. My home. My education. Even the food I ate, it all came from the maiming or death of innocent men. I tried to make it right, I swear. I anonymously contacted the police about the fights. They promised to check out my story. The warehouse was clean, nothing to show I was telling the truth. Like I said, Darius has deep pockets, and isn't above using his influence. And I had no proof. I was shocked, dumbfounded, and it never occurred to me I should have taken pictures. It was the word of an unverified, anonymous source versus that of a well-respected businessman, a multimillionaire with influential friends who'd back him."

"I believe you." Shiloh's quiet, whispered affirmation swept through her like a wildfire, the blaze burning fast and hot, and she realized not all men were liars or cheats or murderers. There was at least one good man still in existence, and he held her within his embrace.

"Good. Fortunately, I do have more than my word. I've got evidence. I feigned ignorance when Darius got home. Pretended I hadn't gone to the depths of hell hours before. He had no clue I'd witnessed his death match firsthand. He scolded me for taking the call on his private line, and then acted like nothing happened. The man I looked at as my father was as big a monster as anything you see in the movies. But I knew I needed a plan to get the proof to shut him down. I might have been young, but I wasn't stupid. It took weeks, but I convinced him I could be trusted with my responsibility. I buttered him up, made him believe I wanted to be his successor in everything, every aspect of his business. Told him it didn't matter if I had to get my hands dirty. I'd grown up in poverty, and I wasn't ever going back. He believed me. Not enough to confide in me about the death matches; that would have been asking too much. But he allowed me more access to his private office, his private files. I hate to admit it, but I think I made a surprisingly good spy. Darius never suspected I put a bug on his private phone line and recorded the calls. Dates, times, locations of the matches. I created logs, documentation. Others coordinated the fights, and Darius only found out the locations the same day as the event, so it was hard to get cameras set up. I had to rely on sneaking in. The guards were increased after I ratted him out to the cops. I took photos on my phone. I climbed up a fire escape at one place, coming in through the huge industrial fans on the roof. Those shots are the best ones, because I didn't have to hide behind corners or try and take the pictures over people's shoulders. The ceiling shots are clear and crisp, and show every detail. Every face. Including Darius and Eileen."

Shiloh lifted her chin with one finger, and she gave him a tremulous smile. The pride shining in his eyes made her feel ten feet tall. "You are amazing, sweetheart."

"Not really. Because there's a problem and it's not a small one. A, Darius and Eileen know about the evidence. That's why they've been hunting me. And b, I don't exactly have access to it. The records I compiled, they're hidden in their house. I didn't have a choice but to leave them behind when I fled. I don't think they've found them yet, or they'd have had one of the mercenaries take me out already."

Shiloh closed his eyes and pressed his forehead against hers. "You don't make things easy, do you?"

"Once they figured out what I'd been doing, I couldn't exactly stick around, could I?" She stared into his eyes, silently imploring him to understand what she'd done. Every day since she'd hightailed it out of Kansas City, she'd berated herself for being a coward, and not fighting for those poor men who'd been slaughtered because of people's depravity and Darius and Eileen's greed and quest for power. And they'd achieved their goal, because some of the guests at these infamous matches were powerful within the government and political circles. How they'd not only stood by, but condoned the loss of life simply for entertainment value, sickened her. Yet she hadn't been able to stop it because she'd been too afraid. Instead, she'd bolted with only the clothes on her back and a bus ticket.

"I can't believe you stayed as long as you did, sweetheart. Knowing what Darius put these people through, it must have been excruciatingly painful to face him day after day.

We're going to find a way to shut him down, and take down the people who've allowed something this atrocious to continue."

"Thank you."

He tilted his head, a questioning expression on his handsome face. "For what?"

"Believing me. My story is so farfetched, and I don't have any proof, no cold hard evidence to hand over, yet you still trust I'm telling you the truth."

A slow smile spread across his face, and in that instant, she saw the real man beneath the surface. The good, kind soul beneath the sometimes stoic personality, and it was beautiful. A lightness spilled through her, a belief things might actually work out for the best swept the doubt and fear away, things she'd lived with so long, they'd become a part of her. Now, a sense of calm and hope took their place, the foreign sensation filling her with warmth and comfort.

Reaching up, she placed her hands on each side of his face and stared, memorizing every inch. The strength and character in the strong bone structure, the dark sweep of his brows over deep chocolate-brown eyes. The slight uptick of his mouth, just a little higher on the right side than the left. Going on her tiptoes, she pressed her lips against his, and a spark of electricity zinged through her entire body. With a sigh, her mouth opened beneath his as he took over the kiss, devouring her lips in a fiery dance of lips and tongues. Just like in the movies, she could picture explosions of fireworks going off around them, the magic of the moment sweeping her under. This kiss felt more than magical—it felt right. Like she'd been waiting her whole life to feel Shiloh's lips on hers, and she never wanted it to end.

Finally, excruciatingly slowly, she eased back from the kiss, taking one final sip at his lips, and dropping her hands from his face. She couldn't meet his eyes, embarrassed to the bottom of her soul.

"I'm sorry," she murmured, crossing her arms across her chest. "I shouldn't have done that."

He shot her a quizzical look. "Why not? I've wanted to kiss you since about five minutes after I met you, except I didn't want to rush you. I'm glad you kissed me. I hope you'll want to do it again."

"Oh...oh, I guess that would be okay. I mean...sometime...if you want to."

He placed a finger against her lips. "I definitely want to. We can take things as fast or slow as you want. There's no hurry."

"I'd like that."

Before he could say anything else, his phone rang, breaking the spell that seemed to have encircled them. This place, this gazebo, surely must be enchanted, because she'd spilled her soul to him. All the ugliness, the painful memories that haunted her, made her feel worthless, and turned them into something special with a single stolen kiss.

She stared at the swirling pattern of flowers climbing the

columns of the walls, the greens and whites and ivory colors a perfect backdrop for the gazebo and wishing well. Shiloh's murmured voice on the phone seemed far away, and she pondered the possibility of having a life again. Being free to move on from Darius, from Eileen, and their hatred and betrayal.

"I'm sorry. I'm supposed to meet Ridge and Lucas in town. You'll be fine here. I won't be too long, and when I get back, we'll start working on a plan to get the evidence against Darius and close down his deadly empire once and for all."

She nodded and he took her hand, helping her step out of the gazebo, and they headed toward the Big House. As they stepped out of the cluster of pine trees toward the house, she turned back, taking a final look at the white flower-covered structure. Such a small, insignificant structure to contain such wonder and magic. It felt like her whole life had diverged onto a new track, headed in a different yet equally exciting direction, and she couldn't help wondering where it would take her.

Was she being given a shot at true happiness, or would her confession lead to her ultimate destruction?

CHAPTER FIFTEEN

After spending the late morning and early part of the afternoon with Renee, Shiloh's head was still reeling with all the information she'd given him. His heart felt shattered into a million tiny pieces, aching for the life she'd endured for far too long. Calling it living didn't encompass everything she'd been through. Shaking his head and muttering a few well-chosen curse words, he strode through the door into Daisy's Diner and glanced around the tables. He spotted Lucas in one of the back booths. Ridge sat directly across from him. He hadn't known his twin would be joining them, but he wasn't surprised.

Ever since listening to Renee, he'd been testy, on edge, and angry. Chances were good his brother picked up on his feelings and headed for Shiloh Springs. Sometimes the whole twin telepathy thing was pretty cool. They'd always had a connection he didn't share with any of his other brothers, in a way that was some days awesome and some days downright creepy. Their special connection usually meant he couldn't keep anything secret from his brother. Today, he felt like a volcano ready to erupt, but he'd managed to contain himself around Renee. Didn't want her to realize how finding out she'd live a life filled with so much emotional turmoil and pain affected him on a visceral level.

He could use the moral support of the two brothers seated at the table, as well as Ridge's analytical brain to figure out how they were going to help dig Renee out of the mess she was neck deep in.

At the Big House, he'd left Renee with Liam and Dane, knowing they'd keep a vigilant eye out on the premises, and make sure nobody got anywhere near her. Liam put the jobsite foreman in charge for the next couple of days. Boudreau Construction had several projects going all the time, well known throughout Texas and even a few bordering states for their quality and dependability. Liam's crews ran like a well-oiled machine, and he'd assured Shiloh taking a few days off wouldn't be the end of the world. He couldn't help appreciating his brother's willingness to step up, but then, all his family did.

"Shiloh, good to see you." Daisy stood beside the table as Shiloh slid onto the red vinyl bench. "Coffee?"

"Yes, thanks. Looks like you're busy today."

"I'm not complaining." Daisy filled his cup, and topped off Ridge and Lucas at the same time. "I might need to get some additional help soon, if things keep going like this."

"That's because people are wising up to your place having the best food around."

"Thanks, Ridge. Can I get y'all anything else, or is it just coffee?"

"Maybe later, Daisy. I need to talk to my brothers for a bit first."

"No problem. Give me a shout when you're ready."

Shiloh took a sip of his coffee as she walked away, eyeing his brothers over the rim of the cup. Lucas looked like he might explode, not that Shiloh blamed him. He'd refrained from asking Renee any questions yesterday, ceding Shiloh the opportunity to get answers, since she knew him better, trusted him the most at the moment. It looked like Lucas wanted to jump out of his skin, his hands balled into fists on the tabletop.

"Well?"

Ridge simply shook his head. He wanted answers too, Shiloh knew. Ridge had done exhaustive searches for Renee, even pulling in his company hacker. Now that she was here, everyone wanted to make her feel like she was part of the family.

"Did you find out who I've got to destroy?"

"Get in line," Shiloh answered. "It's a long story, and it's not pretty."

"Names. Gimme names, bro." Ridge already had his phone in hand, ready to get Destiny on the search, he'd bet. Guardian Security was quickly gaining cachet throughout Texas as one of the premiere security companies around. They provided bodyguards and investigative services, although Ridge usually referred those cases to him. Installing and maintaining high-end homes alarms, cameras, and the full spectrum of security measures garnered a huge chunk of his brother's business, and he even did security checks and backgrounds for his elite clientele. Samuel Carpenter, a friend of the family and owner of Carpenter Security Services, utilized Guardian Security whenever they needed extra expertise.

Shiloh carefully placed his coffee mug onto the table, afraid he'd crush it in his hands by simply thinking about Darius and Eileen Black. He hadn't had time to investigate them; he'd left the Big House to head toward town to meet with Lucas before he'd had the chance. Plus, he hadn't wanted to do it while around Renee. He had a pretty good idea he wouldn't be able to hold onto his temper, and didn't think she needed to see that.

"We're looking at a couple. Darius and Eileen Black. I haven't had time to look into them."

"Give me five minutes." Ridge slid from the bench and headed for Daisy's front door, phone to his ear. Shiloh knew it wouldn't take long before Ridge had Destiny digging into the Blacks. They'd have answers within five minutes, because Destiny was a world-class hacker, although she preferred the term data manipulator extraordinaire. She'd been tapped to work for the government, though she'd turned them down. A relatively free spirit, she didn't like to be tied down with too many rules and regulations, and she worked within the limits of the law. Usually.

"Renee talked to you? Gave you the whole story?" There was an edge to Lucas' voice, like he was barely holding things together. Shiloh commiserated with him. She was his baby sister. He should be the one helping her. The one she came to when needing help. Instead, he'd had to take a step back, allowing another man to become her confidant. It didn't matter that the man was also his brother.

"Yeah. Give her a little time. This whole thing, it's been a lot. Dealing with this on her own for so long, then finding out you're still alive and she has a safe place to land, it's kind of overwhelming."

Lucas leaned against the back of the bench and sighed. "I feel helpless. Terrified if I demand answers, she's going to panic and run. Scared if I don't, these people are going to get to her and I won't be ready."

Before he could answer his brother, Ridge slid back into his seat. "I've got Destiny working her magic. She'll have something for us soon. So far, all I can tell you is Darius and Eileen Black are married and living in Kansas City."

"Kansas or Missouri?" Lucas pulled a pen and paper out, and started jotting down notes. Shiloh knew the investigative report side of his brain had kicked into gear, already looking at angles the rest of them might miss.

"Missouri. He's in his early fifties. Businessman. Well-respected in his community. Attends charity events, and makes the newspapers consistently, both on the society pages as well as business ones. Eileen is younger, late thirties to early forties. Destiny couldn't get a lock on her age. She did text me this picture thought."

Ridge turned his phone so both Lucas and Shiloh could see. The photo showed a couple standing in what looked like a theater. Darius exuded the air of a confident businessman in a dark suit and tie, with a cocky grin. Eileen appeared the perfectly coiffed wife, long blonde hair spilling over her bare shoulders. A strapless sapphire blue dress emphasized a large bust and clung to her curves as though designed just for her. Studying the picture, Shiloh couldn't help but notice though she smiled for the camera, there was a coldness in her gaze he couldn't ignore. Reminded him of a piranha on the hunt for fresh prey. He barely suppressed the chill racing down his spine. Tangling with her would definitely leave claw marks behind.

"They certainly look like they deserve each other."

Before Shiloh could respond to Ridge's offhand comment, his phone rang. Glancing at the caller ID, his body tense. Why would Tina be calling him from Portland? Wouldn't she be calling Renee directly?

Answering the call, he sucked in a shocked breath when Tina's face appeared on the screen. She looked like she'd been in a car accident, her left eye swollen completely shut, the skin all around it blackened, bruised, and swollen. A white bandage was taped to her forehead, and a large bruised area covered most of her right cheek, extending down toward her chin.

"Tina? What happened?"

"Shiloh…is Elizabeth okay?"

"She's fine. I've got my brothers watching over her. Now tell me what happened."

"This dude showed up at work, looking for Elizabeth, I mean Renee. I'm still trying to remember to call her that." He watched her use a bandaged hand to brush the hair back from her face. A sinking feeling thudded in his gut at her words. If somebody'd come looking for Renee, did that mean he'd taken his frustration at not finding her out on Tina? Regret was a bitter taste in his mouth. He should have considered something like this might happen. Taken precautions. Made sure he'd left somebody watching Tina and the coffee shop, at least for a few days, in case some-body'd caught up to Renee.

"He was looking for Renee?" He gently prompted her to continue.

"Big dude. Close cropped hair, kind of military cut, you know what I mean? Dirty dishwater blondish color. Dark eyes. Cold, dead eyes that gave me the creeps. I didn't tell him anything, I swear."

Shiloh turned the phone so Lucas and Ridge got a good look at Tina's face. Both men recoiled at the sight of her bruised and battered appearance.

"Is this guy the one who did that to you?"

"Um, yeah. He must've followed me back to my apart-ment. I wasn't paying attention as I unlocked the door. He came up behind me, forced his way in, and smacked me around a little."

"A little?" Ridge mouthed the words, disgust written on his face. His brother had a real problem with any man putting his hands on a woman violently, probably as much as Shiloh did.

"He told me his name. Bruce something, I can't remember. Said he was a friend of Elizabeth's from Cincinnati. Honestly, I wouldn't have told him anything anyway, but he gave me a really bad vibe. Not like somebody Renee would hang out with, you know what I mean?"

"Tina, I'm so sorry."

"Hey, it's not your fault. I was stupid. Got distracted and didn't pay attention, or I'd have noticed him following me."

"Where are you now?" Lucas and Ridge both nodded at his question.

Tina sighed and then winced, holding her fingertips against her swollen lip. "Emergency room. Don't worry, they aren't admitting me. I told you, it's nothing serious." She turned away from the phone and muttered, "Not like it's the first time anyway," probably thinking he couldn't hear her. He did, and from his brothers' faces, they had, too.

"Tina, listen to me. You can't go back home."

'But—"

"No buts. This Bruce guy might come back. I'm going to contact the hotel where I stayed while I was in Portland. You remember it?" At her nod, he continued, "I'm going to book you a room there. No arguments. When you leave the ER, go straight there and check in. The room will be under my name, okay? I'll set it up for a couple of days, while we make some plans."

"This is stupid. I won't let some bully push me around, disrupt my life."

"Tina, this isn't about an ex-boyfriend shoving you around, this is about a professional looking for Renee. When he can't find her still in Portland, he'll come back."

"When you put it like that…"

"Let the doctors and nurses get you patched up. I'm going to call you back in ten minutes and give you the information, okay."

"I'm a big girl, you know. I can take care of myself."

Shiloh drew in a deep breath, needing a second before answering her. "Tina, I respect you as an intelligent woman, but I want to help. Please, let's get you out of the line of fire, and then you can bash me for being a chauvinist, okay?"

She started to laugh, and then winced. "Ow, ow. Alright. I'll come all the way to Texas to pound on you. Honestly, I'm scared to go home. I'd have probably ended up in one of those roach-trap motels tonight anyway. I should be ready to go soon, so I'll wait for your call. Tell Renee…on second thought, don't tell her anything yet. She's got enough to worry about."

With that, she disconnected the call, and Shiloh dialed the hotel he'd stayed at in Portland, and made arrangements for Tina to have a room available as soon as she got there.

"Alright, you both heard and saw what happened. We need to get Tina secluded some place safe. She's been a good friend to Renee, and doesn't deserve to be used as anybody's punching bag."

Shiloh stopped talking when he heard footsteps approaching the table. Looking up, he spotted Chance. A tiny kernel of an idea began forming in his brain at his brother's approach.

"Spotted you guys when I was walking past. How's Renee?"

Ah, there was his compassionate brother's white knight peeking through. He'd be perfect for what Shiloh had in mind.

"Have a seat, bro. I need to talk to you." Lucas looked at Ridge, who stared back, then both gave Shiloh a thumb's up. Apparently, they were all on the same page when it came to helping Tina. Chance might get the opportunity to play hero if Shiloh could talk him into it.

"Something wrong?"

"Yes. That's why I want to ask a favor."

Chance's gaze moved from one smiling face to the next, suspicion clouding his gaze. "Okay, I'll bite. What kind of favor?"

"Can you free up your schedule for a few days?"

"You've got to be kidding, right? I just cleared my calendar for the next week. No cases for seven glorious days, and I plan on doing nothing but heading to my condo on South Padre Island and not moving a muscle for an entire week."

"But—"

"No," Chance interrupted Shiloh before he could say anything else. "Do you know how long it's been since I've taken a day off? I have burnout with a capital B. Whatever it is, it'll have to wait."

"I wish it could, bro. I just got off a call from Renee's friend, Tina, in Portland. Somebody came around asking questions about Renee, and worked her over pretty good. She's in the emergency room getting patched up as we speak. Dude, she's got a big black eye, bruises down the side of her face, a split lip, and there was a bandage on her forehead. From the way she winced and held herself, I got the feeling she might have a couple of busted ribs on top of that."

Chance's shoulders slumped for a second before he shoved Shiloh, indicating he should slide over. He made room for his brother on the bench seat. When Chance met his gaze, Shiloh knew he hooked him.

"What do you want me to do?"

"Head up to Portland."

Chance gave a dramatic sigh. "How'd I know you were going to say that?"

"Because you're the smart brother?" Shiloh grinned. "I've booked Tina a room at the hotel where I stayed. All you need to do is babysit her for a little while, and keep an eye out for the guy who roughed her up. She said his name was

KATHY IVAN

Bruce something. I'll get you more information as soon as I've got it. We've got Destiny looking into the people after Renee. Names are Darius and Eileen Black from Kansas City."

"Black…Darius Black. Why is that name familiar?"

Shiloh sat up a little straighter at his brother's words. Chance had a mind like a steel trap. Being the distract attorney for the county, he had his finger on a lot of the pulses of what went on in Texas and beyond when it came to criminal activity. Sometimes he imagined Chance wearing a Superman outfit beneath his business suits, because if anybody had a superhero complex, it was his overachieving brother. He'd become a prosecutor because he felt people who were victims deserved justice, and he in turn demanded it for them.

"I'll need to go home and pack. Can you book me a flight? Text me the details. I need to make a few calls and cancel a couple of plans." He glared at Shiloh. "Long-legged, blonde plans."

"Thanks, Chance. Really, I trust you to keep an eye on Tina. I probably should warn you, she might be a bit of a handful."

Chance quirked his brow, a tiny smile lifting the corner of his mouth. "Oh, yeah?"

For a brief second, Shiloh imagined Tina and Chance in the same room, and pictured the fireworks that would fly. He'd love to be a fly on the wall when those two met.

Chance nodded to Ridge and Lucas and stood, heading for the door. Shiloh waited until he'd exited before breathing a sigh of relief. One problem solved. He couldn't stop picturing poor Tina's face, bruised and battered, knew it would only look worse. By the time Chance got to Portland, she'd be a sight to behold, and undoubtedly bring out the white knight syndrome all the Boudreau men seemed afflicted with.

"Timing seems fortuitous, don't you think? Chance happens to take a whole week off, just when another crisis hits. What are the odds?"

"Lucas, I'll chalk it up to fate and leave it at that. Tina doesn't deserve to be drug into the middle of this mess, but since she has, it's good that Chance can take care of her."

"We got hauled off track with Tina's call. What about these Darius and Eileen characters? Did Renee tell you how they're involved, and what they want from her?"

"It's a long story. How about I tell you when we get to the Big House? Don't want to have to repeat it more than once. Dad wants to be there, too."

Lucas made a grumbly noise, but Shiloh knew he'd agree. Besides, he was heading to the Big House anyway to see Renee. Wasn't like he couldn't wait another hour.

Shiloh stood, tossing a twenty on the table. "I'm going to head out. Meet you guys in a while."

He turned and walked out of the diner, waving to Daisy on his way out. The brilliance of her smile always made his day, and he wondered if she was still dating Derrick Williamson. They'd been seeing each other for a few months. Williamson had even brought his young son to meet her. At least that's what his momma told him. He really hoped things worked out because Daisy deserved all the happiness in the world.

There was one more stop he needed to make before heading back to the Big House, and he hoped he would find what he was looking for.

CHAPTER SIXTEEN

Renee stood between two Boudreau men, hiding her tiny smile behind her hand. Did Shiloh really think she wouldn't realize Liam and Dane had been left behind to act as bodyguards? She hadn't been born yesterday, for goodness sake. Guess it was the thought that counted, right?

She knew from talking with Shiloh that Dane handled the day-to-day running of the Boudreau ranch. It seemed like a huge undertaking, from what little she knew about ranching. Most of what she knew had been gleaned from a television cooking show, where the woman lived on a working spread with her rancher husband and kids, and they interspersed the cooking segments with what it was like to live and work on a cattle ranch. Not exactly how Renee would want to spend the rest of her life, but whatever.

Getting up before dawn wasn't her idea of a good time. For as long as she could remember, she'd been a night owl, preferring to stay up late and sleep in the following morning. Of course, it had been a long time since she'd been able to do so. Working at the coffee shop in Portland, her hours had started pretty much at the crack of dawn. While she'd worked there, anyway.

Dane already looked exhausted, and the day wasn't close to ending. He patted the nose of the donkey, affectionately known as Otto, who'd stuck his snout between the rails of the fence where they stood. The obligatory cowboy hat rode low across his forehead, shadowing his face, with a strong jaw and rugged good looks only partially hidden.

Liam seemed the more talkative of the two. Not that either was a chatterbox. Still, it felt nice to have people watching her back. She'd been alone for so long, it was second nature not to trust anybody, to always be looking for the nearest exit, ready to bolt at a moment's notice or at a whiff of danger. She didn't get that vibe here in Texas. Instead, she felt cocooned by people who saw her as simply Renee.

"You guys really don't have to watch me every minute. I know you've got work to do."

"Are you kidding?" Liam's green eyes twinkled. "You are the best thing that's happened around here in a long time." He shot a glance at Dane, who chuckled.

"If you don't count the influx of females recently. It's been pretty much bachelor territory around here forever, and suddenly our brothers are falling like dominos. Must be something in the water."

"Dude, you know you love every one of our new and soon-to-be sisters-in-law."

Renee glanced between the two men, liking the camaraderie they shared. "Shiloh mentioned that Rafe, Antonio, and Brody were engaged."

"Oh, yeah. Rafe's marrying Tessa. She moved here from North Carolina to teach at the elementary school. Almost got killed over an old bond her family owned, because it was worth millions." Liam began counting on his fingers. "Then there's Antonio. He's marrying Selena. She works at the realty company with Momma. She was in witness protection and on the run. Fortunately, Antonio was able to clear all that up and she's safe now."

"Then you've got Brody. He's with Beth. Beth is Tessa's sister, so he's kinda keeping it all in the family." Dane chuckled and ducked when Liam playfully swung at him. "Hey! Cut it out."

"Doofus. Beth's got the cutest little girl. Jamie's part of the family, too. Next, you've got Ridge, Shiloh's twin. He hooked up with Maggie White. She's gorgeous and rich, which makes him one lucky guy." Holding up his hands in front of him, he explained, "I don't mean he's marrying her for her money. I'm just saying Maggie's one of a kind. She's started an organization to help abused women and children—men too—so they have a safe place."

Renee's head was beginning to spin at all the info bombarding her. She chalked it up to the guys not knowing what else to talk about. Their brothers' ladies seemed like a tame subject.

"Next, you've got Lucas." Dane chuckled before adding,

"Course you already know about Lucas and Jill. She's a real sweetheart and bakes like a goddess. Then lastly, you've got Heath and Camilla. Now they're an interesting matchup. Heath works for the ATF, and he's kind of a mountain, tall and broad-shouldered like Dad. He works in D.C. but he's moving back here. Camilla—"

"She's the writer." Renee remembered Shiloh telling her about Camilla, promising to introduce her. "Shiloh told me about her, and mentioned they were moving to Austin."

"Yeah, Heath's gotta be close to the city for his job. Man, you should've seen him when she got shot." Liam stroked his beard. "You know, now that I'm thinking about it, the women our brothers are attracted to all seem to be trouble magnets."

Dane choked on a laugh. "You're just figuring that out? Boudreau men wouldn't be happy with a boring woman."

Renee joined in the laughter, because she could so identify with these women. "Guess I fit right in."

Liam looped his arm across her shoulders and squeezed, giving her a one-armed hug. "Yep."

Warmth filled her, simply from standing between the two men, and knowing they'd already accepted her as part of their family. The Boudreau clan. She'd heard more than one of the men refer to their family by that moniker. Maybe family was more than having a blood tie. While she had one to Lucas, her biological brother, and she already loved him, this was something more. A voluntary choice of picking the people you wanted in your life. Something she'd never been able to do until recently. People like Tina.

"Can you ride?" Dane shifted to lean against the railing, and Otto trotted over again, probably wanting another scratch behind the ear.

"Horses? I've never even seen one in real life, at least not up close. I'm pretty much a city gal."

Dane gave Liam a side-eye glance and turned to Renee with a grin. "Want to meet one?"

"Really? I'd love to!"

"Y'all go ahead. I need to make a phone call, and I'll be right in." Liam pulled his phone from his pocket, and walked away. Renee's eyes followed him for a second, then turned back to Dane when he touched her forearm.

"Come on. I'll let you meet Peppermint. She's a sweetheart."

"Peppermint?"

Dane grinned. "Well, originally she was named Madonna, because she's a lovely chestnut with a white blaze that looks like a Madonna with child. Beautiful mare. Has a bit of a temperamental streak, though." He chuckled and shook his head. "There's an old saying, 'hell hath no fury like a chestnut mare.' Didn't matter to me. When Dad brought her home, I fell in love. Head over heels, couldn't think of anything but that horse. I think I was maybe twelve or thirteen at the time."

"Maybe we should start with one a little more...calm?"

Renee chewed on her lower lip as she stepped into the barn. The scent of hay and leather assaulted her senses, along with the animal smell. Phew, horses smelled awful.

"No, I promise you're gonna become best buddies." He nodded toward the middle walkway area running between stalls on each side of the barn. A couple of heads appeared over the top of the stall doors, obviously attracted by the noise.

"If you're sure."

"Trust me. Anyway, Madonna didn't exactly live up to her name. Nothing peaceful or sweet about her disposition. She was a fiery redhead with a temper to match, but I knew she was something special. I started sneaking out of the house at night and coming to the barn. She'd back away from me, almost like she was afraid. I remember it was December when Dad bought her, because I always carried some of those hard peppermint candies around in my pocket. I loved sneaking them out of the candy dish, and eating them in class."

Renee smiled, imaging a young Dane Boudreau hiding candy in his pockets. She'd bet Ms. Patti knew he did it and never said a word. "I like those too."

"I guess it was about a week after Madonna got here. I snuck into the barn and made my way to her stall. She stood toward the back, tail swishing, and snorted before turning her head away. I knew she wanted me gone, but I loved her. Momma and Dad had talked about her at dinnertime, and

Dad said she was giving him fits. Even at my young age, I knew what that meant. A working ranch can't afford to have a horse that didn't pull its weight. Dad would give her a good chance, but if she didn't come round…"

Renee stopped walking and turned toward Dane. "She'd have to leave."

Dane nodded. "I knew in my gut she was a good horse, and she'd do the ranch proud. I just needed to figure out a way to get close. Let her know we weren't gonna hurt her. To this day, I don't know what made me reach into my pocket and pull out one of those peppermint candies. Madonna still had her head turned away, ignoring me, like she did every night. Until I opened that one piece of candy."

"What happened?"

"Something about the crinkling of the wrapper got her attention. She whipped her head around and watched my every move as I unwrapped it. Her nostrils flared, and I swear there was something about the smell, because she came closer, as if drawn by an invisible magnet. I'd been ready to pop that piece of candy in my mouth when she stretched her neck across the stall door and whinnied. When I held out that piece of peppermint on my palm, she sniffed it and then delicately took it right out of my hand."

"That's such a sweet story."

Dane raised a finger to his lips, then reached into the front pocket of his jeans. He pulled out a red-and-white striped peppermint candy. Almost immediately, she heard the clip-clop of hooves and a red head with a white blaze on its nose appeared over the stall door.

"Works every time. She's spoiled rotten now, and I'm still head over heels about her." Taking a few steps, Dane walked over and scratched the horse behind her ear, and then motioned Renee closer. "Once we figured out Madonna had a fondness for peppermint candy, she became as sweet a horse as I've ever worked with. Got to where I always carry them in my pocket. When I told my dad about what I'd discovered, he decided to change her name to Peppermint."

Renee cautiously reached out her hand and placed it on the side of Peppermint's neck, awed by the power and beauty of the mare. Her tail swished, but she didn't make any aggressive moves, so she grew a little bolder, and scratched behind her ears.

"Here, give this to her and she'll love you forever." Dane handed her the candy he'd taken from his pocket. Unwrapping it, she watched Peppermint's attention shift to her, in gleeful anticipation the sweet treat. Holding out her hand, with the candy on her palm, she waited to see what the horse would do. Soft, wet lips gently plucked the peppermint followed by the sound of crunching.

"That's amazing!"

Dane patted his hand against Peppermint's neck. "She's a sweetheart. So, Renee, what do you think of your first real-life horse?"

"I love it—her—whatever. Do you ride her every day?"

"Not every day, though still pretty regularly. She's going on twenty years old, but there's still a lot of life in the old gal. She'll ride the fence lines with me, because she's got a lot of stamina, but on some of the rougher stuff, I let her sit it out."

"Thank you for introducing me. And, thank you, Peppermint, for being such a beautiful lady."

She glanced up when Liam walked through the doors of the barn. The grim expression on his face spoke louder than words. Something was wrong.

"What happened?"

Liam cut his glance toward Dane for a second, so fast if she hadn't been watching him closely, she'd have missed it. Great, the macho men thought they could protect the little lady. The heck with that.

"Don't look at him. If something's happened, you need to talk to me."

"Lucas and Shiloh are on their way. It might be better if—"

"Whatever it is, I can handle it. I wish you'd all stop acting like I'm a delicate freaking flower. I've survived on my own for a long time. Stop pussyfooting around and just say it."

"Alright, fine. Your friend Tina called and talked to Shiloh. Called him from the emergency room."

The bottom of Renee's stomach felt like it dropped to the ground. A wave of panic swept her, and she grabbed onto the stall door. "Is she okay?"

Liam nodded. "She's gonna be fine." Another glance toward Dane. "Somebody came to the coffee shop looking for you. Roughed her up when she wouldn't tell him where you were. She's alright," he rushed to add at Renee's gasp. "Shiloh already arranged for her to stay in a hotel there, and he's sending somebody to keep an eye on her. Just in case."

"Who?" Dane asked the question before Renee had a chance.

"Chance. He's home packing and will catch a flight out of Dallas."

"Your brother's going to Portland? But isn't he the district attorney? Can he just drop everything and leave?" A million questions raced through her head, fear for her friend utmost in her mind.

"Pretty lucky break, actually. Chance dropped by the diner while Shiloh was there. Turns out he'd just taken all of next week off and was heading down to his beach retreat. Once Shiloh explained the situation, Chance headed home to pack.

"This is my fault. I've dragged everybody into my mess."

"No."

The single word from behind her startled her. Douglas Boudreau stood a few feet away, his size dominating the space, yet he didn't frighten her. Instead, he appeared like a sea of calm surrounding the riptide threatening to drag her into its volatile depths. His determined steps barely made a sound as he walked toward her, placing a calloused hand on her shoulder. That simple touch eased something broken inside, and her breath caught in her chest.

Douglas pulled her against his solid chest, and held tight as her body wracked with sobs. It felt like a dam broke inside her, and all her emotions exploded from her as they breached the fractured walls she'd built. Cocooned in his steadfast embrace, she felt comfort and a steadfast foundation of strength, knowing he wouldn't let go. Her body shook with each sob until dissolving into hiccupping tears.

Opening her eyes, she noted they were alone in the barn. Liam and Dane apparently left when their father showed up.

"I'm sorry."

Douglas cocked his head, his expression tender. "What for?"

"Crying all over you."

He shook his head, a tender smile on his face. "Ain't no shame in crying. God gives us tears to help ease the pain. Do you think I haven't held my wife when she needed to let free the emotions that threaten to choke her? Or Nica? Gal, I've done the same for most of my sons, though they'd probably never admit it. We're human. Tend to bottle up our feelings until they'll tear us apart from the inside if we didn't have an outlet. Tears help."

Renee studied his face, wiping her hand across her cheeks. Douglas was obviously as wise as he was kind, especially since she was practically a stranger. The more she got to know this family, the more she realized how special they were.

"Thank you."

"I know it's going to take a while to sink in, because you've been through things in your life no woman should have to endure, but you're not alone anymore. You've got a family who'll stand beside you and help you fight your battles." He took one of her hands in his, squeezing gently. "Lucas gave me a call and told me about your friend. I'm sorry. I was on my way home anyway to pick up some blueprints I'd forgotten, and decided to check on you."

"I wish I'd never met Darius or Eileen. I know they're behind this. I realize you don't know Tina, but she's...special. A bright ray of sunshine who kept me sane when my world seemed full of craziness. My heart is aching, thinking about her being in pain because of me."

Douglas straightened to his full height, his expression guarded, though his touch remained gentle. "That's where you're wrong, darlin'. It's not your fault. The fault lies solely with Darius and Eileen. Get that through your head."

Renee blinked, realizing he was right. She'd been carrying the weight of their actions for so long, she'd forgotten. The actions and fallout were strictly their own doing, and she didn't need to bear total responsibility. The only thing she was guilty of was trying to live a life outside their sphere of influence.

"Liam said Lucas and Shiloh were on their way home. I

should probably head inside."

Douglas studied her face for a long stretch, and finally nodded. "I've got to head back to the job site. It's been a crazy day, and bound to get worse."

She gave him a spontaneous hug, squeezing tight. "You're a good man, Douglas Boudreau. Thanks for the shoulder to cry on."

"You are most welcome, Renee O'Malley. My shoulder's available anytime you need it."

Giving Peppermint a final pat, she turned and headed out of the barn, Douglas matching her steps. She felt lighter, freer than she'd felt in a long time. Something in Douglas' calm demeanor, his matter-of-fact attitude, and his unconditional acceptance of her as part of his life, his family, gave her the strength and courage to face her final hurdle.

Taking down Darius and Eileen Black once and for all.

Darius glanced at the text message. Closing his eyes, he inhaled deeply and counted to five. It still amazed him that his wife was careless enough, or foolish enough, to think he hadn't duped her phone. There wasn't an incoming or outgoing call, e-mail, or text to that number he didn't get copied to his own. She stupidly thought he didn't know about her relationship with Bruce. Shaking his head, he pocketed his phone, and stepped into their bedroom.

"Hello, darling."

Seated at the vanity, Eileen's gaze met his, and she smiled the seductive smile she used to charm every man she met. It had worked on him for the longest time, too, until he'd looked beneath the surface and discovered the manipulative, power-hungry great white shark lying in wait to devour the unaware and gullible. Honestly, it was one of the things that attracted him in the beginning. She appeared sweeter than honey on the outside, a lovely Southern lady, but deep down she'd been his equal in their quest for money and power. No boundaries were too great they couldn't be overcome together, and they'd amassed a fortune that rivaled the wealthiest men in the state. Too bad her greed seemed to have overtaken her good sense.

"I wasn't expecting you until later."

"I decided to come home early and surprise you." His hands drifted to rest gently on her shoulders, and he found himself wishing he could simply slide them a few inches higher and squeeze them around her pretty little neck. It would eliminate so many of his problems. Too bad he couldn't act on the impulse—at least not yet.

Eileen stood and turned in his embrace, brushing a soft kiss against his lips. "It's a lovely surprise."

"Would you like another?" Sliding his hand into his pocket, he wrapped it around the black leather case he'd picked up on his way home.

"Another surprise? You know I love surprises." Her voice

dripped with sultry innuendo, and she trailed her deep red nails along his jacket sleeve.

"I picked up a little something on the way home just for you."

Her eyes widened at the site of the long black box, greed coloring her expression before she wiped it clean. Snatching it out of his hand, she opened it, and a gasp escaped. Inside it held a sapphire and diamond bracelet he'd had designed to match her eyes. Pulling the bracelet free, she held it out to him.

"Put it on for me, darling?"

"Of course, my love. The sapphires reminded me of the color of your eyes, and I couldn't resist."

She spun around and held her arm up beside her face, turning it back and forth, and watching the gems catch the light. A happy smile lit her face and she turned, throwing herself into his arms.

"I love it. Thank you!" Twining her arms around his neck, she pressed her body against his, the scent of her perfume wafting up and making him want to sneeze. Lately, she'd been drowning herself in the stuff, and being close to her made him dizzy.

"Anything for you, my precious." Dropping his hands to his sides, he perched on the edge of the bed and stared at his wife, noting the fine wrinkles across her forehead. Must be time for her to get another Botox injection. She'd have a royal conniption if she knew he'd noticed any imperfection.

"You spoil me."

"You're worth it. By the way, have you heard from Bruce? He hasn't checked in with me in a while." Time to dangle the bait, see if she swallowed the hook and lied to him, or whether she'd tell him the truth.

"Bruce? No, I haven't spoken with him since the last time. I told you about it."

A lie. He hated it that he wasn't surprised. The text notification of an incoming call to her phone from Bruce had shown up moments earlier. If only this was the first time she'd lied to him, but he knew it wasn't. She still acted all lovey-dovey, so cloyingly sweet it made his teeth ache. She had no way of knowing he'd found out about her affair with Bruce months ago. At least they'd been discreet, hadn't paraded their relationship under his nose.

"Eileen, darling, shouldn't you know by now not to lie to me?"

"What?" She whirled around to face him, her expression wary. "I haven't lied to you."

"Bruce called you not fifteen minutes ago, or did it slip your mind? Was he whispering sweet nothings in your ear, instead of doing the job I pay him for?"

"I don't know what you're talking about, Darius. Bruce and I—"

"Are finished. Done. Am I understood? I've indulged your liaison far too long, turned a blind eye. No more. It's interfering with the job, and I will not tolerate that. Bruce works for me, are we clear?"

Eileen inhaled deeply, and he found his eyes caught on her chest. The plastic surgeons had done a stupendous job, but he simply didn't care anymore. She opened her mouth, and he cut her off with a sharp wave of his hand and pulled out his phone, dialing Bruce's number. He answered after the second ring.

"Hello."

"I want a report on your progress. Now."

"Yes, sir. I actually was going to call you with some good news. I spoke with Elizabeth's friend from the coffee shop. I used a little physical persuasion, but she wasn't talking. A nosy neighbor called the cops, and I had to get out of her apartment. Gal ended up going to the local emergency room. Of course, I followed her. Couldn't have her spilling her guts to the cops. I stayed out of sight, and she made a call to some dude named Shiloh. She asked about Renee. She also mentioned this Shiloh character was in Texas. Wasn't Renee one of the names we're following up on?"

A tingling of Darius' senses spread through him, anticipation building with every heartbeat. Could they finally be close on finding Elizabeth, no matter what name she currently used? She'd evaded him, spiriting away like a phantom every time he gotten close.

"Indeed, Bruce. Tell me exactly what she said."

Eileen moved closer, her expression guarded, though her eyes shot daggers. He didn't care if her feelings were hurt by his confrontation about her affair. If she didn't like it, she knew where the door was. He doubted she'd leave. The ironclad pre-nup made sure of that.

"Like I said, she called somebody named Shiloh. I ain't got a last name, but I'll keep checking. She mentioned something about going all the way to Texas to bash him. Dude's planning for her to stay in a hotel here in Portland, and not go back to her apartment. I'm gonna follow her and find out...Boss, I gotta go, she's heading out the door. I'll call you as soon as I've got a last name for this Shiloh fella."

Darius stood and slid the phone back into his pocket, a feeling of jubilation coursing through him. Maybe today wasn't a total loss after all. Without another word or glance toward Eileen, he walked out of the bedroom. Might be good to let her stew a bit, consider her options. Most of the time she was a smart cookie; she'd make the right choice. She always did.

Now that he had a bead on Elizabeth, he had plans of his own to make—travel plans. He'd always wanted to see Texas.

CHAPTER SEVENTEEN

Shiloh and Lucas piled out of the car the minute he slammed the gear into park. Lucas was a step ahead as they sprinted for the front porch. He hated the fact he'd be bringing Renee bad news about her friend Tina, but he wasn't about to hide anything from her. At this point, she'd already been through enough lies he wouldn't add to them.

Following Lucas inside, he checked the living room and the kitchen, but saw no sign of Renee. He started for the stairs when Lucas' voice stopped him.

"Bro, come look at this."

Heading back into the kitchen, Shiloh spotted Lucas staring out the window over the sink. Standing at his side, he watched Renee walking toward the house beside his dad. There was a lightness in her step that hadn't been there before, and he couldn't help wondering who or what happened to put it there. Whoever was responsible had his thanks.

It took a couple of minutes for them to cross from the barn to the house, and he watched every step, noting the protective stance, the carefully measured strides of his father, and felt a surge of pride. Renee must have said or done something right, because his father's actions were those for someone he cared about.

He opened the door right before they got to it, and Renee smiled at him. The whole world seemed to tilt on its axis at the sight. Sure, she'd smiled a few times since they'd met, but this one was different. There was a carefree, easy freedom to the act, like a weight had been lifted and she felt alive. Whatever, he didn't care how it happened, only that she seemed happy. That was good enough for him.

"Shiloh! I didn't know you were back."

"Just got here. Have you been having fun?"

"It's been great! Dane and Liam showed me around the paddock and the barn. I got to meet Peppermint and gave her some candy. Did you know she's the first horse I've ever seen outside of a movie?"

Her babbling nonsense didn't matter; the glow of happiness surrounding her did. This was the most animated he'd ever seen her since they arrived in Shiloh Springs. He glanced at his father, who watched Renee with a fondness he reserved for family. Somehow, she'd burrowed herself beneath his rough exterior, and found a place in his heart. Didn't surprise him in the least. She was a loveable person.

"I didn't know that. I hope Peppermint behaved herself."

"She was a perfect lady. And my bodyguards behaved themselves, too."

"Figured that out, did you?" Shiloh shrugged. "They

volunteered, if that makes any difference."

"It's fine, I get it." Renee reached up and cupped his cheek, her fingers soft against his face, and he allowed himself a brief second to lean into her touch. Anything to delay telling her more bad news. "What's wrong? You're so tense, I know something's happened. Just tell me."

"It's Tina." Before she could say anything, he hurried to add, "She's fine. Chance is on his way to Portland, and he'll take care of her."

"Dane told me. You wouldn't have sent Chance if it wasn't serious."

Shiloh watched his father nudge Lucas with his shoulder, and jerk his head toward the living room, and they both exited, leaving him and Renee alone. Taking her hand, he led her to one of the kitchen chairs and eased her onto it.

"Just remember, Tina is okay. I spoke with her and arranged for her to stay at the same hotel where I stayed in Portland for the next few days."

"I need to call her." She held her hand out toward him.

"You can't call her. She's at the emergency room." He captured the hand she'd held out for his phone, squeezing it between his. "A neighbor heard noises and called nine-one-one."

Twin trails of tears ran down Renee's cheeks, and Shiloh brushed them away gently with his thumbs. He knew she blamed herself, and there wasn't a bloody thing he could do to change her mind. No amount of talking or explaining or cajoling would manage that. Right now, stating the facts and letting her process the news was his best option.

"Like I said, Tina called me from the ER. She didn't tell the guy anything, so you're safe."

"But she isn't. What's to stop him from going after her again?"

"Chance will be there today. She's not going back to her place until we know for sure she'll be safe, I promise. Nobody but us knows she'll be at the hotel, and once Chance gets there, she won't be alone, okay?"

Renee grabbed a paper napkin out of the holder in the middle of the table and wiped furiously at her eyes. "This has to end, Shiloh. It's obvious Darius and Eileen sent this Bruce person. It was bad enough when they only went after me; hurting my friends, that's the last straw."

He could practically see the rod of steel in her backbone as she sat straighter in her chair.

"Help me take them down."

"Anything you want, sweetheart."

He stared into her green eyes, red-rimmed from her bout of crying, saw the determination in her gaze, and wasn't surprised at the words that followed.

"Let's make a plan and end this once and for all."

CHAPTER EIGHTEEN

B ruce bit back a curse as he watched the pretty brunette pick up her keycard from the front desk. It had been a piece of cake, following her from the hospital to the hotel, and slipping into the lobby right behind her. She'd never even noticed him. He was beginning to think she didn't have two brain cells to rub together inside her head, because she never once looked around to see if she was being tailed. Shaking his head, he wondered if he'd ever understand the female mindset. Oh, well, made his job a whole lot easier when they weren't too bright.

Tugging her purse strap higher on her shoulder, she headed for the bank of elevators off to the right side of the posh hotel's lobby. Didn't seem like the kind of place she'd frequent, after seeing her apartment where she lived. He doubted she had the dough to afford an upscale joint like this place. His gut told him this Shiloh dude was picking up the tab. Might be interesting to figure out who he was, and why his current mark was important to the guy. He'd learned the hard way, a long time ago, knowledge was power. Especially in his line of work.

Something must have alerted her, maybe some sixth sense *finally* kicking in, because she hesitated a brief second before pressing the up button. Her eyes scanned the lobby, and he eased behind a column, but kept his eyes glued to her. There was something unique about her he found fascinating. It wasn't her good looks, because while she was pretty, beautiful women were a dime a dozen. No, it was something else, some intrinsic "yeah, baby" that set her apart. Maybe it was her stubborn refusal to reveal Elizabeth's location. She'd been a regular spitfire, staunchly refusing to answer his questions. It pained him to whale on her. But, a job's a job, and Darius paid big bucks.

Once the elevator doors slid closed, he moved from his shadowed realm and walked over to the reception desk. A geeky-looking male, who didn't look old enough to shave, stood there eyeing him questionably. Time to turn on the charm and find out where pretty little Tina planned to lay her head.

"Good afternoon, sir. May I help you?"

Bruce barely refrained from rolling his eyes at the kid's nasally voice. Good grief, he even sounded like a nerd. It would be so easy to crush him like a bug. It wouldn't take much effort.

Focus, Bruce, you're here to do the job and report back to Darius.

A smile spread across his face at the thought. Maybe he could come back after he'd finished with Tina, and wipe some of the perkiness out of the clerk. Oh, well, the fun and games would have to wait until the job was done.

"Yes, I'm looking for a friend. She was supposed to check in this afternoon. About this tall," he gestured to about shoulder height, "pretty brunette. Name's Tina Nelson."

"I'm sorry, sir, but we're not allowed to give out information on guests."

"I understand, but I thought I caught of glimpse of her a couple minutes ago. We were supposed to meet in the lobby, but I had to take a call, and missed catching up with her."

The nerd looked at Bruce over the top of his glasses and offered, "Perhaps you can call her, and she can give you her room number."

Bruce shrugged and raised his hands, in an 'aw shucks' kind of motion. "See, that's the thing. I broke my old phone this morning and had to get a new one, and lost all my contact information, including her number. Otherwise, I'd have texted her to let her know I was in the lobby."

"I really wish I could help, but as I stated, I can't give out any information on guests without their authorization."

"I get it. I just hate missing her because of a miscommunication."

Walking away, Bruce gritted his teeth, knowing he'd have to figure out another way to get to Tina. But he wasn't giving up. Too much money was at stake. Finding Elizabeth not only meant a huge increase in his bank account, it had become a personal quest. She'd bested him at every turn, making him chase her halfway across the country, always staying one step ahead. He felt like Captain Ahab and she was his white whale.

With a quick glance around the lobby, he headed for the best spot for surveillance. He was a patient man, and given enough time Tina would make a mistake. When she did, he'd have her—and the answers he knew she held. Until then—he'd wait.

"I'm here."

"Any problems?" Shiloh watched Renee and Nica in the living room, seated side by side on the couch, acting like they'd known each other their whole lives. Their unexpected bursts of laughter warmed his heart, and he couldn't stop thinking this was how it should have always been. Close in age, with Renee only a year or so older, his gut told him they'd have been best buds, and up to all kinds of mischief growing up. Another part couldn't help rationalizing this was better, because the feelings he felt for Renee weren't familial, not in a sisterly way. What he felt needed no explanation. He loved her.

"Other than lousy traffic from the airport? No. I'm getting ready to check in." Chance's voice held a hint of irritation. "Everything okay on your end?"

"So far, so good. Renee and Nica are in the living room."

"Probably plotting some diabolic scheme only Nica could come up with, but it'll end up blowing up in her face. Gotta love her, she means well, but things don't work out the way she plans. I forgot to ask. Did you get one room or two?"

"One. You can't keep an eye on her from a separate room. Of course, I haven't told Tina there's only one room. At least there are two beds, bro."

"Great. You left me the dirty work of telling her I'm spending the night. Real classy, dude."

Shiloh chuckled, picturing the scowl on his brother's face. "You're a lawyer. Smooth talk her with all your book learning. You went to the University of Texas, graduated in the top of your class. Surely you're not afraid of one beat-up coffee barista? You'll have her eating out of your hand in no time."

"Jackass."

Shiloh heard muffled voices, and figured Chance was talking to the desk clerk. He glanced toward the living room. Yep, Nica and Renee were up to something. Whatever it was, it would be worth it to see the smile on Renee's face. A few minutes later, his brother came back on the phone.

"I'm heading up to the room. I'll call tonight and give you an update. Wish me luck."

"Good luck. Listen, Chance, Tina might be a bit of a handful, because she's pretty independent and headstrong. But she's been a good friend to Renee, and she wouldn't be in this mess if she hadn't been helping."

"Got it. I'll play it by ear, and sit on her if I have to. Nobody's gonna get close to her on my watch."

Shiloh closed his eyes, grateful yet again for his brothers and their unwavering support, no questions asked. "Did I say thanks?"

"Yeah. Don't worry, you'll owe me. Go and take care of Renee. And Shiloh?"

"What?"

"I've been watching. If you care about Renee as much as I think you do, don't miss out on your chance at happiness, because I think she might feel the same."

Shiloh's stomach clenched. Just like that? No objection? No you-don't-know-what-you're-doing accusations? He choked past the lump in his throat to reply.

"Thanks."

"Talk to you tonight." With that, the line went dead.

"Hey, Shiloh!" His sister's bellow could've been heard all the way to the barn. Quiet she wasn't.

"I'm right here, not Timbuktu. And I was on the phone, pipsqueak." He plopped down onto the ottoman and gave Renee a wink. "What do you want?"

"Can you believe Renee has never had a girls' night out? That's practically un-American. We're going to have to change that ASAP. I'm going to call the ladies, and we'll take her to Juanita's. Tacos and tequila shots. Music and guacamole. Hot tamales and cold cerveza." She held out her hand, palm up. "Gimme your keys, we're gonna have to borrow your car."

He started to give Nica a piece of his mind, because she must have lost hers, thinking about taking Renee out to a restaurant and putting her in the line of fire. While he was fairly sure Darius and Eileen didn't know where she was, was it worth the risk?

When he met Renee's gaze, he caught the mix of barely banked excitement and wariness, reminding him of a puppy, hoping for a treat but expecting a slap. He couldn't do it. He couldn't douse the spark of eagerness for a new adventure, especially knowing how hard she had it. Always moving, always hiding.

"I'll loan you my car on one condition."

Nica turned and high fived Renee. "Told you I could talk him into it."

"He said there's one condition, Nica. Let's see what it is before you celebrate too soon." Renee's voice held affection for his baby sister, and he knew he was definitely a goner. Over the moon, probably never touching down on earth again, gone. She lit every corner of his world, from her intelligence, her naïve innocence, and her unrelenting quiet strength. Come what may, he wasn't going to lose her. He'd found her and she was his.

"Alright, brother of mine, what's your condition?"

"It's actually two parts. Number one, I'm driving."

"But—"

"Number two," he continued as if she hadn't interrupted, "the men are coming with you. All the ladies can sit together and have all the fun you want, and we won't interfere. The men will sit at a different table, on the other side of the restaurant, but we will be there. Otherwise, it's a no go."

"That's not fair, Shiloh. It's not really a girls' night out if all the men come along."

"Sis, think for a minute." He leaned forward, close enough so Nica could read his serious expression. "I'm not trying to rain on your party, but there are bad people out there looking for Renee. I don't think going to Juanita's is going to raise an alarm, but I'm also not letting her leave the ranch without people watching her back. Would you prefer I have Dusty and Jeb sitting in Juanita's, in full uniform, guarding you? Because I'll do it. And I'll call Juanita and tell her to seat them at the very next table."

"You wouldn't!" He merely quirked his brow, and she blew a raspberry at him. "Fine. But separate tables, and no funny business, like trying to horn in on our fun."

"Deal."

When he glanced at Renee, it was to see her body shaking with mirth, her hands across her mouth to contain her laughter. When he winked, she couldn't contain herself, and laughs spilled free. It was the prettiest sound he'd ever heard.

"Come on, Renee," Nica jumped up from the sofa. "We've got to go call the gals and get dressed." She grabbed

Renee's hand, and tugged her toward the staircase. Before heading upstairs, she turned to Shiloh. "Be ready at six thirty. We want to get a good spot."

Shiloh watched the two women disappear upstairs, whispering the whole way. Pulling his phone free from his pocket, he dialed Juanita's restaurant, requesting their two largest tables, across the restaurant from each other. Then he sent a group text to his brothers, letting them in on the plan. Within minutes, he got confirmation they'd all be there.

He glanced up when he heard the front door opening, spotting his mother coming in. Studying her, he couldn't help noticing the slight droop to her shoulders. She wasn't moving with her usual pep and vigor, and it bothered him.

"Momma?"

Watching her, it was like a metamorphosis happened. Gone was the weariness, the slightly rounded shoulders now pulled back, head held high. If he hadn't been looking for something wrong, he'd never had noticed the subtle yet noticeable change. It almost seemed like she put on an outer shell, a façade she wanted the world to see, overlying the actual fact she wasn't at her best.

"Shiloh, honey, I didn't see you there."

"So I gathered. Come here." He pulled her into his embrace, wrapping his arms around her tiny frame, and noticed how frail she actually was. All his life, she'd been bigger than life, small but mighty against all odds, running the family and the ranch with a steel fist in a velvet glove. Today, for the first time, he noticed her vulnerability, and it scared him.

"Thanks, sweetie, I needed that."

"Everything okay?" He studied her intently, not sure what he was looking for. Maybe she'd been working too hard, and adding the worry about Renee on top of things was too much.

Reaching up, she patted his cheek. "Everything's fine. I'm just tired. Rough day at the office. I had two clients who didn't know their backsides from their beehives. Sometimes, I wonder if people have the good sense God gave a goose."

"Why don't you come sit with me in the kitchen? I was just going to grab some sweet tea. Let me pour you a glass, and you can tell me all about it."

The look she gave him would have stopped a polar bear in its tracks. "What in the world is wrong?"

"Can't I just want to spend a few minutes with my mother without something being wrong?"

The only thing wrong is I'm worried about you, Momma.

"Don't think you're fooling me for an instant, young man. But I'd love some tea." With a soft smile, she floated past him into the kitchen and reached into the cabinet for two glasses. He gently took them from her, and motioned her toward the table, surprised she acquiesced without an argument. Oh, yeah, something was wrong.

"Momma, you know I love you. I'm worried about you. If anything's wrong, you know you can talk to me, right?"

She drew in a deep breath, and let it out slowly before

meeting his gaze. "Nothing's wrong, per se. I'm just feeling a bit nostalgic. With Renee finally being home where she belongs, I've been thinking a lot about the boys who didn't make it living here. The young men who never quite fit in, didn't feel like there was a place for them here. Wondering if there was something more I could have done, should have done. If I missed picking up on the signs they weren't adjusting. Everybody deserved their shot, and I've found myself wondering how they're doing. If they managed to straighten out their lives, or ended up over their heads in a system trying its best, but incapable of giving them the direction they needed."

Her head bowed when she finished speaking, and he wondered how she managed to carry the weight of the world on her shoulders. She'd take on heaven itself for one of her kids, and sometimes it was easy to forget she was simply one person. One fragile human being with weaknesses and burdens she shouldered without complaint; a woman who felt things deeper than she'd ever admit. Shiloh reached across the table and clasped her hand in his, searching for the right words. He had no idea she'd worried about the other adolescent youth who'd gotten a huge break by being assigned to the Big House—to Douglas and Ms. Patti. Guys hadn't realized how lucky they were to be given a chance at a real family. Sometimes they were broken in spirit or too rebellious or too stubborn to figure out they'd been given a miracle, and ended up matriculating back into an overcrowded, underfunded child services program. He'd often wondered about a couple of the guys, too. They'd been tough nuts to crack, all brash swagger and harsh attitudes, looking to take on the world and prove they were bigger, stronger, and wiser than anybody.

"I've thought about them, too." He watched her head rise at his softly whispered words. "This ranch isn't like any other place, Momma. You and Dad created a refuge, someplace where the rest of the world couldn't touch us. Not saying we didn't get our share of bumps and black eyes, scuffles and fights. I remember more than my fair share of bloody noses and bruises. I'm talking about more, though. I can only tell you what I feel about it. When my biological mother died, I felt like my world ended. My father was simply a figment, a ghost I never even knew. I knew him here," he pointed to his head, "but I didn't really understand the concept of having a dad."

"Your father was a good man. He loved your mother very much, and even though you hadn't been born yet, he adored you and Ridge. It's a shame you never got to meet him." Her words settled over him like a warm blanket, a weight of love she always managed with simple, yet eloquent words. He wanted to give her back the same comfort.

"She told us about him, showed us pictures of him. Told us he wanted us, right up to the minute he was killed. I do wish I'd had the chance to know him. But this," he gestured around the room, "I wouldn't give this up or change anything. Not one single second. None of us would, Momma. You and Dad gave us all love and support and understanding. And I'm not just talking about those of us who stayed. You gave each of us exactly what we needed, when we needed it. Sometimes, no matter how hard we try, no matter how much we want to, we can't change another person's actions. That's why it's called free will."

Her eyes welled with unshed tears, and he wondered if he'd said the wrong thing. Crap, was he making things worse? He'd never been one for talking about emotions. Too complicated with too many bottomless pits to fall into when you open yourself up and become vulnerable. But he'd do it for Momma, because she deserved to know she hadn't failed them. She hadn't failed any of them.

"Nick and Brian and Gage made their own choices. Something was broken inside long before they came here, and you and Dad did your best to help them heal. You may never know, but I like to think your actions, your love, they carried it with them when they left. That it made a difference in the long run, and helped them find some semblance of peace."

"Thank you, son. You are the best thing in my life, you and your brothers and Nica." She gave a watery sniffle. "And our family is growing. Who knows what's right around the corner? Weddings and maybe babies before too long."

"If it would make you feel better, I can look for them. See if I can find out how they turned out."

She shook her head and stood, walking around the table to put her arms around him and hug him tight. "Thank you, but no. I'd rather hang onto my dreams they turned out okay, than face the reality of something worse."

"If you change your mind, let me know. I'm rather good at digging up information, especially for my favorite gal."

He stood and dropped a kiss on top his mother's head. "By the way, we're heading over to Juanita's later, if you want to come. Nica, Renee and the other women are having a girls' night out. Something about tequila shooters…"

Laughing, she shook her head. "Y'all go and have a good time. I'm going to get supper started for your dad."

He walked out of the kitchen and rounded the corner toward the stairs, stopping short when he spotted Renee standing on the bottom step. How long had she been there?

"You are the most amazing man I've ever met." She came down the final step, putting her directly in front of him. Reaching up, she twined her fingers in his hair, pulling him toward her until his face was inches away from hers. Something blazed in her eyes, making the green color spark with an inner fire. Taking that one final inch, she pressed her lips against his. Fire zinged through him, his entire body burning from within. The softness of her mouth beneath his was an unexpected delight, and his arms slid around her, pulling her closer. She'd initiated the kiss, but he took over, deepening the kiss. Her lips parted beneath his, allowing him access, and he swept his tongue across her lips, loving the feel of her in his arms.

Time seemed to freeze, everything around him disappearing except for the woman he held. Her response both surprised and delighted him. He'd waited, not wanting to rush her, not when she had some many other things to deal with. But no more. No running away or hiding from his feelings. If her kiss told him anything, she was ready to explore something with him. He couldn't wait.

Slowly, he eased back, reluctant to break their impromptu kiss, but a throat clearing from the top of the stairs couldn't be ignored. Nica had lousy timing.

"Come on, Renee, we've gotta finish dressing or we'll be late. Everybody's going to meet up on the patio at Juanita's."

Renee stared into his eyes, a tiny smile lifting the corners of her mouth. "I'll be right there."

"Yeah, right," Shiloh heard her mutter under her breath, but not as quiet as she thought. "Why is it when I finally get female friends around here, they all fall for my brothers?"

Renee's shoulders shook beneath his hands, and he grinned. "I'm not sure what happened just now, but I hope it happens again."

A faint blush bled into her cheeks. "I have the feeling it will. I better go finish getting ready."

"Okay."

She stood silent in front of him, not moving. "I...I really need to go back upstairs."

Running a finger across her cheek, his knuckle brushed

her jawline, her skin like the finest silk beneath his touch. "Upstairs. Sounds like a good plan."

"Yeah." She shook her head, before giving a nervous laugh. "Right. Upstairs. Going now."

Turning slowly, she put one foot on the bottom step and he watched her draw in a deep breath before taking the next step and then the next. On the fourth step, she stopped and turned back to look over her shoulder, her eyes filled with mischief.

"You're a pretty good kisser, Mr. Boudreau."

"You're not so bad yourself, Ms. O'Malley."

Flashing him a seductive smile, she made her way up the stairs and out of sight. Once she was out of sight, he chuckled quietly. "Yep, it's official. I'm a goner."

CHAPTER NINETEEN

S hiloh grabbed the coffee pot being passed around the table and refilled his cup. Man, he needed the extra jolt of caffeine this morning. Whose great idea was it to meet at 6 o'clock in the morning after spending the night at Juanita's, watching the women down tequila shooters? Oh, yeah, it had been his. He regretted that decision now because he wasn't at his brightest with barely two hours' sleep.

Grumbling came from the living room, followed by Brody and Rafe coming into the kitchen and heading straight for the cupboard and pulling down empty mugs. This kitchen was smaller than the one at the Big House, but Dane had volunteered the foreman's house, hoping to avoid interruptions. All his brothers needed apprising of Renee's situation, because they needed to come up with a solution and stop Darius and Eileen from killing anybody else.

"Morning. Glad you made it."

Rafe shot Shiloh a glare over the top of his cup. "This better be good. I pulled a double shift last night, and all I want is to head home and sleep for the next eight hours. And unless you're going to feed me, can we move this to the living room? This kitchen is too small for all of us."

Amidst grumbles and shuffling feet, the men sprawled on Dane's furniture. He wasn't there yet, still out feeding the herd, but Shiloh knew he'd pop in before they were finished. Unfortunately, running a ranch didn't allow for a lot of changes in schedule. When the animals needed to be fed, you got up well before dawn, loaded the feed, and hauled it out to the pasture. It was hard work, and he'd done it enough times while growing up he didn't envy the men out there in the dark, unfurling the hay bales and food for the cattle. He'd decided early on he wasn't destined to be a rancher; he enjoyed his creature comforts too much. Like being able to sleep past sunrise. Dane, on the other hand, had thrived on every aspect of ranching. Said it brought him a kind of satisfaction nothing else had, and he ran the Boudreau spread with a tenacity and determination that rivaled spreads two or three times its size. A couple of the outfits up in Montana had tried more than once to persuade Dane to relocate and manage their operations, but he'd turned them all down, wanting to stay on the family ranch. Shiloh wondered if his brother had ever been tempted to take one of the offers.

"You talked with Renee. Who's after her?"

Shiloh should have known Antonio would get right to the heart of why they'd gathered. He'd been due back in Austin today, but he'd called his boss, SAC Derrick Williamson, and gotten the okay to stay and find out everything he could. Williamson headed Antonio's FBI division, and he'd grown fond of the Boudreaus, even managing to spend time in Shiloh Springs whenever he could. When he'd heard about Renee and her plight, he'd unofficially assigned Antonio to determine the extent and severity of the situation, and report back to determine federal involvement.

"Two people, Darius and Eileen Black. Exceedingly high profile. Located in Kansas City, Missouri. Influential and wealthy."

"Destiny did some preliminary digging into the Blacks," Ridge added without prompting. He shot a glance at Shiloh. "They have connections, political and financial. They're respected in the community as philanthropists, raising hundreds of thousands of dollars every year for numerous charities. A few lawsuits against them, mostly disgruntled employees, which were settled out of court. Nothing that would raise a red flag or put them on any watch lists or federal attention."

"That's because they don't know what Renee does about their so-called pillars of the community." Shiloh set his cup down on the table, the coffee leaving a bitter taste in his mouth. Or maybe it was thinking about the Blacks that did. "The Blacks do run several legitimate businesses, though I'd bet if you dug deep enough, you'd find all kinds of dirty laundry. But they have a...unique...way of supplementing their wealth."

He stood, feeling antsy and needing to keep moving, because the rage inside him needed an outlet, and he didn't want to destroy his brother's home. White hot hatred for people he'd never met coursed through him, and he wanted to scream at the top of his lungs, tear things apart with his bare hands. Instead, he was forced to remain in control, because he needed a plan—a carefully constructed, fully integrated, foolproof plan—to take down Darius and Eileen Black, once and for all.

"Don't just stand there, spill it." Brody's voice remained calm, cool, and levelheaded. That was his brother, the one who held onto his temper the best, didn't let things get to him. Which was good, because once roused, Brody's temper didn't cool until he'd defeated whatever caused his wrath.

Before he could answer, the front door swung open, and Liam and his father stomped through. Shiloh frowned, because he'd asked Liam to keep his father occupied, come up with an excuse to keep him at the job site. As much as his father wanted to be part of this, it was too ugly, and he'd wanted to shield the older man from being tainted. He should have known better.

"Dad."

"Shiloh."

He shot a heated glare at Liam, who stared back, as if daring him to say a word. Knowing his brother, he'd tried to keep their dad occupied, but Douglas Boudreau was like a force of nature, and couldn't be tamed, especially by one of his sons. Honestly, he should have known trying to keep him out of the mix wouldn't work.

"What did I miss?"

"Not much, Dad. I explained a couple named Darius and Eileen Black are the people after Renee. They are known movers and shakers in their city. Ridge had Destiny do a cursory background check on them, and they come up clean."

"She's digging deeper, going into the dark web, and see if she can find anything," Ridge added.

"Why are they after our gal?" Douglas eased onto a chair, dwarfing it with his size. Sometimes, Shiloh forgot how big and powerfully built his father was until he got a visual reminder.

"That's where things get interesting. Have any of you heard of death matches?"

Several indrawn gasps answered him, followed by a flood of curses. Guess that answered his question.

"Renee's mixed up with death matches?" Douglas shook his head, his expression furious. "I don't believe it."

"No, Darius and Eileen Black are. Renee found out what they were doing. She tried reporting it to the police anonymously. Unfortunately, as I stated, Darius had friends in high places, and everything got swept until the proverbial rug. Since she couldn't go through official channels, Renee began collecting evidence about what the Blacks were doing. Locations, dates, times, photographs and even some video."

"That's my girl." Lucas raised a fist in acknowledgement, and Ridge fist bumped him.

Shiloh explained to his brothers and father everything Renee had told him in the gazebo, all the ugliness she'd witnessed firsthand. He'd read between the lines, realizing there was so much Renee hadn't told him. Hadn't wanted to burden him with the totality of the ugliness she'd lived with. Though her life before going to live with the Blacks hadn't been a picnic, he wouldn't wish her tormented soul on anyone.

His brothers and father listened to every gory detail, expressions ranging from stony disbelief to fury with every word. In the middle of telling them, Lucas stood and left the room, heading straight out the front door. Shiloh couldn't imagine the anguish his brother felt, knowing his baby sister's life involved such depravity and disregard for human existence.

"How is this possible?" Liam perched on the arm of his father's chair, face white. "We're talking murder. And for what, fun and games? Public amusement? I'm trying to wrap my head around the logistics of running this kind of nightmare scenario. We're not talking about living in the country or out in the boondocks, where maybe a body turning up could be underplayed. From what you've told us, this happened more than once that Renee saw. How'd they dispose of the bodies? That close to the city, it's not going to be easy."

"Probably why they chose the homeless. Nobody's looking for them. It's unfortunate, but if somebody disappears off the streets, the only people going to raise a fuss are other homeless people."

Ridge shook his head, fists clenched on top of his knees. "There'd still be bodies. If they start popping up around Kansas City, eventually somebody – the press, activists, good cops – are gonna start asking questions." He pulled out his phone and started typing. "I'm gonna get Destiny to check and see if there've been a suspicious number of bodies turn up in the area. Otherwise, we've got another problem on our hands. Without any physical bodies, it's going to be extra hard to prove the killings are happening."

Shiloh blew out an exasperated breath. He hadn't thought to ask Renee about the homeless people they rounded up off the streets, and what happened after the fights. The more they dug into these supposed death matches, the deeper and uglier everything got.

"Renee didn't have any idea how many of these fights happened before she stumbled upon the truth. She knows about at least three that she can prove."

His father stood. "Then we take what she's got to Williamson. Let him present it to his bosses."

"Can't," Shiloh admitted. "She doesn't have it."

"What?"

All his brothers started talking at once, and he slashed a hand through the air. "Eileen caught Renee at the last fight.

She got careless, and Eileen spotted her. Called the guards on her, and she had no choice but get out. They chased her, shot at her when she drove away. Two cars followed her away from the warehouse, and she barely escaped. She didn't have a choice. If she wanted to stay alive, there was no time to go back for the evidence. It's hidden in the Blacks' house."

"Well, now, we've certainly got a crap storm of epic proportions. A couple who have beyond reproach reputations, police corruption, political collusion, kidnapping, and murder. Have I covered all the bases here?" Antonio ticked off each count on his fingers as he listed them. "Unfortunately, we can't simply arrest them on Renee's word alone. With their clout and money, they'd be out before the ink was dry on the warrants. Shoot, we don't even have enough evidence to get a judge to issue warrants."

"I wish Chance was here, he'd know what we could and couldn't do legally." Rafe leaned against the fireplace, coffee cup still in his hand. "Me, I'd swarm the place and toss 'em all in jail. But like Antonio said, they'd be out before the cell door swung shut."

"This is exactly why I called y'all together. We must come up with a *legal* plan, one where we can keep Renee from being implicated in the fallout. I want her protected. She's done nothing wrong, and her life has been in the crosshairs of these despicable people for too long."

"I agree with Shiloh. Whatever we do, Renee stays out of it."

Shiloh hadn't noticed Lucas come back in until he spoke. He met his brother's stare and gave him a nod. On this, they were in total agreement. Protecting Renee came first, no matter what. Glancing around, he noted all his brothers nodding. Good.

Time to get to work. Darius and Eileen Black were going down.

The waiting was interminable. The stupid woman hadn't left her hotel room all night. He'd stayed in the lobby until he'd garnered enough suspicious looks he'd needed to make a strategic withdrawal, at least temporarily. Doubting she'd do something stupid like make a run for it in the middle of the night, he'd managed to snag an empty room under his alias, and paid cash. Ticked him off too, because it ended up taking a big chunk of the money he had on hand. He'd need to hit an ATM soon, and pull out more.

This morning, he'd decided to spend a little more cash in exchange for information. He did a quick scan to make sure nobody watched him, and slipped down the hall toward the kitchen. If he was lucky, he'd find somebody either desperate or greedy enough to take a bribe, and he'd find out what room Tina stayed in. Extra bonus points if she called down for room service. Incapacitating one of the staff delivering her breakfast would be a piece of cake.

Staying out of sight, he surveyed each member of the hotel's delivery staff, weighing their outward characteristics. Studying everything from their haircut to their shoes, it was simple to deduce who might be swayed with a promise of bonus bucks for answering a couple questions. He'd found most people would sell out their next-door neighbor if the price was right.

He chose a tall, lanky blonde male who looked like he was barely out of his teens. Fresh complexion, rosy cheeks, he had the All-American good looks of a farm boy straight from the country, and new to the job. A little raggedy around the edges, but amenable to a quick smile and a bit of conversation. It took less than five minutes to have the lovely Ms. Nelson's room number, and the fact her breakfast tray was being prepared at that moment. How fortuitous.

Slipping down the hall, he headed for the elevators, and pushed the seventh floor button. If his luck didn't run out, he was about to get a second shot at Tina. It was imperative to get the answers for Darius, because he knew exactly what his boss was capable of firsthand. Eileen he could handle. She thought she had him eating out of the palm of her hand. Ha! She 'd been great in the sack, but he didn't follow anybody's orders unless they held the purse strings. Eileen might have money and connections, think she ruled Kansas City, but she was in for a rude awakening, coming sooner than she expected.

The dinging of the elevator brought a cruel smile to his

lips. He loved his job. The thrill of seeing the fear in his opponent's eyes, the stink of flop sweat when they realized the danger he represented. He didn't have a problem whaling on another man, because they had the chance of fighting back, and he always fought fairly. Of course, nobody'd beaten him yet. Hitting a woman, though, he didn't like it, but he'd do it, because it was part of the job.

Halfway down the corridor, he stopped in front of room 716. There it was. Behind the door lay the answers he needed. Darius had held his foot on Bruce's neck for so long, he'd almost gotten used to it. Once he found Elizabeth and delivered her to Darius, he was finished. Done. He'd walk away and never look back, because this payday would put him over the top and he could retire. Find a house on the beach in a country where he couldn't be extradited and live in relative luxury for the rest of his days. Sounded like paradise. The only thing standing between him and his new lifestyle stood on the other side of the closed door of room 716.

The elevator dinged again, and he heard the rattle of a cart rolling across the elevator doors. Perfect timing. So simple pretending to be a hotel guest coming down the hall, the busboy never even looked his way, simply uttered a good morning as he rolled the cart past. With a single blow, Bruce knocked him out cold, and dragged him to the storage area. He doubted anybody would be looking for supplies any time soon. If they did, well, they'd find a surprise.

He walked back to the breakfast cart, and straightened the cuffs of his jacket. Pushing the cart forward, he knocked on the door and announced, "Room service."

"Just a minute," came from behind the door, her voice feminine and sweet. Within moments, the door opened, and Tina stepped back, a hairbrush in her hand. She barely gave him a second glance, and she motioned toward the table by the open curtains. "Just put it over there, thanks." Without a backward look, she walked toward the table.

He rolled the cart into the room and closed the door behind him, silently engaging the security lock. Stepping around the cart, he savored the feeling. She might have been smart enough to have her Texas friend secure her this room, but she'd let a stranger across the threshold. After this, she might think twice before opening the door.

"Good morning, Tina."

She spun around so fast, her robe swirled around her legs, shock coloring her expression. Ah, there it was, the first scent of fear. The recognition of the potential threat he posed. A heady combination. He winced when he felt the hairbrush bounce off his chest. Good, she planned on fighting back. A bit of spunkiness always added a bit of cachet.

"Chance!" she yelled, and he crossed the room, needing to shut her up. It wouldn't do to have her alerting half the floor there was trouble. He grabbed her by her upper arms, shaking her vigorously.

"Shut up. Nobody's going to help you."

"Wrong," a deep voice sounded from behind him. Turning Tina loose, he spun around, only to be met with a hard fist to his jaw. He staggered back, staring at the tall, blond, half-naked man standing there in a pair of boxer briefs, hair damp from the shower. Droplets of water spread across muscles that rippled beneath the skin, revealing he'd put up a fight in defense of Tina. Clever girl, she'd called in reinforcements to protect her. Too bad it wouldn't help.

He dove for the man, grappling with him as they landed on the floor. Trying to ram a knee into his groin, he missed, hitting his thigh. The other man wrested his arm free, and slammed his elbow against Bruce's forehead, and his head rocked back. With a roar of outrage, he swung widely, grazing the blond guy's shoulder. Somehow, using some kind of crazy jujitsu-style move, he wound up with his arm wrenched behind his back, pulled taut, causing excruciating pain to his shoulder.

"Who are you, and who do you work for?" The other man got right into his face, his eyes blazing with anger.

"I'm not telling you nothing. Let me go." He jerked and turned, trying to loosen the man's hold, but couldn't break free. Kicking back, his shoe connected with the other man's shin. A grunt of pain made him kick back again, hearing it hit with a solid thunk. When the other guy's grip loosened, he wriggled free and sprinted for the door, with one last look over his shoulder. The man's expression was calm, hands fisted at his side. He didn't give chase. Guess he realized he needed to stay and protect the little lady.

Bruce slowed his run to a brisk walk as he headed for the elevator. He'd get another chance, and this time he'd be better prepared. The bodyguard piqued his interest, because he'd displayed moves only a professional would know.

He headed for his room to regroup and clean up. This wasn't over. The answers he needed were behind that door, and he couldn't walk away. Darius owned him body and soul until Elizabeth came home, and then he'd be free. Until then, he had a job to do.

CHAPTER TWENTY

"We've got a problem, bro."

Shiloh winced at his brother's voice. When he'd seen Chance's name on his caller ID, he'd left the rest of his family in Dane's living room, working on a plan to take down Darius and Eileen. He didn't need another problem to deal with now.

"What happened?"

"Tina's stalker buddy, Bruce, paid us a visit this morning."

"You're kidding! How'd he find her?"

Shiloh heard Chance whisper something to Tina, and heard her groan in the background. He almost laughed out loud, because he had the feeling those two had butted heads more than once already. If Darius' mercenary had gone after Tina again, Chance's overprotective streak would have come roaring to the forefront, and he'd gone all bodyguard on her.

"Best I can figure, and this is simply an assumption because if it was me, it's what I'd do—he probably followed her from the hospital. She came straight to the hotel and checked in. He was surprised to find me in the room. Guess he wasn't expecting her to have anybody protecting her. Dude's strong, too."

"I hadn't anticipated he'd follow her. I should have."

"Brother, give yourself a break. You've got a lot of balls in the air right now; you can't think of everything. Besides, Tina's fine, although Bruce got away. I called Williamson and had him contact the hotel's front desk. Figured they wouldn't tell me squat, but they'd make an exception for the FBI."

Shiloh grinned at his brother's strategy. "Did it work?"

"There's nobody registered in the hotel with the first name of Bruce. I can't verify if he stayed here, or simply loitered on the premises, looking for an opportunity to get close. Williamson discovered the busboy bringing the room service cart got coldcocked and stuffed in a closet. Tina opened the door for room service while I was getting out of the shower."

Ah, that explained how Bruce the Stalker got in, because Chance wouldn't have opened the door without finding out who was on the other side first. "I'm surprised he got away from you."

Chance muttered an oath. "Guy is strong and fast, and he had on shoes. I was naked except for my drawers. I got a couple good blows in, though. He's gonna be sporting a goose egg on his forehead and a pretty sore shoulder for a while. Meanwhile, I've got a bruise the side of Texas on my shin."

"Ouch."

Shiloh glanced into the living room. His brothers were still arguing back and forth, which meant he had a few minutes. He couldn't leave Tina in the hotel, even with Chance there. If Darius' hired goon found her once, moving her to a different location in Portland was out. Only one option made sense.

"Bring her here."

He could hear Chance's sigh through the phone. "How did I know you were going to say that?"

"Because you're smart?"

"I'll call the airport, see what flights are available, and book us on the next one to Houston or Dallas, whichever leaves first. Oh, by the way, we will be flying first class, and you are picking up the tab."

"Done."

"Call you back soon." Chance disconnected before he could tell him thanks.

He looked up when his father walked into the kitchen. Didn't surprise him, his dad always knew when things were falling to pieces, and was there to help pick up any he missed. If he could be half the man his father was, he'd consider himself lucky.

"Anything I can do?"

"Dad, I don't think a single thing has gone right since I found Renee and brought her home. She's in so much trouble, and I'm scrambling to figure out how to help her.

Tina, her friend in Portland, has been dragged into this mess, because Darius is determined to find Renee. The mercenary that's on Renee's trail roughed Tina up and sent her to the emergency room. I sent Chance to keep an eye on her and play bodyguard if needed. Same guy showed up this morning, I guess to try and find Renee. Chance managed to chase him away."

"So, have him bring her here. We'll keep her safe."

Shiloh shot his father a grin. "That's what I told him. He's booking a flight."

His father straightened and pulled out his phone. "Let me call your momma, and tell her we're gonna have a guest."

Shiloh left him in the kitchen, quietly talking to his mother, and walked back into the living room, inwardly cringing when all eyes turned to him. He was clueless on what their next step should be. He was a private investigator, not law enforcement like Rafe and Antonio. He'd didn't have the expertise to plan and execute apprehension of criminals. Heath was back in DC, finalizing his move back to Texas, or he'd probably be right in the middle of helping Renee. Course, he'd also be a tad peeved when he found out he'd miss out on all the action.

"What have we got so far?" He figured he'd tell them about the latest attack on Tina later. One thing at a time.

Ridge went first. "It's going to be tricky, because there are so many moving parts to this particular puzzle. If it was anybody but Renee, I'd say we'd need to find a way to sneak her back into the house and retrieve the—"

"Nope. Not happening."

"Of course not. No way is she going anywhere near the people who've been trying to kill her," Rafe interjected, playing the role of peacemaker. "We can't serve a search warrant, because that will tip them off, and they'll simply shut everything down."

"At least nobody else would be murdered," Liam volunteered, his expression as closed off as his words.

"We know from what Renee told Shiloh they do these fights three or four times a year. Unfortunately, we have no way of knowing when the last fight was to calculate if another one is coming up. It would be ideal if we could catch them in the act, before anybody else gets hurt." Brody added in his two cents, and walked over to lean against the fireplace, his stance similar to Rafe's. Shiloh kept a smile off his face with difficulty. His two brothers couldn't be farther apart in looks, yet their mannerisms mirrored each other. They could have been contrasting bookends, one dark and the other light. Both good men he was proud to call family.

"Wouldn't that be the perfect scenario?"

"I've got a question," Dane raised his hand before realizing what he'd done, and quickly continued. "Would Renee remember anybody she saw at the fights? Someone important, like a big muckety-muck who might be persuaded to reveal the date and time and location of the next match for say an offer of immunity?"

Every head in the room turned toward Dane when he finished talking, and a flush stained his cheeks at the attention. Shiloh could practically feel the embarrassment pouring off his brother.

"That's actually...brilliant." Rafe grinned and slapped Dane on the back.

"I can ask her." Lucas' quiet statement hung in the air. Shiloh noted Lucas hadn't contributed much to the planning. He'd sat quietly on the sofa, head lowered.

"Bro—"

"I have to do something. I couldn't help her before, but I'm not going to sit quietly in the background because you're all afraid I'm going to rush in blindly and screw up everything. The least I can do is face her, hold her. Be there for her now, when I wasn't before." Guilt colored every word and Shiloh's heart broke for Lucas. No matter how many times he'd been told it wasn't his fault that Renee had been taken away so many years ago, hearing it and accepting it were vastly different things.

"Alright. First thing, we'll find out if she remembers somebody who might suit our needs. Second, Antonio and Ridge, talk to your contacts with the FBI and DEA. I'll catch Heath up to date and have him talk to the ATF. We're going to need a concerted and concentrated federal presence on this, and since we're talking about the government, the wheels move excruciatingly slow."

"Definitely don't want to alert the local law enforcement," Rafe added, "especially if they've got people on the inside covering the Blacks' activities. Do they have somebody in the district attorney's office? We don't know, so our best bet is to have the feds from outside the Kansas City jurisdiction coordinating. Even better if we can pull in everyone from out of state, because who knows how extensive the Blacks' reach is?"

"Agreed. Antonio, Ridge and Heath on government watch. The rest of you, you're on guard duty. Renee, Momma, Nica, anybody at the Big House gets watched twenty-four seven. Oh, and add Tina Nelson to that list." Shiloh updated his brothers on the situation in Portland.

"I've put out a call to a few of my army buddies. They're more than ready to pitch in any way you need them," Douglas offered from the hall. "Gizmo made an offer of any electronics. Pro bono." He grinned at the last words, because they all knew Gizmo, a computer genius who developed extraordinary devices for the military, never did anything free. If there wasn't a profit in it, he'd pass.

"Tell him thanks, Dad, and we'll be in touch." Shiloh glanced around the room at each man there, who were willing to set aside everything they had going on to help Renee, and by extension him and Lucas. Their bond, their kinship, was truer and deeper than any blood connection. This was his family.

"Thank you." He almost choked on the words, emotions welling up within him. At the silent nods from his brothers, he knew they understood. Meeting Lucas' gaze, Shiloh knew they'd have to talk soon, because the way he felt about Renee wasn't going away. Every minute of every day she was in his heart, his thoughts, a part of him he wasn't letting go of—whether Lucas approved or not.

The Big House buzzed with activity. Ms. Patti had come home, mentioned they had a guest coming, and promptly disappeared upstairs. Renee's offer of help had been met with a smile and declined. Nica bumped her shoulder against Renee's and shrugged.

"Trust me, Momma's got this down to a routine. She'll have a bedroom ready and waiting in less than fifteen minutes. Wish she'd told me who's coming, though. I'm not good with surprises."

"I wish Shiloh or Lucas would get here."

Nica made a scoffing sound. "Ha, they're off playing boy scouts, putting their heads together and figuring out all their secretive plans. Did they even stop and think for one minute maybe we," she pointed between herself and Renee, "might have something to contribute? Oh, no, we can't worry the womenfolk, it might offend their delicate sensibilities."

Renee stifled a giggle at Nica's theatrics, though she was right. Every Boudreau male had disappeared before dawn, headed who knew where, though she had a pretty good guess what they were discussing. She should have been there. Nobody knew more about how Darius and Eileen thought, what they were capable of, than her. Besides, she needed to be there when they were taken down. They'd made her life a living, breathing nightmare. She deserved to look them in the eye when they realized she'd toppled their petty empire, crushing it to dust.

"Stupid alpha, macho jerks." Nica grabbed a magazine off the ottoman and flung it across the room. "I wish they'd realize I'm not a kid anymore. I'm as capable as any one of them."

"Honey, you're the glue holding those boys together." Ms. Patti walked down the stairs and pressed a kiss against Nica's forehead. "You can be ninety years old and they are still going to treat you like their baby sister."

"But it's not fair."

"Nobody ever said it was fair. One day you'll appreciate how much they love you."

Nica rolled her eyes. "I love them too, but they are still stupid. Renee and I can help."

Ms. Patti wrapped one arm around Nica's shoulder and the other around Renee's, and led them to the sofa, urging them to sit. "Let's say you were there. What would you do?"

"I…" Nica closed her mouth and glanced sheepishly at her mother. "I bet if I had all the facts, I'd have something to add. I shouldn't be excluded just because I'm a woman."

Her mother patted her knee affectionately. "Sweetie,

your brothers didn't exclude you because you're a woman. I'd bet that never crossed their minds. It's because you're their baby sister, emphasis on the key word baby. They've watched you grow from a newborn dressed in frilly pink to a little tomboy trailing after them across the ranch. You were a gangly, awkward teenager with pigtails and braces. Yes, you're a grown woman getting ready to graduate from college before long, but in their eyes, you're always gonna be the girl with skinned knees and dolls. Even when you're married and with kids of your own, that'll never change."

"Well, they need to realize I'm not a little kid anymore."

Ms. Patti laughed, the joyous sound filling the room. "Spoken like a true adult."

Renee listened to the interaction between mother and daughter, the love and affection they shared, and felt a wistful pang of regret. She'd never had the kind of relationship they shared. For a while, she'd thought Eileen cared for her as a mother did their child. For years, the façade held, until Renee realized she was nothing but a prop, a life-size trophy Eileen could parade around to her society friends, highlighting herself as the perfect stepmother.

"I have to agree with Nica. Making plans, coming up with ways to go after Darius. They don't understand who they are up against."

"My sons won't rush into anything blindly. And knowing them like I do, I can assure you they'll talk to you, get your input before implementing any strategy. Douglas is there, he'll make sure everyone keeps a level head."

"Wait, Daddy's there? I though he and Liam went to the job site."

"For some reason, Nica, your brothers seem to forget your daddy isn't easily fooled. He let them think they were being secretive, having Liam tell him he was needed on the job. They simply drove out to the street, turned around and headed for Dane's house. He'd already planned it before they left, and told me what he was doing."

Nica snickered behind her hand. "I'd have loved to be a fly on the wall when he showed up."

"Me too," Renee added.

"They'll probably be here soon. When Douglas called, they were almost finished with their meeting."

The sound of car doors slamming outside could be heard, and Renee jumped to her feet. Shiloh was first through the front door, his gaze going straight to her. Douglas and Lucas followed behind him.

"Are you okay?"

"Of course, why wouldn't I be?" Renee had a hard time reading his expression. Had something bad happened, and he was afraid to tell her? She watched him glance toward his mother, watched her shake her head, and everything inside her tensed.

"Walk with me?" His voice was low, hand held out to her, and she slid hers into it. Warm fingers wrapped around her hand, and she followed him into the kitchen and out the back door. He didn't seem to have any destination in mind, simply moving forward, each step taking them further from the house. The rock in the pit of her stomach didn't ease, but she'd hold on, keep her patience, and let him tell her whatever was bothering him in his own good time.

They'd gotten to the far side of the pen on the far side of the barn when he stopped. The soft nicker of the two horses inside broke the silence, and she swung around to face him. The lines beside his eyes were deeper, and she wondered if he'd slept at all. Raising her hand, she touched the frown lines across his brow, smoothing them with her fingertips.

"I have something to tell you."

"I guessed that much, since you didn't want to talk in front of everyone. It's bad, isn't it?"

"Yes and no."

She raised her brow at his response. "Just tell me."

"Tina's on her way here."

Every muscle tensed at his pronouncement. "Why?"

"Someone came after her, looking for you. Don't panic, she's okay."

"Don't lie. She's not okay or you wouldn't be bringing her all the way to Texas. Is she hurt?" The sudden picture of her friend lying in a pool of blood popped into her head, and she squeezed her eyes shut, trying to block out the horrific image. This was all her fault.

"I sent Chance to Portland to watch over her. Somehow Darius' guy found them again. My brother managed to chase him away, but we all agreed it would be best for her to leave Portland until we end the threat, once and for all. She should be here later tonight."

"They're never going to give up, are they? No matter how much time passes, or how far away from them I run, they always seem to find me. I am sick of this." She shoved at his chest, pushing him back a step. "I know you and your brothers met this morning. You had no right to do that without me being there. This is my problem, my fight. I will not sit on the sidelines while you try to protect me. If that's your plan, I'm out of here."

"Please don't say that."

She spun around, not having heard Lucas come up behind her. Like Shiloh, he looked tired, carrying his weariness like a cloak around him. His expression was wary, as if he was afraid to reveal too much. Closing the gap between them, she wrapped her arms around him, squeezing him tight against her chest. Without a doubt, she was the cause of his stress, trying to carry the burden of the same guilt she felt from their separation. It didn't matter how many times she claimed it didn't matter, the underlying niggle of doubt remained. Logically, she knew he had nothing to do with their parents dying, the Texas child welfare system snatching them up and pulling them apart. It was a burden neither should shoulder.

"Lucas, I'm not leaving forever. Never again. But I need to stop Eileen and Darius. How many people fought in those matches after I ran? How many deaths? Each one weighs on me, because I should have done something. Said something. Maybe gone to the press. Instead, I only thought about saving my own life. The guilt eats at me. Whatever you're planning, you Boudreaus, I need to be part of it."

"That's why we need to talk. I hate to ask you to relive something so horrendous, and I wouldn't, but it's important."

"Whatever I can do to stop Darius, tell me. I can handle it. I don't want one more death in my ledger. I've done enough damage with my silence to last a lifetime."

Laying her head on his chest, she could feel his heart beneath her ear, the steady rhythm soothing the wildness inside her. This moment, this minute respite, felt like a sea of calm before the monsoon threatening to cut a path of destruction through her life, and she grasped it with both hands.

"You told Shiloh about the evidence you collected. Dates, times, locations, and people."

"Yes, along with pictures and video of both the matches and the crowds. I didn't tape the deaths, though. I couldn't bring myself to do it."

"No, I don't want you thinking about those. You said there were important people paying to watch these matches. Powerful, influential people. Ones who wouldn't want the press or the feds coming down hard on them."

A thrill of excitement coursed through her as she realized

what he was asking. Her mind raced, cataloging anyone who fit the bill. More than one name popped into her head, but one stood out above the others.

"Benjamin Crenshaw."

Lucas stiffened at the mention of the U.S. senator's name. Influential not only at the state level, but a highly ranking official in DC, nobody would have suspected the hardliner of participating in blood sports. She was sure he wouldn't want his connection with illegal gambling and unsanctioned murders to come to light and ruin his esteemed career.

"You're sure?" Shiloh walked back into her line of sight, and Lucas' arms eased slowly from around her.

She nodded. "Positive. I've got a couple of good close-ups of him and his wife, in the VIP seats, right next to Darius."

Shiloh and Lucas exchanged a look, matching grins spreading across their faces. Guess they liked my choice, she thought, watching their growing excitement.

"Lucas, call Antonio and give him the name. Tell him to get Williamson to contact whoever he has to in Washington, and get the ball rolling. If Crenshaw won't cooperate, Renee can come up with somebody else, I'm sure."

"Several."

"I'm on it. Sis, I'm so glad you're back."

Renee smiled at her brother, her eyes misty. "Me, too."

As Lucas walked away, she ventured a question. "If

you're getting the FBI involved, what's going to happen? Make a deal with Crenshaw to testify against Darius and Eileen?"

"We're hoping for more than that. If we offer Crenshaw immunity from prosecution, he'll have to turn over information on the next bout. Date, time, location, and anything else if he wants to stay out of prison. With advance information, and a firm location, we'll set up a multi-agency team with FBI, DEA, ATF, and catch them in the act."

She mulled it over in her head, looking for any cracks Darius might slither through, and off the top of her head she didn't see any. For the first time in forever, she had hope an end might actually be in sight.

Unfortunately, she knew Darius. Knew the way he worked, the way he thought. And knew he'd figure out a way to skate on any charges the feds might bring against him. Unless she stopped him.

It was time to chop the head off the snake, and pray that it didn't turn out to be a hydra.

CHAPTER TWENTY-ONE

I t took two long weeks and enough negotiations with multiple branches of the federal government, but they had a working plan in place. Senator Benjamin Crenshaw fought them in the beginning, refusing to acknowledge his involvement, much less participation, in something as morally reprehensible as death matches. With the looming threat of incarceration and the loss of his political career, he caved.

A team was assembled with the joint efforts of FBI, ATF, DEA, State Highway Patrol, and federal attorneys, and tonight they were raiding the secretly scheduled match. Crenshaw provided the intel, and was isolated at a facility where he would be held until after Darius and Eileen Black, and everyone else associated with the underground fight ring was captured and in custody.

"I can't believe they're finally going to pay for what they've done." Renee's soft voice whispered.

"Because of you. Your bravery in exposing them, fighting for the ones who can't fight for themselves. That's what's shutting Darius down."

"Everyone, get ready. We're moving in five." Williamson's voice echoed in Shiloh's earpiece. The literal extent of the operation was mindboggling. Hundreds of men had been brought in to handle the takedown. The FBI had agreed to allow Williamson to ride point on the mission, since he'd been the one to bring the information to the upper echelon, and coordinated with the task force throughout the subsequent interrogation of Senator Crenshaw and his wife.

Renee insisted on being here. While part of him wanted to refuse, citing the danger as too great, another part realized she needed to witness the events transpiring. Hearing about it secondhand wouldn't give her the closure she'd need to put it behind her. He didn't plan to leave her side for a single second. Let the others be glory hogs, he'd rather have the woman he loved safe.

Darkness had fallen a couple hours ago, and for the last hour, expensive luxury cars and mid-level sedans had pulled up to the derelict warehouse on the northern outskirts of Kansas City. It wasn't the same building where Renee had captured the first fight, but another similar in size. Someone on the task force managed to scrounge up the old blueprints of the building, so they had a fairly good idea of the layout and where everything was located.

The location was abandoned and in one of the not-so-nice neighborhoods on the outskirts of suburbia. It would've been overlooked by most, and deliberately avoided by others. It made it the perfect place to do something ethically and morally abhorrent without prying eyes or nosy neighbors calling the cops.

Shiloh had to admit, they were clever. The attendees turned their keys over to the valets, and went inside like they didn't have a care in the world. The cars were scattered and parked within a couple blocks' radius of the building. He noted a couple of discreetly placed guards on each block, ostensibly watching over the makeshift parking lots to discourage would-be thieves.

He, Renee, and twelve men in flak jackets and body armor were in the back of a panel truck, waiting for the go signal. There were several more trucks parked close enough to the warehouse. When they got word, they'd arrive simultaneously and stop the fight. Placing his hands on Renee's shoulders, he squeezed gently, feeling the bunched muscles beneath his fingers.

"It'll all be over soon, sweetheart. Tonight's the last night you'll have to live in fear."

"It's all surreal. I've pictured this moment in my head so many times, I can't help thinking I'm dreaming, and when I wake up everything will be the same. And another man would have died, because I was too afraid to stand up and tell anybody what was happening."

Shiloh gave her a brisk shake. "Don't ever think that. You tried telling the police, and they didn't act. That's on them. If you hadn't run, chances are good you'd have died." A shudder racked his body at the thought.

"I know you're right. I just—"

"Alpha team, beta team, you're a go!" Williamson's voice was loud and clear in Shiloh's earpiece, and within seconds the engine on their truck revved to life. This was it. Tonight was make or break, taking down Darius' illegal fiefdom. The squeal of tires sounded and the men in the back of the truck jostled around, bracing their hands against the walls of the truck.

Screeching to a stop, the back doors were flung open, and they poured out the back, racing toward the back door of the warehouse. A lone streetlight shone on the broken asphalt of the alley, enough light to illuminate the back door as the agents raced inside. Shiloh climbed down and turned, reaching to help Renee down. He slid his arm around her waist, clamping his hand firmly against her side. Nobody was getting close to her tonight. Not a single hair on her head would be mussed, not while he had breath in his body.

The sound of yells and screeches of outrage spilled through the open doorway, the sounds of chaos evident from inside the warehouse. A few of the agents remained outside, lining the alley, ready to apprehend any who might try and escape out the back.

"I have to go inside."

"Not happening. I can't allow you to put yourself in the line of fire."

"Shiloh, I have to do this. You can go with me, or you can let me walk through the door by myself, your choice. But the one thing you can't do is stop me. I have to see this through, make sure Darius and Eileen pay for what they've done."

Struggling against his instinct, which told him to pick her up and plant her backside in the truck, where she'd be safe, he finally nodded.

"You do not leave my side under any circumstances, got it? The first sign you're in trouble, I'm picking you up and we are out. Done. Finished."

Her shoulders slumped in what he assumed was relief. Guess she'd been expecting him to put up more of a fight. Maybe he should have, but he understood her need to see this through. Guilt was a heavy burden, one he didn't want her to live with for the rest of her life. That was the only reason he was standing aside, and letting her do what she had to do. Because he loved her enough to set her free.

He went in first, shielding his eyes from the flashing lights. The sounds of heavy metal pounded, Nine Inch Nails if he wasn't wrong. Pretty smart move actually on the organizers' part. Any innocent person going past the building would assume a bunch of teens were having a rave or something, and wouldn't give it a second thought. After all, who'd assume death and destruction hid in plain sight?

He managed to squeeze through a hallway filled with people, corralled by a wall of agents applying handcuffs and zip ties to wrists amidst loud and profuse protests. Though they were mostly men, he was surprised at the number of women present. Guess depravity bypassed gender bias.

The end of the hallway opened to a scene resembling a nightmare. Holding a hand over his eyes to block out the flashing lights, he breathed a sigh of relief when they suddenly stopped blinking and changed to white overhead lights being turned on, illuminating the spectacle. It was eerily similar to what Renee had described to him that day in the gazebo. A large boxing or wrestling mat filled the center of the floor, encircled entirely by chain link fencing on all sides and across the top.

Makeshift seating formed an almost perfect circle around the fighting area. Sections cordoned off by velvet ropes highlighted the more exclusive area. If he took a guess, he'd assume it was the VIP area. Dozens of agents attempted to maintain some semblance of order, standing guard at each section, refusing to allow anyone to leave. Several people stood, demanding to call their lawyers, while others simply cried over being caught.

"Over there," Renee pointed toward his left. Seated close to the front was a dark-haired man, an air of power and authority surrounding him. There wasn't any doubt this man controlled everything and everyone around him. Shiloh could picture him seated on his quasi-throne, like a Roman emperor, gazing down on his citizens, deciding who deserved to survive, and who would perish. He wondered if during the death matches Darius sat impervious to the atrocity and destruction, and held out his hand, signaling a fateful thumbs up or thumbs down, ending a person's existence.

"That's Darius. I wonder where Eileen is; she's never far from his side."

Shiloh watched her scan the crowd, and wondered if she'd be able to pick Eileen out of the teaming mass of bodies. When he felt her stiffen against his hand, he knew she'd succeeded. Following her line of sight, he spotted a beautiful blonde woman about six feet from where Darius sat, slowly making her way toward the exit. Only six feet separated her from escaping her fate. He couldn't allow that to happen.

"Will you give me your word you'll stay right here? I'll get her."

Renee nodded. "I promise."

Taking a deep breath, Shiloh began maneuvering his way through the bodies, shifting and shimmying past men in jackets with FBI across the back. Others were emblazoned with ATF. He knew agents had been pulled in from various agencies to handle a takedown of this scope. There was a lot of pushing and shoving, but he doubted many would escape the vigilant agents.

Only a few feet now separated him from his quarry, and he quickened his steps. No way was this big fish escaping the net, though if he didn't make it through this quagmire of bodies, she had a shot. He watched her try to make herself look small and innocent, almost deceptively fragile as she slid past a group of people being secured with zip ties. Another few feet and she'd be out the door. While it was a longshot that she'd elude capture, because outside teemed with more agents and vans and trucks to transport the people detained, Shiloh didn't want to give her any opportunity to slip through their fingers.

A large man stepped into his path, blocking her from sight, and Shiloh shoved him out of the way. Frantically scanning the crowd, he didn't see her anymore! Son of a—he couldn't have lost her. Renee counted on him, trusted him to catch her, see that she paid for the innocent lives she'd destroyed. He raced toward the last spot he'd seen her, skirting around several more agents in the process.

Nothing. Eileen had vanished like a puff of smoke. He craned his neck around, scanning every person. No blonde-haired woman anywhere close. Shoulders slumped in defeat, he turned back, looking at where he'd left Renee. Panic rose in his chest—she wasn't there.

Renee watched as Shiloh made his way through the crowded warehouse. The sounds bombarded her on every side, until she wondered if she'd ever hear normally again. Glancing again toward Darius, she couldn't help smiling when she watched the man who'd introduced himself earlier as Derrick Williamson spin him around and place cuffs on his wrists. It seemed fitting that Darius be treated like a common criminal. He committed heinous acts in his drive for wealth and power. Achieving both hadn't made him feel fulfilled or happy, and she couldn't help feeling that the consequences of his actions fit. He stood tall and proud, never giving an inch, even with his kingdom crumbling around him. The fight club where he'd gained so much of his wealth and privilege was little more than a sham, the illegal gambling that lined his pockets helping tighten the noose, and she couldn't be happier.

Her eyes scanned the crowd, searching for Shiloh. So many people, they all started to blend together, and she shielded her eyes with her hand, blocking out the bright light. She didn't spot Shiloh, but her eyes rested on the face of her nemesis. The woman who'd been more like a big sister than a mother until Renee had discovered the truth. She also knew everyone underestimated Eileen, because she could put on the sweet and innocent act, and could have almost any man eating out of her hand in minutes.

She bit her lip, thinking about the promise she'd made to Shiloh that she'd stay put. But Eileen was getting closer and closer to the door. If she made it through to the outside, Renee knew in her gut she'd get away. Somebody had to do something, and everyone had their hands full rounding up all the audience members. Which meant it was up to her to stop Eileen.

The only way to reach the other woman was to head straight past the combat zone, the one stained with blood from past matches. The cage door had been forced open, and it hung half off the hinges, vacant of the men who'd been forcibly held inside. Thankfully, they'd managed to stop the fight before either had been injured too badly. At least that's what one of the agents told Shiloh earlier.

The smell of blood was strong as she picked her way past, skirting past bodies struggling against the zip ties restraining them. Federal agents were guiding two and three people at a time down the makeshift aisles, and she maneuvered her way one agonizing step at a time, trying to keep Eileen within view.

Darting to the left, Renee spotted an opening and raced toward it, realizing this would be her one and only shot to get to Eileen. Spotting Shiloh in the middle of a throng of bodies, she knew he wouldn't make it in time. It was up to her.

Taking another step forward, she realized Eileen had disappeared. No! Surging toward the exit door, she elbowed and shoved her way through, catching a glimpse of the golden sequined gown Eileen wore and sprinted toward her. The other woman turned to glance over her shoulder, and spotted Renee. Tossing her a smirk, she bounded through the open door and outside.

Renee sprinted toward the doorway Eileen had disappeared through just as Shiloh reached her side. Out of breath, she pointed.

"Eileen...she's out there. I couldn't catch her."

"Come on."

Shiloh grabbed her hand and pulled her along behind him into the humid night air. Flashing red and blue lights formed a nimbus, illuminating the darkness enough she could scan the crowded parking lot. Men in suits stood talking with a couple of the agents, while others loaded cuffed individuals into the backs of trucks like the ones they'd ridden over in with the agents. Others loaded into vans, packed together like sardines in tidy rows.

Movement out of the corner of her eye had her spinning, because of the golden glint. "There she is! She can't get away."

"She won't." Shiloh scanned the area, and shouted, "Antonio—a little help here."

He pointed toward Eileen, and Antonio's eyes widened. Without another word, Shiloh raced toward the fleeing woman, Antonio following quickly behind. Renee wrapped her arms around her middle, her eyes never leaving the scene in front of her. Right as Shiloh and Antonio caught up to her, Eileen's heel caught on a rutted piece of pavement and she tumbled forward, sprawling onto the ground. Her screech had several heads swivel in her direction.

A dizzying relief spread through her when Antonio reached down and grabbed Eileen by the arm, yanking her upright. Though she couldn't hear what he said, she had a pretty good idea he was reading the Miranda rights to her former friend.

Shiloh walked back to her and slid his arms around her.

263

Laying her head on his chest, she savored the feeling of warm seeping deep into her. It was finally over. For the first time in a long time, she realized the good guys did win in the end, and the bad guys went to jail. It was a heady feeling, and she wanted to savor it, relish it, because it had been a long time coming.

"How do you feel, knowing Darius is going to be behind bars?" Shiloh's hand smoothed the back of her head and slid down her spine in a comforting motion.

"I glad it's over. I'll have my life back. Have a future. Figure out what I'm going to do with having choices."

Antonio passed them, his grip on Eileen's elbow strong and sure, and he turned her over to another FBI agent, gave Renee a brief salute and a cocky grin, and jogged away, rejoining the group of agents standing with Derrick Williamson.

Glancing around, Renee laid her head on Shiloh's shoulder. Tonight's raid succeeded in shutting down Darius' operation, and effectively eliminating the threat to her life. Her job was done and she was finally free.

CHAPTER TWENTY-TWO

Renee watched Eileen struggle as the handcuffs clicked shut behind her back. Her carefully coiffed blonde hair hung in clumps around her face and over her shoulders. Mascara streaked beneath her eyes and down her cheeks, her eyes wild as she wrenched at the FBI agent attempting to lead her to a waiting vehicle. She spotted Renee standing beside Shiloh, and her eyes widened, hatred skewing her features into a rictus of ugliness.

"You! This is all your fault. I should have let Bruce kill you when he had the chance, but I was too soft. I let my kindness and affection for you keep me from seeing the real viper in our midst. How could you do this to me?"

"The only thing I'm responsible for is bringing down your den of evil, Eileen. You were my mother. How could you treat people like pieces of trash, to be used and disposed of? They were human beings with lives and families."

"They were worthless street trash, drug addicts and junkies. They jumped at the chance of lining their pockets, at the chance to live like kings on their winnings. Nobody forced them to do anything against their will. And we have signed contracts, absolving us from any responsibility."

"No piece of paper is going to absolve you from committing murder. That's what you condoned here. Greed and corruption fueled these monstrosities. Darius' quest for limitless power got innocent men killed. How can you look at yourself in the mirror every day?" Renee started to turn away, then glanced over her shoulder. "I hope you rot in prison. Think about it, Eileen. No more Botox. No plastic surgery. No tummy tucks or liposuction. The real you is finally going to be on view for everybody to see the underlying ugliness you've tried to hide."

"I hate you!" Eileen screeched the hateful words as the FBI agent shoved her into the back seat, slamming the door and cutting off her vitriol.

Shiloh slid his arm around her waist, and they watched as the combined task force led people out of the warehouse, straight to the vehicles waiting to take them to several different locations for questioning and transport. It was a daunting sight, watching teams from a multitude of government agencies corralling the people who'd willingly contributed money, secrecy, and their silent collaboration of fights ending in tragedy. For what? Entertainment? Morbid curiosity? It turned her stomach that people were inured to the suffering of their fellow man. When had their hearts hardened to the point of not caring?

"You did it, sweetheart. Nobody's going to come out of this unscathed. It's going to turn into a media circus soon, because there's no way the press doesn't know by now. Do you want to stick around, or do you want to get out of here?"

"Have you seen them bring Darius out? I need to see him with my own eyes. Know he's caught, before I can relax. Does that make sense?"

Shiloh raised his hand and waved at Antonio, who came jogging over. "Do you know where Darius is?"

"I don't know, let me check."

She watched him sprint over toward a group of agents, those bright FBI letters standing out on the back of their jackets. Less than a minute passed before he returned.

"He's cuffed in the back of an ambulance. EMTs are treating the injured over there," he gestured toward several ambulances parked in the midst of the chaos, their lights flashing. "Let's go find him."

They walked toward the ambulance, her hand in Shiloh's. As they neared, he squeezed her fingers gently. When she looked at him, he nodded toward the ambulance on the right. "There he is."

Flashes of red and blue cast an eerie glow over Darius' face. An EMT pressed white gauze against his head, trying to staunch the bleeding. Apparently during his apprehension, he'd gotten knocked around and gashed his forehead. A streak of blood trickled down his cheek, stark against his pale skin. He hadn't spotted her yet, and she watched him, wondering how she'd ever looked up to the man. Respected him, adored him as an adopted father. Had he always been like this? Did something in his life change, making the man into a monster?

"I need to talk to him alone."

"Absolutely not." Shiloh clearly didn't want her anywhere near Darius, but this was something she had to do.

"He's handcuffed. There's a policeman standing right there. Darius can't hurt me ever again. But I need answers to questions only he can answer, and if I don't get them now, before they haul him away, I may never get them. Please understand, Shiloh."

Indecision played across his face, but he finally relented. "On one condition." He turned to Antonio. "Can the police officer handcuff him to the ambulance door? I refuse to have Renee anywhere near him without him being restrained."

"Don't think that'll be a problem, bro."

Antonio approached the officer, and she watched as Darius' wrist was secured to the door handle. She hated to admit it, but a wash of relief flooded her at the extra precaution. And the thoughtfulness of Shiloh's action made her love him more.

Slowly closing the gap between her and Darius, she knew the moment he sensed her. He stiffened, then seemed to deflate, like a balloon with the air slowly leaking away. The EMT finished taping a bandage on Darius' forehead and stepped away, leaving her room to move closer.

"Hello, Darius."

"When everything went to hell in a handbasket, I knew

you were behind it, Elizabeth."

"Renee. My name is Renee O'Malley. But you already knew that, didn't you?"

Instead of a sneer, which she expected, he gave her a gentle smile. "I knew. Did you think I wouldn't check every detail of your life before you came into my world? My home? I know you hate me, but I only did what was best for you. Always. Did you know when you were a little girl, the welfare worker never put you into the system?"

"I've known for some time. What I don't know is why."

"That's because I made sure there was no trail to follow." Darius sighed and closed his eyes for a moment, anguish coloring his expression. "I always wanted a child, but Eileen couldn't have children. Then one day, I went to a charity event, and I fell in love with a little redheaded girl I met when she was ten years old. Your green eyes captivated me, the spark of life and intelligence. I couldn't leave you in that place. You deserved more. There was something about you, call it a kinship, an affinity of spirits, but I felt in my heart you were meant to be my daughter. And I made it happen."

"I don't understand what that has to do with my records disappearing."

"I wanted you for my daughter, but I couldn't afford for somebody to come looking for their child later. So I checked out your background, where you came from, who your people were. I have very competent computer people, and they traced you all the way back to when you lived with your parents. Before they were killed. They discovered the social worker for the state never put you into the system. She sold you."

Shock rocketed through Renee. Of all the things she'd wondered about her past, that wasn't even on her radar. She'd been sold? How was that even possible in this day and age? Children didn't just disappear. Yet she had, and she'd gotten an answer of sorts.

"I was sold?"

"It's not as uncommon as you'd think. I've never done it, but with enough money, anything's possible. Unfortunately, the social worker didn't pick the best parents for you. You were too much for them to handle, with the temper tantrums and running away. They in turn rehomed you with people they found on the internet. The rest you probably remember; you were old enough to understand what happened around you."

She did remember, shunted from place to place, never finding a real home. Shaking her head, she blocked out the sordid details from her past. It didn't matter anymore. She had a bright future to look forward to, reunited with her brother and a family who accepted and loved her.

"What about my records? What did you do?"

"That took time and a lot of money, but I made it all go away. Your early years were obliterated from existence, because that child didn't exist anymore. You had a new life and a new family who wanted you. Who loved you. I love you, Eliz—Renee. Despite everything that's happened, you turning your back on your family, involving the cops, I still love you. You are the child of my heart."

"Darius," she started, noting his wince at her using his given name and not calling him Daddy.

"I have the files. Kept them all. Stupid, I know, but I knew someday you'd want to know. Demand answers. Check the safe in my home office. There's a panel in the bottom, underneath everything. You'll find them all there." He glanced toward the policeman standing beside the ambulance door. "Guess it's time."

"I'm sorry. I wish there'd been another way. No, I wish you'd never done any of this."

He gestured toward his Armani suit, then shrugged. "Looks like I'm about to make a fashion statement. Prison orange. Somehow I'll make it work." He stood, and waited as the handcuff was unattached from the handle, and the cuffs were secured behind his back.

"Goodbye, Darius."

Giving her a sad smile, he shrugged. "Be happy. Find your place in this world and make a life. My biggest regret is not letting you go when you found out what I was doing. I thought about it, but by the time I found out Eileen sent Bruce after you, it was too late. Besides, I never intended to go to prison. Figured I'd go out in a blaze of glory if I ever got caught. I would have too, except I saw you standing in the warehouse, your eyes filled with hatred. Too little, too late, I guess, to say I'm sorry."

Without another word, he allowed the officer to lead him to a waiting car. Renee wrapped her arms across her chest, her heart hurting for the father she'd know, not the man he'd become. Strong arms surrounded her, and she was pulled back against a muscular chest. She looked up and met Shiloh's gaze.

"You okay?"

"I think so. I do believe he loved me, but not enough to quench his love for power and money. I'd always come in second place. He did tell me he's the one who erased all the records from when I was little. Had my life changed, molded and manipulated to fit the idea of the perfect daughter he wanted. And he kept the files, told me where to find them."

"Ready to go home?"

She smiled, looking up into the eyes of the man she loved with all her heart.

"As long as you're by my side, then yes, take me home."

The fallout from the raid at the warehouse continued for days afterward. Shiloh had spent most of his days, and sometimes his night, fielding phone calls and dealing with the press. He was bloody sick and tired of the whole mess, wished it would go away. The only bright spot in the whole ordeal? Darius and Eileen Black landing behind bars. Eileen was singing like a bird, and throwing her husband under the bus to try and save her own hide. Personally, he hoped she got the maximum penalty allowed by law.

Well, there was on other bright spot. Renee wasn't in danger any more. She'd been allowed to go back into the Blacks' house, accompanied by several feds, and retrieve the evidence she'd collected before she'd been forced to run for her life. Federal prosecutors were practically giddy when they saw what she had on Darius and Eileen Black. He was so proud of Renee, overcoming everything and coming out the other side without allowing the taint of ugliness to scar her soul.

Once the Blacks were in custody, Renee got a message via e-mail that Bruce, the Blacks' hired mercenary, had terminated the contract and left the country. Any attempt to track the e-mail IP address proved futile, even with his best computer guy searching. Didn't mean he wasn't going to keep an eye on Renee anyway, but the immediate threat was gone.

"Good morning. Did you get any sleep?" Renee walked over and wrapped her arms around him from behind, and laid her head between his shoulder blades. He took a deep breath, loving the feel of her hugging him, knowing she didn't have to run or hide. The change in her ever since the warehouse chaos had been dramatic and instantaneous. Maybe it was the knowledge she was safe. Or maybe it was finally getting to spend quality time with Lucas. They planned on getting away for a couple of days, just the two of them. Chance volunteered his condo on South Padre Island, and they'd taken him up on the offer.

"I did. How are you doing this morning? I saw your light on when I went to bed."

"Tina and I did a lot of catching up, figuring out where we're going from here. So many things have changed. All for the better, I swear." He could hear the smile in her voice, lightening his mood. He loved knowing she was happy.

"Bet it's a weight off her mind, knowing Bruce isn't coming after her anymore."

Renee nodded and stepped around in front of him. "I think this whole thing scared her a lot more than she wants to admit. She jumps at the slightest sound. No matter how many times I tell her it's over, I don't think it's sunk in yet."

"Getting over a trauma doesn't happen overnight. She's more than welcome to stay here as long as she needs. I know Momma and Dad won't mind. Momma already thinks the world of her." Shiloh had a feeling Chance wouldn't be all that upset to see Tina stick around. He'd noticed the way his brother watched the pretty brunette when she wasn't looking.

"She knows. Your mom and dad both told her. Honestly, I don't want to her go back. Selfishly, I want her to stay here, in Shiloh Springs."

"What about you? Are you planning to stick around?" *Please say yes. I want you to stay. Here in town. Here with me.*

She couldn't quite meet his eyes when she answered. "I don't know. I want to, but I guess it would depend on a lot of things. Can I find a job? Where would I live? I want to plant roots, stay in one place, and see if I can make it my home."

"Would it make a difference if I said I want you to stay? Hear me out." Taking her by the hand, he glanced around before leading her to the front porch, hoping his busybody brothers would mind their own business, and let him tell Renee how he felt without interruption.

"Renee, I think—no, I know—there's something between us. Something special. I've felt it since we met. There's a connection I've never felt with anybody else, and I hope you feel it, too."

"Shiloh—"

"Stay here. With me. I know everything's happening so fast, and you've barely had time to catch your breath, but I love you, Renee O'Malley. I can't imagine my life without you being a part of it. Will you think about it? Think about how good we could be together. We don't have to rush things. I'll give you time to get to know me before you make up your mind. But I didn't want to wait any longer before telling you how I feel. I know you want to stay close to your brother and the rest of the family, and I want that, too. My job, my business, it's in San Antonio, and it's doing well. I've thought about opening another branch, and I wouldn't mind moving back here, being closer to family. If that's what you want. I'm probably screwing this up, but—"

"Stop." Her hand landed against his lips, and he drew in a deep breath. He'd scared her. Stupid, stupid, stupid. He'd know it was too soon to tell her how he felt, but if he'd tried to keep it inside one more minute, he'd have exploded. If he had to lose her, at least she'd know she was loved with every fiber of his being.

"You're not rushing me. Yes, it's crazy fast, and yes, we've been through a lot in a really short time, but...I love you, too."

"Really?"

"Really," she smiled as she answered him.

"Seriously?"

"Serious as a heart attack."

Shiloh felt like his heart might explode in his chest from sheer happiness. She loved him! What should he do? He didn't have a ring, but he could still go down on one knee. Or maybe he should make the proposal special with candlelight and roses. And champagne. All women deserved champagne.

"For the love of all that's holy, bro, just kiss her already!" Ridge stood at the edge of the porch, a huge goofy grin on his face.

"Yeah, go on and kiss the girl." Dane pushed his hat further back, lounging next to his brother.

Renee's shoulders shook with laughter when he looked at her hands against her flushed cheeks. Her green eyes sparkled in the sunlight, and he read the love in her gaze.

"Well, you heard your brothers. Come on and kiss this girl."

So he did.

CHAPTER TWENTY-THREE
EPILOGUE

C hance smiled, watching Jamie dance around to the music playing through the speakers they'd set up inside Daisy's Diner. The family rented out her place after hours to hold a celebration, because a cold snap had come through the day before. The engagement party for Shiloh and Renee was pretty much a spur-of-the-moment thing, but the weather decided to throw a wrench into the mix, dropping down into the thirties, and the weatherman predicted possible snow flurries. So, instead of a party on the patio at the Big House, they'd moved the celebration into town.

Daisy hadn't minded having the shindig at her place. Instead, she'd pitched in, moving some tables around and voila, instant party central. The counters overflowed with food and desserts, mostly provided by the guests in a typical potluck fashion. In the center of the spread was the cake Jill made, exquisitely decorated with an abundance of flowers. Friends and family clustered in small groups, catching up on all the things happening, a typical Sunday night in Shiloh Springs.

Jamie grabbed onto Brody's hand, and tugged him to the middle of the diner and did a complicated wiggle thing, hair flailing wildly behind her. Chance guessed it was her attempt at dancing. Brody stood there, indulging his stepdaughter. His brother had taken to fatherhood like he'd been born to have a family, giving Jamie all the love and affection she deserved. Even with the trauma she'd suffered at her father's hands, she'd snapped back happy and filled with joy.

Most of his family was gathered inside the diner. The only ones missing were Joshua and Nica. She'd had to head back to school, frustrated she'd miss the party, but knowing she'd already missed more time than she could afford and still graduate on time. Joshua was off doing whatever Joshua did when he wasn't in Shiloh Springs. Chance had to admit, he was worried about him; he'd been gone more and more over the last year, and when he was home, he was distant, withdrawn. Not his normal self. Maybe he should give his brother a call, see if there was something he could do.

"Nice party."

He hadn't heard his father walk over. "It's nice seeing Shiloh so happy. Renee seems to be thriving since Darius and Eileen's arrests. I can't imagine living like she did, always on the run."

"That wasn't living; it was surviving. Now she's getting a chance to really live. She's with people who love her. It'll make a difference. Plus, she's got Lucas to help if things get rocky."

"It's funny, watching my brothers falling like a row of dominos. They're lucky to have great women who love them." His gaze swept past Rafe and Tessa, his brother's arm around her shoulder. Brody and little Jamie stood beside Beth, her face glowing as she looked at her husband. Ridge laughed at something Maggie said, and a pretty blush spread across her cheeks. Lucas handed a plate to Jill, his gaze filled with love. Antonio and Serena hadn't been able to make it to the celebration. The whole situation with the Blacks and their takedown had Antonio up to his eyeballs trying to straight out the whole deplorable mess. Chance was thankful he didn't have to prosecute any of the multitude of people involved. The logistical nightmare was only beginning, and he knew the next few years would see more evidence unfold surrounding the fallout from Darius and Eileen's horrendous fight club.

"Your brothers have been blessed to find wonderful women who'll stand by their sides, support them, and love them." His father's attention turned from scanning the room to him. "You never know when the right woman will come along. One day when you least expect it, she'll fall into your lap, and you'll know. When it's the right one, like me and your Momma, you will know deep inside she's the one."

Chance shook his head, not wanting to think about falling in love. His career was on track, doing a job that made a difference, and there was lots of time to think about marriage and starting a family later. Without realizing it, his gaze shifted to Tina. The thorn in his side. Ever since he'd gone to Portland, the perky brunette had alternately fascinated and infuriated him.

His father nodded toward Tina. "She's gonna be leaving soon. Told your momma she couldn't stay here much longer. I know Renee was hoping she'd want to stick around longer, maybe move to Texas. Looks like that isn't going to happen."

"She's got a life and friends in Portland. Now that the danger's past, and it's safe to go back, there's nothing keeping her here." And why did thinking about her leaving make his stomach clench into knots? There was nothing between them. He admitted she was a beautiful woman, anybody with eyes could see that. Plus, she was funny, full of life, and didn't seem to back down from a challenge.

"Son—"

"Dad, would you mind giving my best to Shiloh and Renee? I've got to turn in early. I've got a full day in court tomorrow. Give Momma my love."

His father studied him and Chance couldn't meet the man's gaze, because he'd just lied to him. He did have court in the morning, but that wasn't why he was leaving. No, something far more intriguing waited for him.

The investigator's report on one Tina Nelson. In all the chaos and frenzy surrounding Renee and the subsequent FBI raid on the Blacks fight club, nobody'd thought to see if Renee's friend was really the sweet, no-nonsense woman who'd given her shelter at a time she needed it the most, or if there was more beneath the surface than met the eye.

He'd gotten a text from Destiny that she'd e-mailed him a report on Tina. Ridge's pet hacker was the best in the business, and he'd hired her to do a deep dive into all things Tina Nelson, after Destiny reassured him she wouldn't tell Ridge anything about her off-the-books foray to gain the information Chance desired.

With one last glance at Tina standing by Renee's side, her eyes sparkling, her head thrown back as she laughed, he couldn't help thinking how beautiful she was, how captivating and alluring. But beneath the surface, he sensed there was more to the beguiling brunette than met the eye, and he meant to find exactly who the real Tina Nelson was, because in his gut he sensed trouble with a capital T.

Whistling, he climbed behind the wheel of his car, and headed for his apartment. He loved delving into a mystery, and Tina Nelson might prove to be a delicious puzzle to solve. Only time would tell.

Thank you for reading Shiloh, Book #7 in the Texas Boudreau Brotherhood series. I hope you enjoyed Shiloh and Renee's story. I loved writing their book. Even though Shiloh proved to be a handful, Renee proved to be woman enough to tame him.

Want to find out more about Shiloh Spring's district attorney *Chance Boudreau* and the excitement and adventure he's about to plunge headfirst into? Will he find discover there's more to Tina Nelson than meets the eye? Why can't he stop thinking about the perky brunette? Keep reading for an excerpt from his book, Chance, Book #8 in the Texas Boudreau Brotherhood. Available at all major e-book and print book stores.

CHANCE

(Book #8 Texas Boudreau Brotherhood series) © Kathy Ivan

LINKS TO BUY CHANCE:

www.kathyivan.com/Chance.html

C hance laid his briefcase on the desk and rubbed a hand across the back of his neck. He hated mornings like this. Most of the cases he prosecuted in Shiloh Springs weren't major crimes. He couldn't remember the last time he'd done anything more intense than burglary with the use of a firearm when a couple of stupid teens decided to rob Jimbo's Grocery. The evidence had been cut and dried, to the point he was surprised the guys wanted to go through with the case and not plead out. Guess everybody wants their day in court, and they'd ended up being found guilty and got a much harsher sentence than if they had simply pled and took the deal.

Which should have happened this morning. The case was cut and dry, without a shadow of a doubt Marshall Goodman was guilty of assault. Marshall had a list of priors a mile long, a repeat offender who'd been out on probation when he beat the stuffing out of his ex-girlfriend's new fella. Eyewitnesses came forward, and there was even video footage from multiple bystanders. He'd worked out a plea deal with defense council, hammering out every little detail, and headed into court this morning, expecting to be in and out in under an hour. Instead, he'd been blindsided when the defendant decided to toss the deal out the window, opting for a jury trial. Idiot.

The rest of the afternoon had been arranging for the court date, then moving around another case he'd been working on, shoving it off onto the assistant district attorney. It wasn't like they had a ton of court cases every day. Usually, two days a week, he'd have to show up either in front of the bench or behind the scenes in the judge's chambers dealing with the small stuff. Shiloh Springs wasn't exactly a hotbed for criminal activity. The most excitement they'd had in a long time had been when the high school had been locked down with a hostage situation. That case was pending before the county court, and he couldn't wait to sink his teeth into a nice, juicy gun running, multiple counts of kidnapping, and a variety of other charges. For once, he'd get to hone his skills on a meaty offense.

Shrugging off his jacket, he folded it and laid it across the back of a chair and loosened his tie. Time to get comfortable, since he didn't have to go back to court this afternoon. Opening his briefcase, he pulled out his laptop and moved around to sit at his desk. He had converted an entire bedroom in his place to a home office, and that's usually where he spent his evenings, buried in work and research. Today, his attention wasn't on work though. Well, not in the traditional sense.

Clicking on the mouse, he opened the e-mail from Destiny, his friendly neighborhood hacker. He'd hired her off the books, because looking into Tina's background wasn't for any professional case he was prosecuting. No, this was personal. He'd read through the e-mail at least a dozen times already, and studied the attached photos, yet he found himself coming back again and again, searching for clues. Nuances and kernels of truth were contained within the dossier; he just had to weed them out one by one. Destiny had done her usual excellent job of digging out information others would have overlooked, or never found in the first place. She was just that good.

Clicking on the first photo, a pretty, smiling brunette popped up on screen. Head thrown back, she was laughing at something her companion said, her eyes shining with life. His chest tightened at the sight of her vivacious, infectious smile. She'd wormed her way into his head, haunted his thoughts from the moment he'd met her. Their first meeting had been eventful, to say the least. Darned woman tried to brain him with the hotel ice bucket.

Tina Nelson. The woman he'd been tasked with babysitting in Portland, and later brought into his parents' home here in Shiloh Springs. In a pinch, she'd watched out and protected his sister when she'd been hiding from the people hunting her. Taken a beating when their hired mercenary wanted information on how to find Renee. She'd refused to tell him where Renee was, even though it meant she'd endured physical pain. Admiration for the spunky brunette warred with the facts on the page. The ones that troubled him, making him wonder if she could be trusted.

Clicking on another picture, he studied the man seated

beside Tina. He carried himself with an air of somebody who came from a privileged background. The picture had obviously been taken at a business dinner or event of some kind. The sandy-haired man sported a tux, complete with cummerbund, but Chance could tear his eyes away from Tina. Her dark hair had been longer then, falling in waves past her shoulders. The royal blue gown hugged her curves in all the right places, displaying a lush body any woman would envy. Though she smiled at the camera, her eyes told the truest picture. They were haunted, filled with anguish clearly visible to anybody looking beneath the saccharine smile. Her arm was entwined with the taller male's, his fingers resting atop hers in a possessive move.

Chance blew out a deep breath. Maybe he was trying to see something into the picture that wasn't there. While he had made a career of being able to read people, from their facial expressions to their mannerisms, Tina remained an enigma.

Moving the mouse to the next picture, he clicked it, and expanded it onto his screen. Here she was again with the man from the previous photo, but there was a world of difference between the two pictures. In this one, she appeared beaten down, her vivacious spirit extinguished. Shoulders slumped, she appeared withdrawn, as if trying to appear smaller, not wanting to draw anyone's eyes to her.

Checking the metadata between the two photos, he not-ed they'd been taken about three months apart. Such a short period of time, yet the differences were night and day. What happened to the woman he'd spent the last few weeks with?

The final picture showed a woman almost unrecognizable. The long hair she'd worn was cut into a modern edgy style, buzzed on the left side close to the scalp and colored a platinum blonde, so white it almost appeared to have no color. The quirky grin he'd come to know since her days at the Big House was the most recognizable thing about her. He knew women liked to do makeovers, update their looks with new hairstyles, new makeup and clothes, but this? It almost appeared like she was trying to reinvent herself.

Or maybe change the way she looked, so she could hide in plain sight.

LINKS TO BUY CHANCE:
www.kathyivan.com/Chance.html

NEWSLETTER SIGN UP

Don't want to miss out on any new books, contests, and free stuff? Sign up to get my newsletter. I promise not to spam you, and only send out notifications/e-mails whenever there's a new release or contest/giveaway. Follow the link and join today!

http://eepurl.com/baqdRX

REVIEWS ARE IMPORTANT!

People are always asking how they can help spread the word about my books. One of the best ways to do that is by word of mouth. Tell your friends about the books and recommend them. Share them on Goodreads. If you find a book or series or author you love – talk about it. Everybody loves to find out about new books and new-to-them authors, especially if somebody they know has read the book and loved it.

The next best thing is to write a review. Writing a review for a book does not have to be long or detailed. It can be as simple as saying "I loved the book."

I hope you enjoyed reading Shiloh, Texas Boudreau Brotherhood Book #7.

If you liked the story, I hope you'll consider leaving a review for the book at the vendor where you purchased it and at Goodreads. Reviews are the best way to spread the word to others looking for good books. It truly helps.

BOOKS BY KATHY IVAN

www.kathyivan.com/books.html

TEXAS BOUDREAU BROTHERHOOD
Rafe
Antonio
Brody
Ridge
Lucas
Heath
Shiloh
Chance (coming soon)

NEW ORLEANS CONNECTION SERIES
Desperate Choices
Connor's Gamble
Relentless Pursuit
Ultimate Betrayal
Keeping Secrets
Sex, Lies and Apple Pies
Deadly Justice
Wicked Obsession
Hidden Agenda
Spies Like Us
Fatal Intentions
New Orleans Connection Series Box Set: Books 1-3
New Orleans Connection Series Box Set: Books 4-7

CAJUN CONNECTION SERIES
Saving Sarah
Saving Savannah
Saving Stephanie
Guarding Gabi

LOVIN' LAS VEGAS SERIES
It Happened In Vegas
Crazy Vegas Love
Marriage, Vegas Style
A Virgin In Vegas
Vegas, Baby!
Yours For The Holidays
Match Made In Vegas
One Night In Vegas
Last Chance In Vegas
Lovin' Las Vegas (box set books 1-3)

OTHER BOOKS BY KATHY IVAN
Second Chances (Destiny's Desire Book #1)
Losing Cassie (Destiny's Desire Book #2)

ABOUT THE AUTHOR

USA TODAY Bestselling author Kathy Ivan spent most of her life with her nose between the pages of a book. It didn't matter if the book was a paranormal romance, romantic suspense, action and adventure thrillers, sweet & spicy, or a sexy novella. Kathy turned her obsession with reading into the next logical step, writing.

Her books transport you to the sultry splendor of the French Quarter in New Orleans in her award-winning romantic suspense, or to Las Vegas in her contemporary romantic comedies. Kathy's new romantic suspense series features, Texas Boudreau Brotherhood, features alpha heroes in small town Texas. Gotta love those cowboys!

Kathy tells stories people can't get enough of; reuniting old loves, betrayal of trust, finding kidnapped children, psychics and sometimes even a ghost or two. But one thing they all have in common – love and a happily ever after). More about Kathy and her books can be found at

WEBSITE: www.kathyivan.com

Follow Kathy on Facebook at facebook.com/kathyivanauthor

Follow Kathy on Twitter at twitter.com/@kathyivan

Follow Kathy at BookBub
bookbub.com/profile/kathy-ivan